Beltway Justice

A Tale of Political Civility

D.B. Moffatt

BeachHouse Books

Chesterfield Missouri USA

Copyright

ISBN 9781596300859

LCCN: 2013934865

BeachHouse Books

www.beachhousebooks.com

an Imprint of

Science & Humanities Press

PO Box 7151

Chesterfield MO 63006-7151

636-394-4950

beachhousebooks.com

Prologue

The meeting was held in the shrouded entrails of the United States Capitol building.

The ad hoc confab had been convened to resolve the current stalemate surrounding raising America's debt ceiling. Presiding over the forum was the Vice-President of the United States, Frank Bentklin. Prior to becoming the "second in command," Bentklin had dwelled in the United States Senate for nearly forty years. As to be expected, the Vice-President was well acquainted with the machinations of Congressional "protocol." However, the immediate crisis menacing the people in attendance that morning was not so much about policy as it was about their very political survival in Washington D.C. Bentklin fully realized the mortal political wound that would be inflicted upon each and every one of those present, should the American people be allowed to stop borrowing money they neither had, nor could ever hope, to repay.

To the Vice-President's left sat Morey Drainer, the Senate Majority Leader. Drainer had tenaciously held onto his Senate seat for nearly a quarter of a century. His fellow Senate members knew all too well Morey's surgical skill and unflappable will as a congressional legislator. "IF IT DON'T COST, IT DON'T PASS" was the motto engraved on the plaque prominently displayed on the desk in his office.

Seated across the table from the Senate Majority Leader was Steve Middleton, the Senate Minority Leader. "Pitch" Middleton had flourished during his thirty years in the Senate by mastering the art of compromise. He had realized, early in the game, that if compromise could be achieved, decisions relative to substantial change would inevitably bog down in perpetual committee. This, in turn, would ensure that supremacy of the Washington D.C. status quo be preserved.

The Speaker of the House sat to Middleton's right. It had taken Jim Spendforth over twenty years in the House of Representatives, to attain his current position. As a politician, his ultimate aspiration had always been to become Speaker of the House. He had long savored the fantasy of holding the "People's Gavel" firmly in his hand. His party's victorious results in the previous year's election had made Spendforth's wish a reality. To his chagrin, the dream so deeply coveted and so richly deserved had, almost immediately, mutated into an unholy nightmare!' A faction of his own caucus, his own caucus! was refusing to toe the party line by automatically raising the national debt ceiling. The federal borrowing of money, from whatever source and, for whatever reason, had always been a mere formality during Spendworth's ten terms in the House of Representatives. Therefore, this unprecedented rebellion was not only an unnecessary inconvenience; it was an escalating international embarrassment for all of Washington D.C. to endure. In fact, there were growing rumblings of the "treason of traitors!" It was this outrageous behavior that had necessitated the current conclave. Clearly, Speaker Spendworth was under the most pressure of those present that morning.

Vice-President Frank Bentklin called the meeting to order.

"Okay, we all agree that getting this debt ceiling thing put to bed before our traditional August recession is priority numero uno, opened Vice-President Bentklin.

"Hear, Hear!" filled the room in unanimous, bi-partisan agreement.

"Well, we wouldn't be here cutting the baby in half, in the first place, if Jim could simply keep his troops marching straight," snorted a contemptuous Drainer, Senate Majority Leader.

"Morey, are you suggesting I haven't been trying?" asked a dumbfounded Speaker of the House.

"Obviously, not hard enough," rebuked the Senate Majority Leader.

"Morey, I've offered these kids everything! Accelerated rankings, plum committee positions, enhanced staffing funds. Why, I even put three windowed offices on the table!" bemoaned Spendworth.

"And all of that isn't enough for these newbies?" asked a now shocked Senate Majority Leader.

Spendworth continued. "Morey, that's not the half of it! They actually believe that they are here to make good on promises made to the people who sent them to Washington!" Spendworth tried to explain.

"The young fools are not factoring re-election into their absurd equation," dismissed the Senate Majority Leader, derisively.

"That is the very crux of this stunning dilemma, Morey. This faction of my caucus expresses absolutely no interest in being re-elected! ," revealed the Speaker.

"Then what the hell are they doing in this beautiful town we call our Washington D.C. in the first place!" bellowed a now outraged Vice-President Bentklin.

"There's something else," continued Spendworth, his voice beginning to crack and his eyes starting to mist. "They won't stop using the "C" word," he choked.

The dreaded "C" word was code for: "Cuts in Spending, No new Taxes." "They demand an immediate, unilateral reduction in spending, period," stammered the Speaker.

The, heretofore silent, Middleton, Senate Minority Leader, weighed in.

"Jim, that's simply not how we handle things here in Washington D.C. You, of all people, should know and appreciate that," counseled Middleton.

"I do, Steve" was the Speaker's meek reply. His cheeks were moist with tears.

"Jim, Jimmy boy," soothed Morey Drainer. "We're all players on the same team at the end of the day. "We'll work something out. We always . . ."

Suddenly, the door to the room flew open!

Standing at the entrance was a woman of middle-age. She sported a tasteful, well-tailored business suit and wore a wide, vacuous, toothy smile.

"Sorry I'm late guys. Have I missed anything?"

"No Fanny, you haven't missed a thing," answered Speaker Spendworth, dabbing his eyes.

Fanny NoGosi was the Minority Leader in the House of Representatives. She had been a member of Congress for well over two decades. During that tenure, she had managed to achieve something no woman before her would have dared to dream. She had risen to the title of Speaker of the House! Unfortunately for Fanny, a sudden wave of public ignorance had unceremoniously deposed her of that lofty perch. Although no longer the Speaker, NoGosi had not lost her voice. She took a seat to the left of Drainer.

"What the hell is up with the F.A.A.?" fumed the Minority Leader of the House. "They had us in a holding pattern for nearly half an hour! And once we managed to land my jet, I ended up having to walk to my limo! Double Dip Recession, my paduza!"

"Fanny," Drainer cut in. "Jim has been updating us on the problems he's having with a rogue element within his own caucus," began the Senate Majority Leader.

"Let me guess, Morey," interrupted NoGosi. "The Herbal Brigade is up to its usual, anti-Washington Establishment bull crap!" she said with practiced disgust.

"Bonzo!" corroborated an animated Bentklin. "These terrorists are actually trying to make hostages of us!" decried the Vice-President.

NoGosi studied the anguished expressions on the faces of her long time Congressional friends as she mulled the grim scenario.

"Listen, boys, these bumpkins are new to Washington D.C. and naïve to the way we conduct business in our town. "Give them time and they'll come around. Trust me."

"Unfortunately, Fanny, we don't have that kind of time," lamented House Speaker Spendworth.

"And why the hell not?" interrogated NoGosi.

"Because, the Big Guy went directly to the people and told them that if the debt ceiling isn't raised by next week, the country's entire economy is going to go over the cliff," interceded Senate Minority Leader Middleton.

"And, who gave him that bright idea?" demanded, NoGosi.

"He did it on the fly," confessed the Vice-President. "He was en route to The Vineyard for a little R&R," confirmed Bentklin.

"Oh, that's rich! That's so regally royal," hissed NoGosi.

Fanny NoGosi began to violently swivel to and fro in her leather-backed seat. Finally, she came to an abrupt halt. She fixed her venomous glare upon Spendworth.

"Mr. Speaker, NO spending cuts without HIGHER TAXES!" she screamed.

Once again, Spendworth's eyes began to mist.

For the first time during the morning's session, Pitch Middleton relaxed. He found the room's escalating rancor to be a calming relief. Finally, it was his moment to enter the game. He took the "Hill" with confidence.

"I have an idea," he tossed out. "One that might save everyone seated at this table come next year's election.

"Bring it on, Stevie man!" rooted a now animated Vice-President Bentklin.

Middleton went into his stretch. "The President shall receive his requested line of credit increase of $2.3 trillion, effective, immediately," began the Senate Minority Leader. "Pitch" paused to let the enormity of the concession take root. He continued.

"Secondly, there will be no new, apparent tax increases. Thirdly, we, the people present at this morning's meeting shall empower ourselves to create a new committee; a bi-partisan group charged with the task of discussing possible future spending cuts at some time in the future." "Pitch "Middleton had just thrown his best stuff down the center of the aisle. The room fell silent.

The first to speak was Senate Majority Leader Drainer. "I like the idea of another committee, Steve," conceded the Senate Majority Leader.

Fanny NoGosi spoke next. "Steve, what exactly do you mean by "future" spending cuts?

"Fanny, I mean future spending cuts that you, as House Minority Leader, and Morey as Senate Majority leader can slip through the cracks without jeopardizing your re-election efforts.

NoGosi and Drainer looked at each other. They nodded in agreement. All eyes turned towards Speaker Spendworth.

"Jim, can you get your hostage takers to agree to this most generous compromise" asked a hopeful Vice-President Bentklin.

"Yes, I think with these magnanimous concessions, they'll go along," said a relieved Spendforth.

"Good," voiced Bentklin. "Now that the people's work is completed, why don't we allow them to pay for cocktails and lunch!"

"Hear, hear!" was the unanimous bi-partisan cheer of compromise.

Chapter One

That evening's Georgetown gathering was not a mere dinner party but, as always, a Washington D.C. gala event. Expense was never a concern, therefore, never spared.

The Great Room was impressive. The ebony paneling was rich and exquisitely refined. The Fereghan Sarouk rugs were plush in depth and layered design. And the Renaissance chandeliers reflected the wealth and arrogance of their mirrored merrymakers. The spangled gowns adorning the women were worn solely to impress only those who could afford commensurate designers. The lines of the men's costly suits were interrupted only by inconvenient "bulges of prosperity." The omnipresence of expensive scents pervaded the room with obnoxious indifference.

All things considered, it was a well-deserved celebration for another Congressional victory in the name of the American people. Earlier, that very day, both houses of Congress had sagaciously compromised to raise America's national debt ceiling; thereby, saving the country from "certain economic calamity." The legislation guaranteed that the people in attendance that night, as well as their esteemed Congressional colleagues in absentia, would be legally empowered to continue to spend money that was not their own; money that, in point of fact, did not even exist!

This was a vintage Washingtonian D.C. celebration. After all, who better to kick the champagne glass down Pennsylvania Avenue than those who drank so profusely from it? The cocktail hours droned into dinner finally being served. The food was haute cuisine. Although some considered it a bit too "Continental," it was obviously expensive and, therefore, acceptable. The banal conversations were interrupted only by the intermittent cackles of hyenas.

As after dinner drinks were being poured, the key note speaker sat at his table reviewing the speech notes he had prepared earlier that day. A busboy arrived at his side to replenish a water glass. Accidently, the server spilled some water on the man's papers.

"You clumsy jack-ass, get the hell out of my sight!" screamed an incensed Master of Ceremonies.

"I'm terribly sorry, Sir."

"You're going to be a hell of a lot sorrier after I report your ineptness! Now get lost!" The young man cowered and then retreated back to the kitchen.

Red Party Congressman Barry Sooner was the evening's keynote speaker. At the age of sixty, he had spent twenty-four of those years representing his home state in Washington D.C. Although never considered a true insider by the "truest" of Washington D.C insiders, Barry was, nevertheless, valued as an essential role player. His uncanny ability to garner votes from either side of the aisle depending upon what the situation called for at the time had endeared him to both major political parties. During the course of his twelve terms in Washington D.C., Sooner had gradually assumed the unofficial title of "Congressional Social Host" for many of the parties, events and outings that were constantly being planned for and then enjoyed by the Members of both Houses. In fact, in recent years this "growing responsibility" had usurped the vast majority of Barry's time. Short, stocky, and florid of complexion, Sooner was recognized as a "good guy" by everyone in Washington D.C. and a threat to no one in Washington D.C.

As he rose from his seat, Sooner walked with unsteady steps. Approaching the podium, he awkwardly clawed at his throat. Lurching forward, he slammed into the podium and then crumpled to the floor.

Knowing smiles and upwardly rolling eyes suggested that the honorable Congressman had, once again, imbibed too enthusiastically from the grape.

A catcall from the back of the room, "he's fallen in the polls, again" was received with raucous laughs of heart felt empathy! Sooner was on his back and motionless. The once ruddy skin tone had been replaced by the wan color of chalk. The eyes stared vacantly at a Renaissance chandelier; reflecting only his

8

incapacitated state. A small trickle of deeply darkened blood oozed from the corner of his mouth. Barry Sooner would never again rise in the polls, or anywhere else for that matter.

The Congressman was dead.

.

Chapter Two

Immediately following the Senate vote to raise America's debt ceiling, Bill Ryder scuttled out of the Rotunda. His limo was in its usual parking space, waiting to whisk him off to that night's rendezvous. Yes, he had been invited to that evening's Georgetown festivities. However, at the last possible moment of social etiquette, he had declined the invitation. This was the result of an already planned tryst; a meeting that would prove to be far more entertaining for the man from the Mid-West region of the country.

Blue Party Senator William Ryder was in high spirits, indeed. He had been instrumental in securing enough Red votes in the United States Senate to demonstrate a "truly" bi-partisan compromise in the Blue Party controlled Senate. That was a homerun for everyone who was anyone in Washington D.C.

But, in that day's Senate triumph, Ryder had achieved something far more meaningful for himself than mere escalation of the nation's debt ceiling. His victory in the previous year's election had been his ticket to a fourth term in the United States Senate. That, coupled with the day's earlier voting coup, made him a virtual lock to be inducted into the most exclusive clique the world's most elite country club had to offer; The Gang of 20/20! Only, those, who had served at least twenty years in the Senate and had successfully sponsored or co-sponsored at least twenty bills that had passed both Houses of Congress could even be considered for membership. That afternoon's vote had been Senator William Ryder's fait accompli! An exaltation to be relished in the manner of a roi!

The Senator's limo glided to a halt at the front doors of the Tangerine Oriental Washington, the hotel of his destination. After his passenger door was dutifully opened, the Senator emerged and walked to the entrance. The doorman held the door open.

"Good evening, Senator," the employee welcomed his important guest.

"Yes it is," smiled the politician.

Ryder glanced at both the bell-hop station and the front desk, as he strolled towards the elevators. All nodded in deferential recognition.

Once inside his penthouse suite, the Senator greeted the well-stocked bar. He built himself an obelisk-like cocktail. Strolling across the living room, he flung open the glass sliders and stood proudly on the expansive marbled terrace.

"Now, this is my town!" crowed the triumphant Senator.

He drained his drink and returned to the bar for a refill. There was a sudden, rude, knock on the door.

"Enter," snapped the Senator. A bell-hop opened the door holding Ryder's valise.

""Where would you like this Sir?" asked the young man.

"In the master bedroom," replied the annoyed Senator.

After following his instruction, the bellhop re-entered the living room and tentatively approached the hotel guest.

"Is there anything else I can do for you this evening, Sir?" The employee hesitated momentarily, expectantly.

"No, that will be all," snapped the Senator.

"Very good Sir, I hope you enjoy your stay."

And with that, the bellhop departed, closing the door behind him.

Ryder picked up his drink from the bar, and made his way towards the master bedroom. "Time to dress for dinner and then dessert," he smiled to himself.

Chapter Three

The young man strode down Maryland Avenue with purpose.

He was of average height, rather thin, and sported longish, dirty blonde hair. His complexion was fair and the features somewhere between handsome and pretty. His driver's license claimed a date of birth of twenty-one years. However, with Chinese companies cranking out authentic looking dupes, his actual age was anyone's guess. The fashionable carry-all slung over the left shoulder contained just about anything that might be required to please the whims and demands of that evening's host.

As he crossed the street, the young man gazed up at the building of his destination. Its sight always gave him a rush. It was one of Washington's most posh and expensive hotels.

"Someday," thought Terry, "I am going to walk into this place not as a guest, but as a member of the "Club."

That was Terry's lifetime goal, his one burning ambition. Tonight's engagement was merely a means to that end; no more, no less. As he entered the Tangerine Oriental, the concierge winced a glance of recognition but, not one of welcome. The front desk noted his arrival but, in no way, acknowledged his presence. Terry sauntered to the elevators, waggling both his ass and adolescence in defiance.

"I make more in one night than those losers do in month! ," he seethed to himself.

Entering the elevator, he hit the penthouse button with anger. Who was anyone to pass judgment on him? The door opened. Terry marched toward the door of his future. Quietly, he slipped his card key into the accepting lock-slot. Voila! Once again, he was inside the magical world of wealth; a place where dreams really could come true!

As Terry entered the foyer, he was surprised not to see his influential host seated at the bar. Was he running late? He most definitely would not have forgotten!

"Silly Billy, are you playing hard to get tonight?" he asked in his most coquettish voice.

No answer.

With familiarity, Terry made his way to the master-bedroom. The door was open and the lights were on. Senator William Ryder was sprawled on the king-sized bed. He was on his back and motionless. Terry moved closer.

"Time to wake-up to get it up," cooed the would be seducer.

No response.

Although Terry had never seen a dead person before, he was certain the Senator was a corpse.

Ryder was clad only in an aqua blue bra and panty ensemble. The panties were crotch-less, thereby, revealing that which was to have been the life of the party. There was no sign of physical violence save for a small trickle of blood caked to the corner side of his mouth.

Terry freaked!

His first instinct was to run. But no, that was not an option. The losers downstairs had not only seen him, they knew who he was going to see! Terry bolted from the master bedroom!

Standing in the foyer, he weighed his choices. Unfortunately, there existed only one. With reluctance, Terry pulled his cell phone and hit 911. He then moved into the living-room and stood in front of the glass sliders. Ironically, his thoughts were not about the dead Senator. Nor, were they about a possible criminal link to the death.

"How am I going to explain this entire situation to mother?" he mused to himself.

Chapter Four

The phone call came at just after two a. m. The man sat up in bed and reached for his cell.

"Yes," was the response. It was not so much a question as it was a directive. He listened intently for several seconds.

"Pick me up in twenty minutes," was the command. He eased out of bed and headed for the bathroom.

The woman sleeping by his side had also been woken by the call. She leaned over and switched on a night table lamp. Turning on to her side, she propped her head on her left hand.

"What's up?" she asked in a surprisingly crisp voice.

"Not I," was the irritable reply.

"I already know that, dear. Who called?

The man stopped and leaned over his shoulder.

"It wasn't your obstetrician sweet heat," he responded with affectionate sarcasm. He continued towards the bathroom.

In mock anger, she picked up and hurled Jodi Picoult in the general direction of his backside. He had already disappeared into the shower.

Within minutes the man re-emerged from the bathroom. He crossed the bedroom and gently held the woman's head in both hands and kissed her. He began to dress quickly.

Nick and Leigh Cuffington had been married for thirty-four years. They were both in the second half of their fifties. Nick was the Senior Ranking Inspector, in homicide, for the D.C.P.D. Leigh was a writer of literary fiction.

"To answer your aforementioned question, it was Fuentes," said Nick.

"I figured as much," sighed Leigh. "So do tell."

"Not much to tell. Something went down at the Tangerine, that's all I know," confessed Nick.

"Oh, another swank Washington toilet, the usual D.C. suspect," was Leigh's bored response.

"It's that flush that keeps us such, dear," noted her husband.

"I'm surprised the damn bowl still works.

"Why don't you try to go back to sleep," coaxed Nick.

"Not likely." She got out of bed.

Nick peered out the bedroom window and saw the already waiting car.

"Crime time," he said resignedly. Again, he kissed Leigh and was out the door and down the hallway stairs.

"Hey Nick, watch your back," she called out.

"Always," was his promise. He stopped in the kitchen and grabbed a cold one from the refrigerator. In the foyer, he retrieved the jacket he had deposited in the closet mere hours before. Nick exited through the front door. Even at that early morning hour, the D.C. summer heat was intrusive.

"Should've brought two for the ride," Cuffington lamented to himself. He reached the idling, prominently unmarked police car and slid into the front passenger seat. Fuentes was behind the wheel.

"Where to, Inspector?" was the driver's first question.

"Oh, how about a nice, posh D.C. hotel that neither of us can afford," was the glib rejoinder.

"I know just the place," retorted the driver, as the car eased into non-existent traffic.

Inspector Nick Cuffington genuinely liked Detective Maria Fuentes. She was young, bright and, above all else, damn good at her chosen profession of law enforcement. At the impressively young age of twenty-nine, she had ascended to the level of Ranking Detective; no small accomplishment for a woman dealing in the predominantly male oriented world of bad deeds. Maria was tall and slender. She wore her thick black hair at shoulder length. The complexion was a light olive. Her comely face featured highly set cheek bones, a finely sculptured nose, and a full mouth. But the most striking facial attribute was the emerald eyes; eyes that could either melt or pierce, at will.

Fuentes' family lineage was Cuban. Her grandfather had immigrated the familia from Santiago de Cuba to Miami in the late 1950's, just prior to the "emancipation" of Cuba's middle-class wealth.

Together with his two sons, abuelo had forged impressive business enterprises that were both profitable and widely respected in what had become known as, Calle Ocho. Little Havana had become big business for not only the Fuentes family, but for a large segment of South Florida, as well.

From her earliest days, Maria's parents had insisted upon academic excellence.

"You learn the language of our new country and absorb all the knowledge it has to offer," was the mantra demanded of the young girl. She had responded. Maria not only attended the finest schools America had to offer, she had excelled at each institution in multiple fields of study. It was for this reason her parents were mortified the day she informed them that a career in law enforcement was her chosen path of endeavor.

"The illegal activities of the few should never be allowed to endanger the benign innocence of the many," had become Detective Maria Fuentes' career motto.

Chapter Five

It was a twenty minute ride from Cuffington's house to the hotel in question.

"So, bring me up to date, Maria," requested Cuffington.

"What I told you on the phone is all I've got," replied Fuentes; "suspicious death, at the Tangerine Oriental."

Nick took a sip from his can and stared out the window.

"Who'd you speak to? " asked the Inspector.

"I presume Metro Central," replied Fuentes. "They are the only ones that have access to that particular line. It didn't occur to me to request a badge number," she added, cynically.

"Less evidence," was his equally sardonic retort.

They both laughed.

"It's odd, that's all," Cuffington mused, aloud.

"What's odd, Nick?" countered Fuentes. "That the hot shot Head Inspector of Metro has to drag his important ass out of bed at this ugly hour? "Poor, baby!" She patted his shoulder with theatrical consolation.

"It's not that, it's something else," his voice trailed off; thinking more to himself than speaking to his Detective.

Their car pulled to a stop in front of the Tangerine Oriental.

"Speaking of suspicious activity, allow me to bag and tag yours."

Maria took the empty can from Nick's hand, slipped it into a plastic baggie, and deftly deposited it underneath the driver's front seat.

"Now, that's a niece piece of undercover work, Detective," smiled Cuffington.

"I am learning from the best," was Fuentes' sincere come-back.

What struck them both was the noticeable absence of activity that generally swarms the scene of an unexplained death in a public domain. No flashing red, white, and blue lights of responding emergency vehicles. No bustling throng of first responders and ghoulish onlookers. No corridors of yellow tape demarking the area of suspected violation. Not even the omnipresent lens of an insatiable Washington D.C. media. Now that was weird!

Cuffington and Fuentes entered the hotel's lobby. The concierge glanced up from his newspaper, asked no questions, and returned to the sports section. As they passed the front desk, the two employees took them for cops and nodded towards the elevators. Nick pushed "P" for penthouse. The elevator door opened and they entered. Once, again, Nick pressed "P" and the vestibule silently soared skyward.

"This place isn't much on security, is it?" observed Fuentes.

"Maybe, they've already lost their jobs," conjectured the Inspector. The elevator's door slid open.

Once in the hallway, they surveyed the numbered plaques, and headed in the direction of the stipulated suite. As they approached the designated apartment, they noticed two sentries on post, in front of the closed door. One was from Metro Police. The other was from United States Capitol Police. Nick and Maria glanced at one another, in silent acknowledgement:

"If Capitol Police was on the scene, it could only mean one thing; whatever had taken place behind that closed door, it was a sure bet a member of Congress was deeply involved."

The Metro cop, recognizing his Inspector began to open the door.

"ID!" demanded the U.S. Capitol officer.

The cop from Metro rolled his eyes.

"You want some ID, puppy boy?" fumed Fuentes. "Here it is!"

She pretended to fumble around inside her purse and then came up flipping the bird to a now, visibly flustered young man.

"Irrational exuberance," ran through Cuffington's mind, as he flashed his badge and entered the now opened doorway.

"Asshole," muttered Fuentes as she followed the Inspector inside.

They found themselves in a foyer. Three people were in the adjoining living room. Standing in the center of the next room was a man speaking inaudibly into a cell phone. Seated at a bar, was a woman pecking away on a laptop. And standing in front of a set of sliding glass doors was a young male who appeared to be talking to his own reflection. The man in the center snapped his cell phone and approached Cuffington.

"Nick, what brings you to a place like this?" he said smiling and extended his hand.

"You do," he replied dryly, as he accepted the man's handshake.

Fuentes tensed. That was the voice that had summoned them to the Tangerine!

Captain Patrick "Killer" Killingsworth was Cuffington's counterpart at U.S. Capitol Police. He was around fifty years of age. The Captain was about six feet tall with a firmly stout frame. The eyes were clear, the jaw rugged, and his full head of salt and pepper evenly seasoned. Killingsworth had spent the bulk of his professional career with the United States Secret Service. However, as the years passed and the promotions mounted he found himself becoming increasingly further removed from that aspect of the job he enjoyed the most, field work. It was for this reason that when the position of Head of Field Operations for U.S. Capitol Police presented itself, he jumped on it. The only person Killingsworth answered to at U.S. Capitol Police was the Chief himself.

"You must be Fuentes," concluded Killingsworth.

"Detective Fuentes," was the curt reply.

"Of course," he acknowledged with a smile. "Ginger, come over here. I want you to meet someone," ordered the Captain.

The woman seated at the bar looked up from her computer. She stood, smoothed her skirt, and leisurely high-heeled it towards her Captain. Ginger walked with the conviction that she was far more attractive than reality would otherwise suggest. She was fortyish. Her height was average and she maintained a reasonably proportioned figure. Ginger kept her blonde hair cut short. Her oval face was fair, but slightly puffy.

"Hi, I'm Ginger Snapp; Lieutenant Ginger Snapp," she added for Maria's benefit.

"Ginger, this is Inspector Nick Cuffington and Detective Maria Fuentes," recited Killingsworth.

The women exchanged plastic smiles. It took a mere femma second for each to decide she hated the woman standing in front of her. What Nick noted immediately about Ginger Snapp were her eyes; they never stopped fluttering.

"Pat, what are we dealing with?" asked Cuffington with professional nonchalance.

Killingsworth turned his undivided attention to Cuffington.

"One dead United States Senator," responded the Captain with equal professional detachment. "William Ryder; white, male Caucasian, age fifty-two," he continued.

"Cause of death?" inquired the Inspector.

"TBD," answered the Captain.

"Who's that?" questioned the Inspector, nodding towards the young man standing in front of the terrace windows.

"Terrence Frailey. He is, ah, was the late Senator's invited dinner quest," revealed Killingsworth.

Nick took another look at the effeminate looking youth.

"I get the picture," he said wearily. "Where's the Senator?"

"He's reposing in the master. C'mon, I'll give the guided tour," prompted Killingsworth.

They entered the bedroom. There were two U.S. Capitol forensics techs busily going about their business. They reminded Cuffington of drones, buzzing around their queen bee. The Senator remained in the same supine position that Terry had originally found him, with one notable aberration. Washington's Muses of Fate had not been able to contain themselves, given the irony of the circumstances. Rigor Mortis had set in. Senator William Ryder had risen to the occasion of his final call to duty.

"It would've been a short party, anyway," concluded Fuentes.

20

The Inspector gave her a stern look.

"Put a sock in it, Detective."

"Forever the bridesmaid," she sighed, whimsically.

Cuffington took another sweep of the room.

"Alright, I've seen enough," as he headed back to the living room.

Chapter Six

Cuffington stared implacably at Captain Killingsworth.

"What *don't* I know, Pat?" was the measured query.

For the first time since their arrival, Killingsworth appeared ill at ease. He glanced at Terry, who was still gazing into the glass doors.

"Lieutenant, would you please escort Mr. Frailey to the front door," was the Captain's directive.

Snapp took Frailey by the arm and walked him into the foyer and out the front door.

"Frailey's a person of non-interest," informed Killingsworth.

"And why's that?" asked the Inspector.

"We've already gone through the front desk's journal," answered the Captain. "Given the time he was logged and the time he pushed the panic buttons, there was absolutely no time for foul play on his part."

Lieutenant Ginger Snapp returned to the living room.

Killingsworth continued. "Nick, there was a second incident last night, involving another member of Congress. A sudden rap on the suite's front door interrupted him.

The U.S. Capitol sentry opened the door and entered the foyer, closing the door behind him.

"The ambulance unit has arrived," he reported.

Without prompting, Lieutenant Ginger Snapp walked to the master bedroom and disappeared inside. Within seconds, she re-emerged and signaled the OK for the paramedics' admittance. There was a changing of the guard. The forensics team exited and the EMT unit entered the bedroom, gurney in tow. Moments later, the gurney was rolled out with what, to the unsuspecting eye appeared to be a rather small pup tent. They disappeared into the early morning.

That left only the four officers inside the suite.

"Maria, dismiss our outside post," ordered the Inspector.

"Ditto for ours," added Killingsworth.

Maria nodded, and headed for the front door. She dismissed the sentries and returned.

"What sort of incident, Pat?" resumed Cuffington.

"Congressman Barry Sooner dropped dead while giving a speech at some high-brow dinner party," revealed Killingsworth.

"Cause of death?" pressed Cuffington.

"We don't know yet. The presumption is natural causes; heart attack, stroke, something along those lines," concluded the Captain.

"But you don't think so?" probed Cuffington.

"Nick, I don't know what I think right now! But as a cop, I've never bought into the convenience of coincidence."

When it came to coincidence, Cuffington had long maintained a very similar professional credo.

"Pat, what do you need from my end?" asked the Inspector, with empathy.

"Look Nick, at this point, I have no basis to assume the two deaths are in any way connected. Furthermore, I don't know if either is even a possible homicide," conceded Killingsworth. "But, should it turn out that they are, I want to. . . ," his voice trailed off.

"Spend our time tracking rather than competing," finished Nick.

"So you want to establish a temporary, bi-partisan exploratory committee," dead-panned Fuentes.

"Something like that Detective," nodded the Captain from U.S. Capitol Police. Killingsworth had fully picked up on Maria's not so subtle sarcasm. Her reference had been to the legendary territorial turf wars that invariably flared up between the myriad of Washington law enforcement agencies, whenever, evil darkened the door step of the nation's Capital City. However, despite Fuentes' earlier confrontation with the U.S. Capitol Police sentry, those rivalries had, for the most part, waned. The current volume of criminal activity energizing D.C. had transformed Washington into an Equal Opportunity Provider. The rampaging avarice was more than adequate to satisfy the demands of those seeking career advancement, financial reward, and above all else, coveted Media Face Time!

"Pat, is there anything else I should know involving last night's events?" implored Cuffington.

"You're on the ground floor, Nick. You are as up to speed as I am," avowed Killingsworth.

"Where did you have the bodies transported?" the Inspector wanted to know.

"Metro Morgue," replied the Captain.

"Who is going to perform the autopsies?" ventured Nick.

"Doc Savage," was the reply.

"Sound choice," agreed Cuffington.

"The only choice, given the possible ramifications," insisted the Captain.

"Do you have a time regarding the preliminary findings?" asked the Inspector.

"Nick, I don't even have an ETA on Savage!" bemoaned Killingsworth. "It's August. Like everyone else in this damn town, he's on vacation!"

"Have you spoken to him, personally?" Nick inquired.

"Yea, by now he should be en route from Ocean City via the copter I requisitioned for him," relayed Killingsworth. "He's not a happy chopper."

Nick began to smile. "Did he invite you to the festivities?"

"Are you kidding me?" as the Captain began to grin. "I'm not going to be anywhere near Metro Morgue when the sick little bastard starts serving hors d'oeuvres!"

Both men broke into unprofessional laughter. Detective Fuentes glanced uneasily at Lieutenant Ginger Snapp. She fluttered her response. Neither woman could understand what possible humor could be derived from the evisceration of human cadavers.

Then again, neither woman had ever met Doc Savage.

Chapter Seven

Cuffington and Fuentes traversed the lobby of the Tangerine Oriental and departed into the humidity of the pre-dawn morning. It had been decided that Killingsworth would contact Nick as soon as he had heard from Doctor Savage.

Once in the car, Fuentes turned towards Cuffington.

"Where next?" she asked.

"Foggy Bottom," replied Nick referring to his home's D.C. neighborhood.

They rode in silence for several minutes.

"What's your take on the night's events Nick?" as Fuentes kicked off the conversation.

"I think we have one dead Senator and one dead Congressman," surmised the Inspector.

"No, that's not my question. Why did Killingsworth bring us into the situation in the first place?" was her skeptical inquiry.

"More likely than not, to cover his ass, Detective, responded Cuffington. "Lest you forget this is Washington D.C."

"What's to cover?" scoffed Fuentes. "Two middle-aged guys croaked; one of a heart attack, stroke or whatever, and the other OD'd on some exotic male enhancement drug when the moment was right."

The Inspector suppressed his smile.

"Yes, but both men are, or were, members of the United States Congress. Add to that, the fact that they both died on the same evening and in the same town creates a plausible red flag" countered the Inspector.

Fuentes brooded. She chose her next question with care.

"Nick, are you convinced that Captain Killingsworth is telling us everything he knows?" posited Maria Fuentes.

"I have no reason to assume he isn't. Otherwise, why include us at all to begin with?" reasoned the Inspector.

"Like you just said Nick, to in some way cover own his ass."

Their car glided to a silent stop in front of the Cuffington home.

"I'll call you when I hear from Killingsworth," said Nick as he opened the passenger door to get out.

"Aren't you forgetting something, Inspector?" asked Maria as she dangled the earlier morning's bagged "evidence."

"How would I survive without you," he smiled.

"Let's hope you never have to find out," was her somewhat enigmatic answer.

Nick entered the side door leading into the kitchen. He perused the downstairs of the house. It was dark, save for the crack of light emanating from Leigh's closed library door.

"She's up and writing," thought Nick. "I won't disturb her."

He returned to the kitchen, procured a beer and went out to the small, secluded backyard patio. He took a cushioned seat at the table and began to evaluate the situation in which he was now involved. He lit a cigarette. It was the strike heard "round the world!"

"How many does that make today, Nick?" Leigh was standing in the kitchen's doorway. She was clad in a long bathrobe with her arms crossed in scowled disapproval.

"It's my first cigarette of the day," was his defensive answer.

"Well, considering it's five in the morning, I suppose that's a step in the right direction for you," was her dismissive rejection.

"The thousand mile journey begins with the first step," was his lame riposte.

"Spare me!"

Mrs. Cuffington disappeared into the kitchen. Nick took another drag an exhaled in resigned acceptance.

"The only thing more dangerous than a wife's anger, is a wife's disappointment," he mused to himself. He continued to inhale more of both.

Leigh opened the kitchen door and walked towards Nick. She planted an affectionate kiss on his cheek and sat down in a chair facing her husband. She placed a mug of coffee in front of her.

"So?" she asked with genuine concern.

Nick leisurely finished and snuffed his smoke.

"So, what we're dealing with is the deaths of two members of Congress," answered Nick.

"Two?"

Leigh removed her reading glasses and placed them on the table. She sipped from her mug.

"Pray tell, who were they?" the eagerness in the voice betraying her morbid sense curiosity.

"One Congressman Barry Sooner and one Senator William Ryder," he replied with indifference.

"Hmm," mulled Leigh. "I'm not familiar with the name Sooner, but Ryder rings a bell."

Nick's interest was piqued.

"Why Ryder, Leigh?" insisted the Inspector.

"Oh, it's just gossip, honey," was her off-handed explanation.

"Pray tell, what sort of gossip," mimicked Nick.

Mrs. Cuffington flashed Mr. Cuffington the always dreaded marital look. Nick smelled danger. Having already crossed the DMZ twice in ten minutes, he retreated.

"Leigh, I was only trying to be funny. It was my clumsy attempt at humor. If I upset you, I'm sorry."

She studied his face to confirm the veracity of the apology. Satisfied, Leigh continued. "The scuttle-butt is that Senator Ryder enjoys, ah, enjoyed a rather flamboyant social life. Granted, it's only rumors, but they are persistent.

The Inspector did not respond.

"How did they die, Nick?" ventured Leigh.

"Presumably, Sooner of a heart attack or stroke and Ryder of an overdose," he related.

She surveyed his expression.

"But you have your doubts, don't you."

"Leigh, what I have is two dead members of Congress who happened to die on the same night, in the same town; no more, no less. I'll wait for the medical evaluations and proceed from there."

The early morning sun began to grin it's all too warming smile. Nick drained his beer and stood.

"I need some sleep. Are you coming up?" he yawned.

"No, I'm up for the duration. Besides, I've left Henri in the lurch," she admitted.

Henri Nom de Plume was the gumshoe protagonist of her latest fictional endeavor. "Obviously, Nom de Plume needs you more than I."

Nick smiled, kissed Leigh and headed off to bed.

He slept soundly until nearly noon. The lone interruption had been Leigh's whispering something to him that he couldn't remember. After dressing, he went downstairs. Once in the kitchen, he found a note from her, informing him she had gone to some sort of literary book signing and luncheon. He extracted two large water glasses from a cabinet. Putting ice in both, he filled one with water and the other with grapefruit juice. Nick walked to his office. Sitting in front of the computer, he scanned the morning's messages. None were urgent or for that matter, in any way, out of the ordinary. For some inexplicable reason, this disquieted the Inspector Next, he swept the morning's headlines.

"No screamers," he nodded to himself.

Nick then began to peruse D.C.'s major newspapers. The first mention of the prior evening's occurrences appeared on a page three:

"Congressman Barry Sooner collapsed of an apparent heart attack while attending a dinner function. Present condition unknown."

Cuffington continued clicking. It was pretty much the same from the other papers that reported the incident.

Nick finished his water, picked up his juice and moved on to the bloggers. The name of his cyber quest was nowhere to be found. The late, great Senator William Ryder was not riding the information highway.

"The Killer," is keeping that body bag tightly zipped," he concluded.

Cuffington was impressed. His phone toned. It was Leigh.

"Hi honey," her voice overwhelmed by social din.

"I can't hear you," shouted Nick. "Can you find a phone booth?"

Seconds later, Leigh called back. "Can you hear me now?

Nick smiled. "Somewhere, Superman is alive and well," he reassured himself.

"Nick, what I had to tell you, is that Sooner's name came up in conversation! Everyone here is quite certain it was a heart attack," she said with finality. "Ryder's name has not even been mentioned."

"Well, if his name does happen to pop up, can I be assured you will inform me, before telling Non le Plume," jested, Nick.

"Oh, I can't tell Henri anything. He's in jail!" confided Leigh, with feigned secrecy.

"On what charge?" demanded the Inspector.

"Sexual assault," revealed the author.

"Alas, in the end, it's always the overly amorous Frenchman!

Cuffington's house phone caller ID registered an incoming call.

"Little one, I've got to cut."

Killingsworth's call came in at two-thirty p.m. "Nick?" his voice chalked with sleeplessness.

"Pat, what's the latest," requested the Inspector.

"I just got off the phone with Savage. He tells me he'll have both prelims no later than four p.m. I suggest we meet at Metro Morgue at four-thirty."

"I'll be there at four-thirty," confirmed Cuffington.

Chapter Eight

After dropping off Inspector Cuffington, Detective Fuentes drove to her DuPont Circle condominium to catch some sleep. Once inside, she scavenged the always nearly empty refrigerator and retired to the bedroom. Having set the wake-up for eleven-thirty, Fuentes descended into welcomed oblivion.

Maria lived alone. DuPont Circle had not been her first choice for a neighborhood. Upon graduating from Georgetown, she had preferred Adams Morgan, the Hispanic cultural Mecca of D.C. However, mother had insisted upon "The Circle" address for investment reasons. Maria had had little to say in the matter. After all, the condo was mommy's graduation gift. Seven years later mother, as always, had been proven right.

The eleven-thirty a.m. imposition summoned, obnoxiously. Fuentes rose, showered, and dressed. Over coffee, she scanned her messages; responding to a few and deleting the rest.

"Plain vanilla," she concluded.

Out the door, Maria was on her way to grab something to eat.

Adams Morgan was an adjacent neighborhood to DuPont Circle. As she walked down Columbia Road, Fuentes felt at ease. She was home. She opted to lunch at Cabana Village. Although the nite club's opening hour to the public was five p.m., the kitchen was always open to family. Maria entered a side door of the now, dimly lit establishment. She claimed a stool at the first floor bar. The dozen, or so, patrons gathered there, paused to scope out the new arrival and, in familiar recognition, resumed their prior conversations.

An elderly bartender approached.

"Maria," he smiled warmly.

"Hatuey," was her response to his unasked question.

The man returned with a chilled bottle of beer and placed it in front of Maria, sans glass.

"Comida?" he inquired.

"Si"

The man scurried off to the cocina to order that afternoon's special.

Maria took a sip and reached for a copy of Granma, Cuba's official newspaper. Everyone in the place knew Maria's chosen profession. They also knew she was a Fuentes. That, in their minds, made her one of them, before it made her a cop.

Her meal arrived. She ate leisurely, and continued to read the paper. Intermittently, acquaintances stopped to say hello and make small talk.

Maria's visit to Cabana Village had been purposeful. Her intent was street noise. If anyone present in that room knew of anything related to the previous night's events that might prove beneficial to both parties concerned, they would be forthcoming. She finished lunch and another Hatuey; Nada. She paid the bill and left.

On the walk back to her condo, the Smartass phone summoned.

"Nick" she answered.

"Pick me up at Foggy Bottom, four p.m." He clicked off.

Maria was neither surprised, nor offended, by the Inspector's terse phone call. She had served as his lead Detective for nearly one year. Initially, Fuentes had attributed Cuffington's avoidance of electronic communications to his disdain for the "intrusion upon the human condition," as he phrased it. However, as time passed, she was more convinced it had something to do with his abrupt transfer from the N.Y.P.D to Metro seven years earlier; a relocation that not even the influential Fuentes family had the resources to explain.

Chapter Nine

Fuentes pulled to a stop in front of the Cuffington home at four p.m. She idled for several minutes and then shut the car off. Walking to the side of the house, she entered the backyard and made her way to the patio. Nick was seated at the table, pecking away at a laptop.

"Nick, are you ready?" she asked peering over his shoulder.

"Anything useful from Salsa Strip," he inquired, without looking up.

"Dick," was her admission. "You come up with anything?"

"Less," was the answer, as he shut down the P.C., stood up, and smiled at the Detective. "We're meeting Killingsworth at Savage's office to review the good doctor's prelims."

"Did he tell you anything else?"

"Just that we're meeting at four-thirty," shrugged Cuffington.

They walked around the side of the house towards Fuentes' car.

"Nick, aren't you going to shut the garage door?

"Hell, no! That's my home security system. Who's going to leave an empty house with the garage door wide open? Besides, it drives Leigh nuts.

Maria shook her head in dubious disagreement.

They climbed into Fuentes' cruiser and headed across town towards Metro Morgue.

"Nick, explain to me, again. Why is Metro even involved in these two deaths? It's clearly, Capitol Police's domain. The fact Killingsworth contacted us, in the first place, is really bothering me.

"I thought we already covered this, Detective," was Cuffington's dismissal.

"Something just doesn't add-up, Inspector," remonstrated Fuentes.

"Maria, this is Washington D.C. More times than not, the numbers never add-up."

Fuentes turned onto Massachusetts Avenue and trolled for an available parking space. Finding none, she slipped into a "No Parking Zone" in front of Metro Morgue. Getting out of the car, Maria slapped a parking violation summons under the windshield wiper.

"That should keep them unemployed for a while," noted the Inspector, with admiration.

Standing in front of Metro Morgue's main entrance was Captain Killingsworth and Lieutenant Ginger Snapp. Cuffington appreciated the Captain's professional courtesy of waiting for their arrival, before entering the building.

"Nick, Detective, glad you could make the party," greeted the Captain.

"We've never been invited to attend a joint session of Congress. The Detective and I wouldn't have missed it for the world," replied a sardonic Cuffington.

The four officers entered the building. They were immediately greeted by security. Two guards were posted. One operated the X-Ray conveyor belt, the other monitored the walk-through scanner. Cuffington and Killingsworth complied with the mandates, which included removing their fire arms. Ginger Snapp readily followed their examples, and fluttered through the obligatory process. Fuentes was more defiant.

"What are you going to do? Scan my gun, see that's it's loaded and then give it back to me?" demanded the Detective.

"The rules is the rules, honey," droned the female security guard, snapping her chewing gum and bulging out of her blues.

"Estupidez!"

After non-verbal tongue lashing from the Inspector, Fuentes acquiesced.

The people behind the reception desk motioned them to the elevators without further incident. The Office of the Chief Medical Examiner was located at the far end of the top floor. Cuffington opened the O.C.M.E. door and entered the reception area. The other three followed. A woman was seated at the front desk. Cuffington had met her on several prior occasions.

Betty Ann Norge was around forty. Her brunette hair was streaked with gray and pulled tightly in a ponytail. She wore thickly lensed tortoise shell glasses. Her frame was ample. The florid face was oval and distinguished only by its simplicity.

"Hi Betty Ann, is the Doc ready to see us?

"No Inspector, he's still chilling in his man grave!" "HAA HEE, HAA HEE"

Betty Ann had abruptly convulsed into a bray of uncontrollable, self-appreciative laughter.

"Get it?" she gasped, between her spasms of guffaw. "Grave, Cave?"

"The very first time, Betty Ann," admitted Cuffington. "You're the same old card you've always been!"

"HAA HEE!"

Betty Ann wiped the tears of laughter from her mascara strewn face, composed herself, and picked up the phone.

"Doc, they're here." She listened in silence. Betty Ann looked at Cuffington.

"He wants to know if you guys want to meet him downstairs," informed Betty Ann.

Killingsworth looked at Nick, shaking his head.

"Out of the question"

Cuffington , suppressed his smile.

"Betty Ann, tell him we'll be waiting in his office," was the Inspector's decision.

"Doc, they want to wait up here. Okay, I'll tell them. Listen, Doc, don't forget to turn on the lights before you leave." She put down the phone.

"He'll be up in ten. C'mon, I'll show you in."

Betty Ann rose from her desk and lumbered them into Savage's office.

"Make yourselves comfortable," she insisted.

Betty Ann Norge closed the door behind her. The office was semi-dark; its only illumination emanating from a green shaded banker's lamp perched on the Doctor's desk. The room was small and windowless. On the right side wall stood a stuffed bookcase. On the left side, was sofa and coffee table. The most curious aspect of the room, however, was the shelves mounted behind the Doctor's desk. Each shelf supported glass canisters that contained, what appeared to be internal human body organs, suspended in a translucent liquid. The four officers stood awkwardly in the center of the office. Cuffington was the first to speak.

"Pat, I can't believe a big, bad, former Secret Service agent gets spooked by a little old post-mortem lab."

He was smiling.

"Screw you, Cuffington! It's not the lab, it's the guy. He gives me the yips. I'll be the first to admit it."

With that, the office's door opened. The hallway's light elucidated a silhouette. The shadow stepped forward.

"Why are we standing in the dark?"

The voice was a crisp staccato, tinged with an Eastern European dialect. The overhead lights snapped on.

"There, now isn't that more comfortable?"

Doctor Seymour Savage was a diminutive man. He stood five feet-five inches tall. His frame was thin. The head was bald. The eyes were dark and deeply set, accenting a hawkish nose. The goatee was a black-forest. But, it was his teeth that riveted one's attention. They appeared to be oddly predatory; not quite Halloween costume material, but an unsettling close facsimile. Savage was wearing a white lab coat. Surgical fly glasses sat atop his head. He was holding a glass canister in one hand. He had neglected to remove his neoprene gloves.

The Doctor marched past his appointed guests to the shelves behind his desk. With deliberate care, he arranged the newest addition to his collection, just so. Satisfied, he sat down behind his desk and pressed the intercom button.

"Are my papers prepared?"

"Yes," responded the voice.

The door opened, and Betty Ann proceeded to Savage's desk. She handed him a folder and turned to leave. She looked at Cuffington, and winked.

"Grave, cave," she muttered, to herself.

The door, once again, closed behind her.

Savage flipped through his notes.

"What's the bottom line, Doc?" implored the Inspector.

Savage finished scanning his papers, set them to the side, and fixed his stare at Cuffington.

"Neither individual died of natural causes," was the grim assessment.

"So, you mean they were poisoned?" asked a now rattled Killingsworth.

"I mean, that their central nervous systems ingested the same toxin and the result was death in both cases," responded the Doctor.

"So they were poisoned?" persisted Killingsworth. "

"I did not detect the scent of bitter almond," was Savage's cryptic answer.

The Doctor's allusion referenced the ability of some professionals to pick up the smell of cyanide when emitted from a corpse.

"So, you don't know what the hell killed them, do you?" scoffed Killingsworth.

"Captain, I am a pathologist, not a toxicologist," lectured the Doctor. "I have already had samples sent to those better equipped to handle the identification process. Besides, the name of the substance should be of secondary concern," advised the medical professional.

36

"And why is that, Doctor?" interjected Cuffington.

"Whatever the substance, it is a nasty little devil, indeed! Once ingested, I estimate it takes no more than fifteen minutes to spin its lethal web. Actually, the microbe is quite fascinating; no outward signs of internal bodily distress, until death.

"But why shouldn't we care about identifying the name of the poison, Mr. Doctor?" fluttered Lieutenant Ginger Snapp.

"Because, we've got two different scumbag killers on our hands!" was Fuentes' succinct conclusion.

"Precisely," concurred the Doctor, approvingly.

Savage examined Fuentes, as if noticing her presence for the first time.

"Impressive. I am rarely impressed. Is she one of yours, Inspector?" probed the Doctor.

"Her name is Lieutenant Maria Fuentes, and yes, she's with Metro," confirmed Cuffington.

"I shall keep her name in mind," noted Savage.

Instinctively, Fuentes made an almost imperceptible move towards her recently returned loaded firearm.

A low, slow, atavistic wail of despair escaped the lungs of Captain Patrick Killingsworth. His knees buckled, as he floundered for a desk chair, in which to collapse. His suddenly wan face glistened with the perspiration of desperation. He looked, skyward.

"Sweet Jesus, Joseph, and Mary!"

The enormity of the implication had, literally, staggered the big fellow.

Immediately, Cuffington turned to face the Doctor.

His demeanor had changed. No longer a passive listener of facts, he had assumed the role of a steel hardened Washington D.C. law enforcement professional.

"How long can you keep these findings buried? " was the Inspector's first question.

Doctor Seymour Savage, appreciating the gravitas in Cuffington's voice, continued with a succinct explanation.

"Alas, Inspector, Metro Morgue is a privately owned enterprise. As such, we do not enjoy the same latitude in the interpretation of Federal Regulation, so well enforced by our governmental counterparts."

"Cut to the chase, Savage!" demanded Cuffington.

The good Doctor carried forth.

"By federal mandate, any and all autopsies performed during a twenty-four hour cycle must be duly logged prior to the ensuing cycle," explained the Doctor.

"Meaning what?" implored Cuffington.

"Meaning that, at the stroke of mid-night, Cinderella's carriage turns back into a pumpkin; or, in this case, a socio-political nightmare."

Chapter Ten

The four law enforcement officers stood on the sidewalk, in front of Metro Morgue. Captain Patrick Killingsworth was still visibly unnerved by Savage's autopsy revelations. Lieutenant Ginger Snapp appeared to be oblivious to her Captain's sense of imminent calamity. Detective Fuentes maintained a veneer of self-absorbed retrospection. And Cuffington, always stoic, took command.

"Pat, obviously, we have to talk. I don't think that either of our offices would be appropriate, right now. There's a place one block down. C'mon, I'm buying." It was more dictum than invitation.

They entered a tavern and claimed a stake in a cushioned booth in a room just outside the establishment's main bar. Brewster's was a typical D.C. bistro; an equal complement of Metrocats and Bureaucrats. The place was packed. The noise level was tolerable. A young cosmopolitan waiter accosted their booth.

"Would you care to see my specials?" he inquired, eagerly.

"Not this evening," grumbled Killingsworth.

"Maria, what are you drinking," asked Cuffington.

"Hatuey"

"Oh, I'm sorry princess, we don't carry that particular brand of beer," lamented waiter boy.

"Gringo"

Cuffington hastily intervened.

"The lady and I shall have a couple of Buds."

"And what can I get for you, madam?" asked the waiter.

Ginger Snapp looked at Killingsworth.

"Captain, are we officially off duty?" she fluttered.

"Quite off duty, Lieutenant," was his dire assessment.

"In that case, I'll have a white Zin," as her shoulders giggled.

"Jameson," ordered the Captain. "Make that both brothers!"

"Ooh, party carnivore!" smiled the server.

Killingsworth's glower prompted the young man into a hasty disappearance.

"When did you first know, Pat!" was the Inspector's unfettered demand.

The Captain stared directly into Cuffington's eyes.

"If you're question is when did I know with absolute certainty, it was same time you found out; at Savage's office," was his avowal.

"If you had such strong suspicions, why did you feel compelled to contact me in the first place?" was Nick's next inquiry.

Fuentes broke in.

"To cover his in big time troubled ass!"

Killingsworth stared at Fuentes with silent, oblique indifference.

Despite her best effort, Maria found herself uncharacteristically ill at ease under the Captain's gaze.

The waiter returned with the drinks. He served them in silence and departed.

Killingsworth continued.

"You're mistaken, Detective, not even the highly regarded Inspector, here, could in any way help cover my ass, as you so eloquently phrased it, given the magnitude of what we are now facing."

Killingsworth took a long deliberate pull from his glass and resumed.

"The media maelstrom that is about to consume this town is going chew up far more important asses than mine!"

The Captain drained his cocktail and waved the emptied glass as if it were a dinner table bell. Their waiter reappeared.

"Hey party mule, let's do this again," grinned Killingsworth.

The young man did not make eye contact. He simply bowed, then hurried off to comply with the request.

"To answer your question Nick, I called to get you involved as soon as possible" explained Killingsworth. "I wanted you in on the ground floor."

"And how do I know this is the ground floor, Pat?"

"What, do you think I'm withholding something from you? That I've got information I'm not sharing with you? Christ, you don't know how much I wish I was!"

Their server arrived with the Captain's refill and hovered.

Inspector Cuffington glanced at Detective Fuentes.

"Maria, you okay?"

"Yes."

"Ginger would you care for another?"

"Oh, no, I'm already a little lightheaded," she fluttered.

'I'll say," corroborated Fuentes.

"I'll have one more," requested the Inspector. The waiter vanished.

"Look Nick, all I've got is what you now have. Two members of Congress killed on the same night, in the same town around the same time. The type of poison used in both murders identical and, at this point, unidentifiable. And, if Doctor Psycho and Detective Pit Bull, here, are right, two different assailants!"

The waiter returned with Cuffington's beer and left.

Inspector Cuffington scrutinized the face of Captain Killingsworth with instinctive doubts.

"Look Nick," he beseeched. "I've been swimming alone with the sharks most of my life. But this thing, I mean the possibilities are overwhelming! I know I need an ally; someone I can count on regardless of how big this monster turns out to be!"

"Who else knows everything the four of us seated here right now know?" queried Cuffington.

"To the best of my knowledge, just Savage," replied Killingsworth.

Nick sipped his beer as he analyzed the situation.

The Captain continued.

"I still have some pull with the Service. However, after that it's a crap shoot. Once the cavalries get involved, who knows? F.B.I., N.S.A., C.I.A. this thing could easily turn into a boiling pot of alphabet soup that spills over the stove and onto both floors of Congress" shuddered Killingsworth.

"And that would not be mmm, mmm, good, now would it Patrick!" smiled Cuffington.

"Hell, no!" agreed a looser Killingsworth.

Simultaneously, both men broke into laughter.

"You know what they say, if you can't stand the heat," began a still laughing Cuffington.

"Get the hell out of the House and Senate," finished a nearly choking Killingsworth.

Both men raised their glasses and toasted. Once again, the two women watched their male counterparts and looked at each other in silence. Neither could discern anything, at all, humorous about the situation, at hand. Furthermore, neither had any interest in trying to understand the puerile male sense of humor. Nonetheless, Inspector Nick Cuffington and Captain Patrick Killingsworth were now comrades in arms.

Chapter Eleven

Killingsworth stared across the booth's counter at Cuffington.

"How do you think we should proceed from here?" ventured the Captain.

"I know where I'm going to proceed," announced Fuentes, as she stood up.

"I'll go with you, Maria," chimed Ginger Snapp.

The men rose to allow egress.

Reseated, the Inspector spoke.

"I think we should go on offense," was Cuffington's conclusion.

"Exactly, what do you mean by offense, Nick?" questioned Killingsworth.

"Assuming the public reaction we both anticipate, I think a joint news conference should be scheduled as soon as possible."

"And tell them what Nick?" demanded the Captain. "That we have absolutely no idea what the hell just went down?"

"No, we'll tell them that Capitol and Metro are working jointly and treating the two incidents as one investigation," explained Cuffington.

"And when the question of "suspect" rears its ugly head, what is our answer going to be?"

Killingsworth studied the Inspector's impassive face, anxiously awaiting his decision.

"That we believe the deaths to be related; and that the assailant is still within our jurisdiction."

"Whoa!"

Killingsworth motioned his hands as if an athlete requesting timeout.

"Assailant, Nick, we know that's not the case," objected the Captain.

"All we know is that Savage and Fuentes presume there to be more than one killer; no more, no less," countered Cuffington.

"Damn it, Nick, you know, as well as I do, they're right," insisted Killingsworth. "Which means, that if we follow your proposed course of action, ultimately, we're going to be nailed for obstruction!" fumed the Captain.

Before Cuffington could respond, Fuentes and Ginger Snapp returned to the table. Both men slid over to accommodate their respective associate.

"Have you two Sherlocks solved the crimes?" fluttered Lieutenant Ginger Snapp.

"No, lamented Killingsworth. Truth be known, the Inspector here, is plotting another one."

"Oh," was the Lieutenant's vacuous reply.

Fuentes remained silent.

"Okay Pat, I'll defer. You take the lead on this one. And, when the question of suspects rears its ugly head, answer with the exact words you fed me when we first sat down," conceded Cuffington.

"Refresh my memory, Inspector. What exactly were those words?" demanded an obviously annoyed Captain.

"That all you have are two members of Congress killed on the same night, in the same town, around the same time. The type of poison used in both murders is the same, and at this point, unidentifiable. Oh, and yes, dispensed by two different assassins."

Cuffington motioned the waiter for a check.

The four officers stood on the sidewalk in front of Brewster's.

"Listen Nick, I'll give what you said some thought," offered a somewhat subdued Killingsworth. "I'll sleep on it," he promised.

"I know you will, Pat. Good night Ginger," were the Inspector's parting words.

Cuffington and Fuentes were in their vehicle and headed towards Foggy Bottom.

"Do you mind telling me what that was all about?" hazarded Fuentes.

"Simply a difference in perspective as to the navigation of heretofore unchartered waters, Detective."

"Well, thank you, Nick. That was illuminating," dismissed the facetious Detective.

The Inspector turned towards his Detective.

"Essentially, Captain Killingsworth feels it's in everyone's best interest to handle the entire matter strictly by the book," clarified Cuffington.

"And you don't?" shrugged Fuentes.

"Maria, I, for one, don't believe the book has yet been written about what is currently taking place here in Washington D.C.," confided Cuffington.

"Now, *I'm* getting the yips," smiled Fuentes.

"Well, if it's any comfort to you, I rather doubt we are going to be significantly involved in these investigations," revealed the Inspector.

"And why is that?"

"Because my recommended course of action unsettled Killingsworth more than the actual situation he is facing," concluded the Inspector.

Fuentes pulled to a stop in front of the Cuffington's residence.

"So?"

Maria looked at the Inspector for a directive.

"So, it's nearly eight in the evening. Why don't you take some down time?"

Fuentes hesitated.

"Look Detective, technically, we have no jurisdiction over the events that have taken place. The protection of members of Congress and their families is the primary domain of U.S. Capitol Police."

"And that's, that?" she asked with disappointment.

"No. Between now and the next time we touch bases, I would like you to research the political career of Congressman Barry Sooner," instructed the Inspector.

Cuffington got out of the car. He turned to Maria before closing the door.

"Sooner was a member of the House for nearly twenty-five years; so I am quite certain you will have a long but entertaining voyage. In particular, I want you to focus on any links that might relate him to Senator William Ryder either directly or indirectly involving proposed joint legislation."

"So, you're not going to play it by the book, are you, Inspector?" she smiled.

"As I said earlier, Detective, that book is being written as we speak."

Chapter Twelve

Nick entered the house through a side door. The kitchen's only light was the stove's overhead He walked to Leigh's library. Its door was slightly ajar, emitting lamp light. He tapped twice on the door.

"Come in, Nick"

Leigh's back was to him.

She was seated at her desk, which faced the room's only window. Mrs. Cuffington was self-absorbingly typing at the computer's keyboard.

Nick approached from behind and kissed his wife affectionately on the neck.

"Is it still safe to walk the streets of Washington D.C.?" she asked without looking up.

"Only if you're not a member of Congress," was his assessed reply.

"Well that does sound like a step in the right direction."

Leigh held up an empty wine glass. Nick took the glass and started towards the door.

"I'll be outside"

He re-entered the kitchen and opened the refrigerator, extracted a bottle of white and a beer and headed for the patio. Nick took a seat at the table and lit a cigarette.

Leigh flowed onto the patio and wrapped her arms around his shoulders.

"Are you okay?" was her first question.

"Never better," was his Spartan response." My concern is for Inspector Nom de Plume. Have you bailed him out of jail?"

"Yes"

"Is he innocent or guilty of such an egregious crime?"

"I haven't decided," was her shrouded answer. She kissed Nick and sat down. He poured her some wine.

"So Nick, what's the story with Congressman Sooner and Senator Ryder?" was her feigned, not at all interested, dying to know question.

"They were both murdered," was his terse revelation.

"No, I'm serious Nick."

"So am I."

Leigh Cuffington sat in stunned silence.

The Inspector filled the void of her unspoken shock.

"They were both poisoned. The toxin has not yet been identified. Most importantly, they were killed by different individuals," was his dire summation.

"My God, do you have any idea how all of Washington D.C. is going to react to that news?" she asked in a near whisper.

"No dear, I don't. Why don't you fill in the lines for me," was his sarcastic rejoinder.

"Nick, I didn't mean it like . . ."

The front door bell rang.

"Who in the world can that be at this hour?" wondered Leigh.

Nick stood up.

"I ordered a pie. I'll be right back."

Moments later he returned armed with a pizza box and paper products.

"What kind did you get?"

"Half plain, half garbage."

"Yuck!"

Leigh made a face of distaste.

"I've never understood your fascination with house specials," was her comment, as she opened the box to claim a slice of plain.

They munched in silence. Leigh spoke first.

"Listen Nick, I didn't mean to imply, in any way, that you are not completely aware of the impact this bombshell is going to have on the city; city, hell, the entire country! It's just that, well, it's just that the whole damn notion is so mind-blowing!" exclaimed Leigh.

"It is a bit out of the ordinary," admitted Cuffington.

"So, what are you planning to do?"

Cuffington looked at his wife and smiled.

"I'm planning on eating more garbage" He hoisted another slice.

"Nick, you know exactly what I am asking."

"Let me put your mind at ease, little one. I have no official involvement in these pending investigations" Nick informed her.

"And that's supposed to make me feel all warm and fuzzy?" she asked in disbelief.

"No. It's to let you know that this entire matter is the jurisdiction of U.S. Capitol Police," was the non-pulsed response.

"So why the hell did Killingsworth contact you to begin with?" was her objective inquiry.

"As it turns out, it was simply to get my perspective on the situation. I was merely a U.N. observer; there to witness but not to act."

"I take it he did not like what you had to say" she surmised.

"No, he did not," confirmed the Inspector.

"And what is your perspective, Nick?" she pressed.

"That the situation, at hand, mandates a somewhat unorthodox approach," he stated with conviction.

"You mean an approach that conveniently ignores the rule of law!" Leigh scathed.

"Something along those lines," he stated with conviction.

"My estimation of Captain Killingsworth has just risen immeasurably," decided Mrs. Cuffington.

"Well I'm gladdened by the fact he, at least, gives you a warm and fuzzy feeling, dear."

Leigh shook her head in annoyance.

"I keep forgetting! To ask the great Inspector Cuffington to play within the rules is simply too outlandish a request to hope for!" she sneered.

"This is Washington D.C. If you play by the rules here, you're usually attending a party of one. The best you can hope for is the short end of the stick. And, as a general rule, I know exactly where, that stick, more times than not, ends up."

Nick stood, gathered the remnants of their meal and headed for the kitchen door.

"You know Nick, if you'd learned to play by the rules, we might still be living in New York."

The Inspector did not respond.

Chapter Thirteen

The first mention of the two Congressional murders hit the Net around two a.m. the following morning. Traveling at 4G speed, the news rapidly morphed into a monstrous cyber mushroom cloud rising over a shell-shocked Washington D.C. Cuffington's phone toned a little after four a.m. The now awakened Inspector pawed for its location on the night table.

"Yes?"

"Nick, is that you?"

"Yes"

"It's Pat, did I wake you?"

"Yes!"

"We've got to talk!" implored Killingsworth.

"What are we doing now?"

"I mean in person."

"Where are you now, Pat?" as he sat up and swung his legs out of bed.

"Fifteen minutes from Foggy Bottom."

"Give me thirty," requested the Inspector.

Cuffington hit off, and then speed dial.

"Hi Nick"

Fuentes' voice was clear as a bell. It was if, in lieu of sleep, she opted to stay up, waiting for his phone call.

"Be at my place, in thirty minutes."

"I'm on my way!"

Leigh slid out of bed and into a bathrobe.

"I hear we have company arriving," she yawned.

"Yes, we do," confirmed Nick.

"I'll go downstairs and start the coffee."

Nick headed towards the bathroom to shower.

"Mr. Cuffington, may I tell you something?"

Leigh approached Nick and kissed him.

"I love you very much."

"In spite of the fact we no longer live in New York?" he smiled.

"In spite of even that"

Once in the kitchen, Leigh turned on the counter television and found her cable news station.

Cuffington shaved, showered, and dressed. He descended the stairs and entered the kitchen. The aroma of strong java permeated the room.

"I'm assuming no coffee for the Inspector."

"Caffeine is the Devil's brew," contended Cuffington.

"That's right; tar, carbon monoxide and nicotine are the only true assurances of entering the Pearly Gates," agreed Leigh.

"Be still woman. You're making far too much sense, far too early in the morning," he smiled. "We have some pizza left, maybe I should throw it into the oven," suggested Nick.

"I think not," objected Leigh. "My zucchini cake will be far more appropriate. Besides, these poor bastards are going to get their fill of garbage by the end this day," she reasoned.

"Touché!" was Nick's fervent acknowledgement.

Headlights streamed through the house's front windows.

"Our guests have arrived," observed Nick. "I'll greet them at the front door

"I'll go with you."

Detective Fuentes pulled to a stop and got out of her obviously unmarked cruiser.

Immediately, a second car sped into the driveway and screeched to a halt. Captain Pat Killingsworth clamored out of the driver's side door. The passenger door opened and Lieutenant Ginger Snapp stepped out.

"He did sleep on it," mused the Inspector.

"What did you say, Nick?"

"Nothing dear, nothing at all"

Lieutenant Fuentes was surprised, but not shocked by the presence of U.S. Capitol officers.

"Good morning Captain, Lieutenant," was Fuentes' stiffly formal greeting.

"Detective," was Killingsworth equally crisp response.

Nick opened the front door.

"Come on in," beckoned Cuffington.

The three officers entered the foyer. Nick handled the introductions.

"Leigh, you remember Captain Pat Killingsworth," he prompted.

"Of course, how are you Captain?" greeted the hostess.

"I've been better," admitted the Captain.

"Leigh, this is Lieutenant Ginger Snapp," continued Nick.

"A pleasure to meet you, Lieutenant," beamed Mrs. Cuffington.

"And, of course, you already know this reprobate," Nick finished, smiling at Fuentes.

"The only reprobate I recognize in this room is you, Inspector,"she bantered. "I have coffee waiting in the kitchen. Please, follow me."

Once in the kitchen, Leigh proceeded to pour coffee into ceramic mugs.

"There is milk and sweeteners on the center aisle" she motioned.

Killingsworth stared at Cuffington.

"Nick, we have to talk."

Under the glare of the kitchen lights, the Captain looked haggard. Sleepless and, at odds with himself, Patrick Killingsworth was a dispirited man who had obviously been "spiritually" attempting to remedy the unfortunate circumstances that he was now being forced to address.

"I'm all ears, Pat," prodded Cuffington.

The Captain surveyed the three women in the room uncomfortably.

"It's rather sensitive, Inspector," cued Killingsworth.

Cuffington stood motionlessly staring at the Captain.

The kitchen fell into awkward silence.

Leigh Cuffington, forever, her husband's ambassador to the rest of the world, quickly tried to bridge the gulf between Nick's resentment and Killingsworth's , uneasiness about witnesses.

"Nick, why don't you and Captain Killingsworth go outside and chat on the patio?

"That's a Capitol idea!" agreed Lieutenant Ginger Snapp.

The Inspector looked long and hard at the Captain.

"Pat, both my wife and my Ranking Detective know everything I know about the situation, currently at hand. Furthermore, if I was to find myself officially involved in any aspect of the impending investigations, I would continue to keep both my wife and my Ranking Detective apprised of everything. Therefore, unless Lieutenant Ginger Snapp lacks the required U.S. Capitol security clearance level, I would suggest you either start talking the talk or walking the walk."

Killingsworth studied the countenance of Inspector Nick Cuffington. Finally, he picked up his coffee mug, and with anguished resolve slumped into a chair at the kitchen table. He looked at Mrs. Cuffington.

For the first time since his arrival, the Captain smiled.

"Leigh, might you have a different type of sweetener for the coffee, one that might chase the clarity from the caffeine?"

"That happens to be Nick's particular area of expertise," smiled Mrs. Cuffington with clenched teeth.

"I'll see what I can come up with," volunteered Nick as he disappeared into the den.

Returning, he placed an unopened bottle of Tullamore Dew in front of Killingsworth. The Captain appraised the bottle with admiration.

54

"During all my years of service, in Washington D.C., I never realized Foggy Bottom was so uptown when it comes to fine Irish Whisky!" confided the impressed Captain.

"Only when your presence demands it's need," smiled the Inspector.

Chapter Fourteen

Killingsworth absently stirred the new contents of his coffee mug. At last, he looked up and said to no one in particular:

"To describe the initial blowback from this nightmare as extreme would be doing the monster a disservice. I would more accurately describe it as a savagely surreal predator."

The Captain took a sip of Irish. He focused his gaze on Cuffington.

"I've already gotten the call."

Nick understood, immediately, what the call was and who had placed it. When Captain Killingsworth made his transfer from the Secret Service to U.S. Capitol Police, the official explanation had been "to continue active field service." Inspector Cuffington had come to learn that such was not the case. As it turned out, while commanding a Secret Service detail in South America, it had come to light that certain agents of that unit had conducted themselves in a "less than professional manner" with some of the local working girls. Because there was no evidence that Killingsworth himself had acted improperly and in consideration of a long and distinguished career with the Service, the transfer was expedited. And although it was true that he reported directly to the Chief of U.S. Capitol Police, Killingsworth was, nonetheless, on a very, very, short leash.

"So, what did the Chief have to say, Pat?" challenged Nick.

Killingsworth glanced at the women.

"I don't think I shall repeat it, verbatim. Let me just say, he is none too happy about working the graveyard shift."

Killingsworth drained his mug.

"May I get you more coffee, Captain?' offered Mrs. Cuffington.

"Yes. Thank you, Leigh."

"Well, from where I'm seated Pat, this is obviously a strictly Capitol Police affair," concluded the Inspector.

"Yes, it is," lamented Killingsworth.

Leigh returned with a fresh mug of coffee. Killingsworth returned to the Tullamore Dew.

"Listen, Nick, I've been giving some thought to the approach you outlined last evening," confessed Killingsworth.

Leigh Cuffington winced. She began to busy herself around the kitchen, while parsing his every syllable.

"I knew the initial reaction to the deaths of two members of Congress, occurring on the same night, was going to be intense. However, I underestimated the speed at which, it would become public realization that both members of Congress were murdered," confessed the Captain. He continued.

"I now agree, that if it becomes known both Sooner and Ryder were assassinated by different assailants, it would transform an already out of control situation into Armageddon. My God, the very fabric of Washington D.C. would be torn asunder!"

Cuffington digested both the Captain's words and his appearance. Clearly, Killingsworth was emotionally over-extended.

"The fabric of Washington D.C. has been fraying for quite some time," noted the Inspector. "Patrick, you and I both know that."

Captain Patrick "Killer" Killingsworth looked sheepishly at Cuffington.

"Yes, that's true. But Nick, why does the Mask of the Clown have to be ripped from its face on my watch! he bemoaned." "I've got exactly three years, two months, and one week standing between me and full pension and lifetime medical benefits! Nick, that's all I've got, man!" wailed the Captain.

"That's not all you have," fluttered Ginger Snapp.

Killingsworth gazed upon his Lieutenant. He drained the remainder of the contents in his mug.

"More coffee, Captain," asked Mrs. Cuffington.

"No thank you, Leigh. I've chosen to forsake protocol."

He poured the Tullamore.

"Pat, what exactly what are you saying?" pressed Cuffington.

"I'm saying that your law enforcement instincts are still intact," replied Killingsworth. "I'm saying that we should handle this thing, in the manner you suggested from the very beginning," sighed the Captain.

The heretofore silent Detective Fuentes erupted.

"We?" she spat with venom. "Don't you mean Metro, Captain? Don't you mean the local yokels are the ones you expect to enter this mess and suffer its consequences by Washington D.C. execution?" hissed Maria.

Cuffington turned his undivided attention to his Detective. He said nothing. Fuentes had never before seen such an expression on the Inspector's face. It was placid and totally devoid of emotion. But the eyes, the eyes were riveted upon her with an indifferent ruthlessness; as though, calculating their next decision. Inexplicably, Maria's mind raced to Cuffington's unexplained New York past. She fell into an acquiescent silence. Killingsworth shifted, uncomfortably in his chair.

"Listen to me Nick, I'm not here to hang anything on you or yours," acknowledging both Leigh and Maria. "I'm here to tell you I don't think I'm up to tackling this monster by myself. I'm running damn scared, and man enough to admit it!"

"How much does Chief O'Toole know, Pat?" began Cuffington.

O'Toole was the Chief of the United States Capitol Police.

"Only that we're meeting later this morning to review my preliminary findings," revealed the Captain.

"And, what are those findings, Pat?" continued Cuffington.

"He is unaware of certain material details regarding the homicides, if that's your question Nick," attested the Captain.

"What time is your meeting with O'Toole?" pursued the Inspector.

"High Noon, my man!" chortled the Captain. "You know, not even the worst of fictioneers could come up with such campy timing," grinned Killingsworth.

"Oh, Patrick, you might very well be surprised," smiled Nick, as he tossed an affectionate wink towards Leigh.

In spite of, herself, and the menacing circumstances, Mrs. Cuffington began to smile.

"What time is it now, Pat?" tested Cuffington.

The Captain navigated his wrist watch.

"A little past six am, give or take, a tick or tock," concluded Killingsworth.

"Pat, you will hear from me no later than nine am," committed Cuffington.

The Inspector stood up. Meeting adjourned.

"Lieutenant Snapp, I do not want the Captain driving this morning. Is that clear, Ginger?" directed the Inspector.

"Yes sir, quite clear, sir," was the Lieutenant's crisp comply.

"Leigh, why don't you point our guests homeward," suggested Nick.

"Of course," the hostess replied.

"You know, Ginger, it was so nice to meet you. I wish the occasion had been a more pleasant one," Leigh's voice trailed off, as the trio disappeared into the foyer.

Detective Fuentes stood in the middle of the kitchen staring at Cuffington.

"So?" she asked with suspicious resignation.

"So, what is your primal question, Detective?" was the Inspector's cut to the chase non-answer.

"Are you going to get us entangled in Killingsworth's career ender, she demanded."

"Inevitably, Capitol's current dilemma is officially going to become Metro's future dilemma. Therefore, our involvement is merely a question of timing," deduced Cuffington.

"I still can't shake the feeling that Killingsworth is, in some way, trying to set you up, Nick," worried Fuentes.

Cuffington's expression softened.

"I don't think so Maria, not in this case. I do believe he's legitimately running scared. Besides, he's on the other side of the mountain, career wise. His D.C. big game hunting days are behind him. No, I think he's simply looking to protect and preserve that, which he feels his rightfully his," conjectured the Inspector.

"We'll see," was her wary evaluation.

"Why don't you go home and get some sleep. I'll call you when I have decided the proper course of our direction," urged Nick.

"I think I will."

She began to walk out of the kitchen.

"Maria," summoned the Inspector.

She stopped and turned.

"Whenever you find yourself embroiled in a conversation like the one that took place this morning, never let anyone in the room know what you are actually thinking. That way, you will always leave yourself more options, and less likely to find yourself in front of a Washington D.C. firing squad," admonished Cuffington.

"I'll keep that in mind," Inspector.

Fuentes turned, and left the room. She exchanged brief pleasantries with Mrs. Cuffington. The Detective departed for home.

Nick pulled out two glasses from a cabinet. Filling both with ice, he poured water into one and grapefruit juice into the other. He made his way into the early light of the patio. Several minutes later, Leigh appeared and sat down next to him. She was clutching a coffee mug.

"Well, that was the strangest coffee klatch I've ever attended ," she said, shaking her head.

"Now, you have a clearer understanding of why I never touch the stuff," explained Nick.

"So, what do you make of all this, Inspector Cuffington?"

She sipped her coffee.

"It's too soon to even hazard a guess," he concluded.

"How are you going to deal with Killingsworth," she wanted to know.

"I don't think I've left myself much choice, given the fact it was I who initially introduced the possibility of obfuscating material evidence," he concluded.

"Nick, I owe you an apology. My crack about New York was way out of line. I'm sorry.

"To be honest with you Leigh, I haven't had a chance to give it a second thought. However, I do appreciate your ongoing concern for my, oh so fragile emotional psyche."

Cuffington smiled, and put his arm around his wife.

"If it's any consolation, Mrs. Cuffington, if my hunch is right, we are experiencing only Act I of a rather long play, he revealed.

"Well, thank you, Nick for that bit of uplifting insight. How in the world would I ever survive without your eternally optimistic outlook on the human condition?" she jested.

"In this town, you probably wouldn't."

The Inspector was no longer smiling.

Chapter Fifteen

Cuffington phoned Captain Killingsworth at eight-thirty that morning.

"Pat, where's your meeting with Chief O'Toole scheduled to take place this noon?"

"United States Capitol Police headquarters," he replied. "Nick, does this mean you are officially in?"

"Yes Pat, I'm officially in the game," pledged the Inspector. "Who else is slated to be in attendance?"

"Just the Chief and myself, that's it," confided Killingsworth. "And now, you," he added.

"Any objection if I invite another guest," tested Nick.

"And who might that be?" was his wary response.

"Teasedale," was Cuffington's answer.

He was referring to the head of Metro Police, Chief Emma Teasedale.

"Have you already spoken to her, Nick?" questioned Killingsworth.

"No."

"What's your game plan, Inspector?"

"I'm thinking that if Chief O'Toole has any qualms about suppressing evidence, Chief Teasedale might be able to provide him with some moral support," reasoned Cuffington.

"And what makes you think that she will agree to the deception?" reasoned Killingsworth.

"I don't know that she will," admitted Cuffington. "However, I do know that when Emma decides she wants to bury something, there is no one better in the business. Besides, if only one of the two Chiefs agree to play along, the other will have no choice but to fall in line."

"The old suicide squeeze play," chuckled the Captain. "I like the call!"

"Something like that," confirmed Cuffington.

"But, what if they both give it the thumbs down?" ventured, Killingsworth.

"Then, it's in their hands. Don't forget, they are the ones that are going to be taking the heat directly from on High. And at that point, all you and I will be able to say is, "we warned you.""

"If nothing else Nick, you carry brass in pocket! I've got to give you that much," extolled the Captain.

"Patrick, it's less about brass than it is about approaching an almost surreal situation with an eye towards the pragmatic," concluded the Inspector.

"I'll drink to that!" responded the Captain.

"Killingsworth, you'll drink to anything," countered Cuffington.

"I'll drink to that too!" chuckled the Captain.

"Pat, listen to me, cautioned Cuffington. I want you to meet me outside U. S. Capitol Police headquarters at twelve-fifteen. Is that clear?"

"Nick, the meeting is on the docket for twelve sharp! Chief O'Toole is a stickler for punctuality," complained Killingsworth.

"Twelve-fifteen," insisted the Inspector.

"When you play Nick, it's most definitely hardball," groused the Captain.

Cuffington had already disconnected.

The Inspector of Metro placed his second call of the morning.

"Hello Nick, I was beginning to think you'd forgotten about me," complained the sultry voice.

"Emma, you are the one woman, always on my mind," he riposted.

"Cut the crap, Cuffington! Who, what, why, and where is Waldo?" demanded the Chief of Metro Police. "I already know the when!"

"As we speak, not yet in custody, Chief," answered the Inspector.

"And don't call me Chief! "

Both Teasedale and Cuffington broke the tension with half-hearted laughter over the half-hearted attempt at humor.

"No, really Nick, you wouldn't believe how I am being bombarded with outrage over these unprecedented Congressional murders! " complained Emma Teasedale.

"So, the cat is out of the bag?" downplayed Cuffington.

"Cat, no the rat is out of the bag, Inspector," admonished the Chief of Metro.

She continued.

"For me, the only saving grace to this political maelstrom is that it falls within the jurisdiction of U. S. Capitol Police. And if they can't catch the rat, it will become the nightmare of the Secret Service!" gloated Teasedale.

"So, you're relieved, not to have any official responsibility in the pending investigation?" confirmed Cuffington.

"Relieved? I'm absolutely ecstatic!" exclaimed the Chief of Metro Police.

"Then you won't have any objection if I attend a U.S. Capitol Police briefing later this morning?" probed the Inspector.

There was a momentary silence on Teasdale's end of the phone.

"And what meeting might that be, Inspector?"

"The one to discuss the, who, what, why, and where is Waldo," he asserted.

She paused for a moment.

"And how are you privy to such a meeting, Inspector?" she challenged.

"Let's just say I have been asked to be present in an "unofficial" capacity, if you will," revealed Cuffington.

"And who is going to be in attendance?" asked Chief Teasedale.

"Chief of U.S. Capitol Police, O'Toole and Head of Field Operations, Killingsworth," baited Nick.

"And where is this meeting going to be held, Inspector?" asked a now interested Chief of Metro.

"At U.S. Capitol Police headquarters," divulged Cuffington.

"Have I been asked to participate?" she continued.

"Not officially," replied the Inspector.

Chief Emma Teasdale calculated the proposition proffered by her Inspector.

"Nick, do you know whether or not the media is aware of this little get together?" "You are quite aware of how loathe I am to attention and the camera!"

"Quite aware, Emma," attested Cuffington. "But, answering your question, to my knowledge, the media has received no advanced official word of the meeting. That said, what doesn't the Washington D.C. media already know?" posited Cuffington.

"Good point, Inspector."

Again, the Chief of Metro pondered the circumstances, as presented.

"I've made my decision. I shall attend this conclave; in an unofficial capacity, of course."

"Of course, Emma," agreed Cuffington.

"What time would be appropriate for my arrival?"

"The briefing is scheduled for today at noon," confirmed Cuffington. "And it's been brought to my attention that Chief O'Toole expects promptness."

"And I don't?" huffed Chief Teasedale. "I'll expect you to greet me at U.S Capitol Police headquarters at twelve o' clock sharp!" ordered the Chief. "And Nick . . ."

Inspector Cuffington was already long gone.

Nick's third call of the morning was to Detective Fuentes.

"Yes Inspector?"

"Pick me up at eleven-thirty," was Cuffington's directive.

"And, our destination Sir?" asked the Detective.

"Armageddon"

"I knew it! You simply couldn't help yourself, could you Nick?"

"As I already told you, Metro would have been ordered to get involved at some point in time anyway," he tried to convince the both of them. "Besides, the wheels are already in motion."

"And what if I refuse to pick you up and thereby avoid getting involved in this ruse?" she threatened.

"Then I shall see to it that you are immediately promoted," threatened the Inspector.

"Screw that!" she spewed. "Eleven -thirty it is."

Chapter Sixteen

Inspector Cuffington turned off his office desktop and walked the house's downstairs hallway to Leigh's library. The door was closed. He tapped twice.

"C'mon in, Nick," beckoned her muffled voice.

He opened the door.

Leigh, per usual, was seated at her computer drumming on the keys of fiction.

He crossed the room and kissed the back of her head. He began to scan the words on the monitor. Alas, he hovered an instant too long.

"Hey, no peeking!"

With emoted theatrics, she placed both hands over the screen to conceal the written words.

"Leigh, I was only trying to find out whether or not Inspector Nom de Plume was guilty as charged," was the other Inspector's defense plea.

"The jury is still weighing the evidence," was the extent of her revelation.

"Then there is still hope for de Plume," he grinned.

She did not answer his question.

"Speaking of suspect Inspectors, what does your agenda look like on this day of reckoning?" she asked quietly.

"It starts with a meeting at U.S. Capitol Police headquarters. In fact, Maria is due here any minute," answered Nick.

"And who's going to be in attendance?"

"As far as I know, only Chief O'Toole, Chief Teasedale, and Captain Killingsworth," he responded.

"And then what?" pressed Leigh.

Cuffington looked at his wife with solemn candor.

"I have no idea."

His phone chirped.

"Fuentes is here. I've got to go."

Nick kissed Leigh and started towards the door.

"Hey Cuffington, watch your back," she cautioned, reciting her standard farewell.

"Always"

The Inspector slid into the passenger seat of Detective Fuentes' cruiser.

"Good morning Maria," was his banal greeting.

"And what's so good about it?" she demanded. "Have you caught any of this morning's media coverage?"

"No"

"I find that to be impossible!" she exclaimed. "The media are everywhere!"

"What did you come up with on Congressman Sooner?" asked Cuffington, abruptly changing the subject.

"Well, when it comes to the late Congressman Sooner's Congressional career, you were right and you were wrong." You were right in the fact that his career was long, very long. You were wrong about the fact it would be entertaining."

"Well then, cut to the highlight reel," requested the Inspector.

"There really are no highlights to speak of, Nick. It appears to me Congressman Sooner devoted the vast majority of his time in Washington D.C. involved in social events," concluded the Detective.

"Explain," pursued the Inspector.

"Ostensibly, Congressman Barry Sooner immersed himself in the conception, planning, and execution of social activities."

"Activities?" questioned Cuffington.

"You know what I mean Nick; dinner galas, cocktail parties, fund raisers, victory celebrations, PAC bashes, vacation trips, international travel, weekend junkets, golf outings, football games, tennis matches, baseball games, and every now and then an excursion into the arts," dutifully reported the Detective.

"So what you're telling me is that Congressman Barry Sooner was essentially a business as usual type member of the United States Congress, concluded Cuffington.

"Precisely," concurred Fuentes.

"Tell me about his dealings with Senator Ryder," continued Cuffington.

"As far as any legislative connections between the late Congressman Sooner and the late Senator Ryder, either direct or indirect, I came up with only one match," informed Fuentes.

"And what was that?" asked a now hopeful Inspector.

"Back in 04', Sooner and Ryder co-sponsored a piece of legislation that, if passed, would have automatically increased the salaries and pension benefits of every member of Congress. The bill passed unanimously, in both Houses."

"Well, that doesn't exactly shorten the list of potential suspects, now does it, Detective?"

"Absolutely not, sir"

Fuente's phone chimed. The Detective checked caller I.D.. It was Captain Killingsworth. She handed the phone to Cuffington.

"Yes," he answered.

"Nick, it's Pat. Where the hell are you!" demanded the Captain.

Cuffington glanced at their current location.

"About ten minutes from U.S. Capitol Police headquarters," asserted the Inspector.

"Ten? Damn it Nick, it's twelve-fifteen. O'Toole has already called me demanding to know where the hell you are!"

"Traffic," was the Inspector's convenience.

"Listen to me Nick, the front entrance of U.S. Capitol headquarters is bedlam! It's a media zoo without cages! I actually got bushwhacked by the old *60 Minutes* "gangster interview" assault!"

"I would like to avoid that same welcome. Do you have any suggestions for an alternate point of arrival?"

"Yes," affirmed Killingsworth. "Approach U.S. Capitol headquarters from the rear of the building. In the back parking lot, you will see a secured checkpoint entrance for authorized vehicles. Enter there. I will notify the security detail of you impending arrival. I will meet you at the side entrance. Got It?"

"Yes," confirmed the Inspector. "Pat, how the hell did you manage to get your ass ambushed?"

"I ventured out the front entrance to find you. Last time I'll ever do that. Looking for you is looking for trouble!"

Chapter Seventeen

As they approached U.S. Capitol headquarters, traffic began to snarl.

"Maria, what's the delay?" inquired the Inspector with impatience.

"Protestors," was her succinct explanation.

"Does this have anything to do with the two Congressional murders?" asked Cuffington.

"No," was the Detective's answer.

"Then what are they protesting?" demanded the Inspector.

"Everything!" acknowledged Fuentes with fervor.

"Everything "covers a lot of turf, Detective," cautioned Cuffington. "Why don't you start with who are they?" he suggested.

"This particular group refer to themselves as the Squatting on Whore Street Movement," informed Detective Fuentes.

"By *this* movement, are you suggesting that there are other traffic stopping protest movements currently a foot in Washington D.C.?" continued the Inspector.

"Yes," assured his Detective.

"Then why don't you start by explaining this particular group?" insisted Cuffington.

"As I said Inspector, the Squatting on Whore Street Movement is protesting everything! Lack of social justice, lack of social equality, and lack of social mobility!" implored Fuentes.

"As you describe it Detective, it sounds to me that these people are just trying to be social, concluded Cuffington.

"Nick, you are missing the point! These folks are venting their anger and frustration at the very inequities America has shackled them with; college tuition loans rammed down their throats, mortgage payments on houses they could never afford to begin with, and yes, no artificial shovel ready jobs!"

"I'm beginning to understand their disillusionment," admitted Cuffington.

"Nick, that's the least of it," fumed Fuentes. "The Squatting on Whore Street Movement holds its greatest resentment towards America's banking elite; in particular the gluttonous money-changers of Wall Street!"

"Wall Street," contemplated Cuffington. "When it comes to that street, I'm afraid the Squatting on Whore Street Movement is going to find it to be a rather wide strip to straddle," hedged the Inspector.

Fuentes' cruiser entered the rear parking lot of U.S. Capitol Police headquarters.

The Check Point Charlie, already alerted of their impending arrival, waived them through and pointed towards the "Visitors Only" parking area.

As instructed, they walked to the side of the building.

Confronted with a steel fortified non-entry door, Cuffington tapped twice, as was his wont.

The door opened and Captain Killingsworth ushered them inside U.S. Capitol headquarters.

Lieutenant Ginger Snapp was standing in the hallway.

Killingsworth measured Cuffington with dubious resignation, and shook his head.

"The only consolation I have for you being so late is that both O'Toole and Teasesdale have you in their line of fire!" admitted the Captain.

"It's given them more time to get reacquainted," shrugged the Inspector.

"The Chief's elevator is this way," motioned Lieutenant Ginger Snapp.

Once onboard the Otis, Killingsworth was the first to violate the ritualistic silence of staring vapidly at illuminated ascending floor numbers.

"Nick, as far as I'm concerned, you're spear-heading today's little get together. After all, you're the one that came up with the idea to begin with," concluded the Captain.

"Pat, I couldn't agree with you more," smiled a now relaxed Cuffington.

The elevator's door opened. It deposited them directly into Chief O'Toole's administrative assistant's office. A young man sat behind a desk hunched over a desktop. He glanced up from the monitor. Immediately recognizing Killingsworth he silently nodded them to the Chief's closed door. Killingsworth knocked.

"C'mon in Pat," commanded a voice.

The four officers entered O'Toole's office. The room was spacious and impressively windowed. Chiefs O'Toole and Teasedale were occupying the two desk chairs that were located in front of O'Toole's desk.

"Well, Inspector Cuffington, Chief Teasedale and I were beginning to think you had completely overlooked today's little meeting," announced the head of U.S. Capitol Police with unveiled acrimony.

Chief Henry "Hammerin Hank" O'Toole appeared to be in his early sixties. His height was short and his frame rather bulky. The thick silver hair was brushed with an eye for detail. His crimson, pock-marked face reflected the confidence of authority.

"Forgetting about you O'Toole could be a distinct possibility. However, forgetting about Chief Teasedale would be an utter implausibility."

Smiling, Nick crossed the room towards Teasedale extending his hand.

"It's always a pleasure to see you," he grinned'

Chief Teasedale accepted Nick's hand without reservation.

She rose from the chair.

"Emma, you remember Detective Maria Fuentes," cajoled Cuffington.

"Why of course I do!" insisted a now beaming Chief of Metro. "So good to see you again, Detective," she said extending her hand.

The always charming Chief of U.S. Capitol Police finally followed Chief Teasedale's societal protocol and begrudgingly lumbered to his feet.

Emma Teasedale was a strikingly handsome woman. She was tall, slender, and possessed elegantly chiseled facial features. The short cropped hair was raven in color and the amber eyes constantly on alert. Her age was a Washington D.C. mystery; guesstimates ranged from forty to A.A.R.P. territory. Teasedale's always sharp looking choice of attire was trumped only by a sharper wit. Emma was the first female to become Chief of Metro Police. While serving as second in command, her predecessor had unexpectedly succumbed to a massive heart attack. Emma had been the first to "find" the then Chief of Metro lying dead on the couch in his office.

"Why don't we officially convene this meeting at my conference table," directed Chief O'Toole.

He walked back to the mammoth slab of ebony that anchored the left side of his office.

Chief O'Toole assumed his traditional seat at the head of the table.

Captain Killingsworth sat down to the immediate right of O'Toole. Lieutenant Ginger Snapp took a chair to the Chief of U.S. Capitol Police's left.

Chief Teasedale claimed the seat at the far end of the table directly facing O'Toole.

Cuffington and Fuentes seated themselves to their Chief's right and left.

Chief O'Toole picked up the only phone on the table.

"I'm going to summon my secretary Roland to join us and record the minutes of this meeting," informed the Chief.

"I'd think twice before placing that call," advised Cuffington.

"And why the hell is that!" demanded a now clearly enraged O'Toole.

"Because I don't think you are going to like what Roland is going to hear," the Inspector replied with indifference.

O'Toole gripped the phone with shaking anger.

Chief Teasedale intervened with the professional diplomacy that had enabled her to become the first female Head of Metro.

"Hank put down the phone. Why don't we listen to Inspector Cuffington before taking any further initiative?" soothed the Chief of Metro.

O'Toole slammed the phone back onto its cradle.

"Okay Cuffington, why did you orchestrate this unprecedented forum?' demanded O'Toole.

"Because the situation you and the U.S. Capitol Police are now confronted with is unprecedented," retorted the Inspector.

"I'll be the judge of that Cuffington! Don't forget, you will ultimately answer to me in this matter!" he yelled.

"Well, in that case here's my ultimate answer. I'm out of here."

Cuffington rose and started to exit the room. Detective Fuentes immediately jumped out of her chair to follow the Inspector. Once again Chief Teasedale interceded.

"The ultimate be damned! You, Inspector, report to me! Therefore, I am ordering you to return to this table!

Cuffington stopped and turned. He first looked at his Chief. He then eyed O'Toole. With reluctance, he reseated himself. Fuentes obeyed her Inspector's unspoken directive and also returned to the table.

"Okay Nick, cut to the chase," Teasedale demanded with professional equanimity.

"Okay Emma, the chase is at least two different assassins roaming at large in Washington D.C., murdering members of Congress," answered the Inspector with commensurate aplomb.

Chief Henry O'Toole's crimson tide receded into a pale face of despair. He silently slunk deeper into his over-stuffed leathered chair.

He chose not to pick up his phone.

Chief Emma Teasedale's calmly collected manner did not waver.

"How do you know this to be fact, Inspector?" she continued.

"Doctor Seymour Savage," was Cuffington's terse reply.

"Savage; he's at best, an eccentric weirdo with a penchant for the macabre!" insisted a now recovering O'Toole.

Emma Teasedale calmly assessed the words of her lead Inspector.

"Be that as it may Henry, Savage is the best medical examiner in Washington D.C. when it comes to unearthing death by foul play. The man simply possesses a rare nose for it," conceded Chief Teasedale.

The six law enforcement officials seated at the table remained silent.

Teasedale got out of her chair and walked to a window facing the front of U.S. Capitol headquarters. She surveyed the overwhelming throng of frenzied media activity unfurling beneath her very eyes.

"How much do they know, Inspector?" she asked with oblique calculation.

"I don't know with any degree of certainty," he admitted. "Why don't you go downstairs and ask them?"

Chief Teasedale turned to face the Inspector. The amber eyes had turned to ice.

"Don't ever try to get cute with me Cuffington! "

Teasedale returned to the table and sat back down. She thought momentarily and then fixed her aim at Chief O'Toole.

"Well Henry, it strikes me that this entire matter resides squarely within the domain of U.S. Capitol Police. As such, it appears that you are calling the shots," asserted Teasedale.

The Chief of U.S. Capitol Police shifted uncomfortably in his chair. He thought for several seconds and then turned to Captain Killingsworth.

"Pat, you're far more current on this entire situation than I am, what course of action are you suggesting?" as he quickly passed the buck of responsibility.

Captain Patrick Killingsworth sat in his seat sweating profusely. His head was faced downwardly, avoiding eye contact with all those present at the table.

"I am suggesting that we listen to what Inspector Cuffington has to say," he mumbled. "It was Nick's belief that this meeting would be a good idea."

With that, Cuffington stood up and walked to the window Teasedale had just viewed the media ferment below. He looked at the spectacle that was growing rabid on the front stairs of U.S. Capitol Police headquarters. He pulled a cigarette from his pocket and lit up.

"This is a governmental non-smoking designated building Inspector!" erupted Chief O'Toole.

"Sorry O'Toole, I didn't see the sign," he exhaled.

"Damn it man, put that thing out, immediately!" shrilled the Captain of U.S. Capitol Police.

Cuffington continued to gaze at the chaos burbling beneath him.

"What's going on down there is going to be far more difficult to extinguish than what I have burning up here," concluded the Inspector, as he let out a blue plume of toxin in the general direction of O'Toole.

Chief Emma Teasedale sat with practiced patience, considering both the scene playing out in front of her and the one below.

"Nick, what are you proposing?" she asked with concealed trepidation.

"Proposing? Emma I am not proposing, merely flirting," smiled the Inspector.

Chapter Eighteen

Chief O'Toole was the first to speak.

"And what exactly are you flirting with Inspector, another career move?" smirked O'Toole.

Cuffington took a final drag on his cigarette and dowsed it in an unattended coffee cup perched on the window sill. He returned to the table, sat down, and looked at the Chief of U.S. Capitol Police.

"I'm flirting with three indisputable facts O'Toole," declared Cuffington.

"And would the good Inspector be kind enough to enlighten us, post haste, as to what those three indisputable facts are?" responded the Chief, facetiously.

"That's why I'm here O'Toole," said Cuffington in an intentionally condescending tone.

Chief Henry O'Toole stared back at the Inspector with authoritarian smugness.

"So let's hear them damn it!" he bristled.

"Fact number one; two members of the United States Congress were murdered inside Washington D.C. on the same night."

"Well, you really have uncovered something there now haven't you Cuffington," snickered O'Toole.

Cuffington's "March to the See?" moved forward.

"Fact number two; the initial reaction to these two heinous crimes from both the Washington Establishment and a Maniacal Media has been more than shock; it has been unprecedented awe."

"Once again, what ever would we do without Inspector Cuffington continually enlightening us to the already known and obvious?" opined O'Toole with unctuous sarcasm.

Inspector Nick Cuffington turned towards Chief Teasedale and smiled, shaking his head.

"Fact number three; both assassinations were carried out under Chief Henry O'Toole's watch; the person ultimately responsible for the security and well-being of all members of the United States Congress," concluded the Inspector.

O'Toole stared at the Metro Inspector with scornful disbelief.

"These tragic events could have been carried out under anyone's watch," dismissed O'Toole.

"Very true, O'Toole, unfortunately for you, however, they were executed under *your* watch," emphasized Cuffington.

O'Toole paused to collect his thoughts.

"No rational individual could possibly decide to lay the blame for these murders on any negligence stemming from my office," he tried to convince himself.

"I tend to agree with you Chief," admitted Cuffington. "However, what was the last rational decision you recall being made here in Washington D.C.?"

Chief Henry O'Toole began to slowly realize the enormity of his involvement in the Congressional murders. Cuffington rose from his seat, extracted another cigarette, and walked to the same window facing the front of U.S. Capitol Police headquarters. He lit his smoke. Once more, he gazed down upon the media mayhem burgeoning beneath him.

"Would you care to hear my first suggestion O'Toole?" he asked with patient indifference.

"No!" was the Chief's blunt answer.

"I'd be most interested in that suggestion Inspector," insisted Chief Emma Teasedale.

She rose from the table and joined Cuffington at the window.

"Now Emma, you should know better than this!" chastised Cuffington. Hasn't OSHA made you duly aware of the hazards of second hand smoke in the workplace?"

"Please," as she rolled her eyes in derision." Now out with it Inspector!"

"It strikes me that when it becomes public knowledge that the two members of Congress were murdered by at least two different assassins, this town is going to go *Neddy in the Woods!*" he concluded.

The Chief of Metro stared at Cuffington and shook her head.

"Nick, do you think you are telling me something I don't already know?" she demanded.

Teasedale extracted the cigarette from Cuffington's fingers and began to smoke it.

"What would be your recommended approach to these investigations, Inspector?" was the Metro Chief's next question.

"It is my belief that if full disclosure of all circumstances surrounding these Congressional killings goes any further than this room, any hope for an effective and ultimately successful murder investigation will be rendered an impossibility," surmised the Inspector.

Teasedale finished the cigarette and tossed into the coffee cup. She and Cuffington returned to the table and sat down.

"Okay Nick, put your proposal into words," instructed Chief Teasedale

"One word is all that I require," revealed the Inspector.

"And what is that?" pressed Teasedale.

"Obfuscation"

Both Chief Teasedale and Inspector Cuffington turned to face Chief O'Toole. He was slouched in his chair. He appeared to be preoccupied with things other than the matters at hand. Instinctively, he straightened his posture and riveted his eyes upon Cuffington.

"Obfuscation, Inspector? Wouldn't **obstruction** be a more appropriate choice of word? In fact, wouldn't "obstruction of justice" be an even more appropriate phrase?" challenged the Chief of U.S. Capitol Police.

Cuffington momentarily remained silent, weighing his course of rebuttal.

"There exist unique circumstances, where the canon of justice supersedes the rule of any given law. I believe we are now faced with one of those ambivalent situations," reasoned the Inspector.

80

Chief O'Toole shook his head with disapproval.

"Cuffington, you've always struggled with the concept of law; more specifically, the fundamental understanding of law enforcement. Perhaps, you would have been better suited as a judge. In that role, you would be free to interpret the law in any way that might suit your fancy," scoffed the Chief of U.S. Capitol Police.

Cuffington studied the Chief with amused disdain.

"O'Toole, as usual, you are way behind the curve. Today, judges no longer interpret the law. Today, judges make the law," dismissed the Metro Inspector.

The Chief of U.S. Capitol glowered at Cuffington. His scowl had transformed from professional disapproval to one of personal loathing.

"To borrow a most appropriate phrase from Chief Teasedale, cut the crap Cuffington," invoked O'Toole. "Listen to me Inspector, what you are suggesting everyone in this room to do is lie, pure and simple!" thundered O'Toole. "At least be man enough to come out and say it!"

Cuffington surveyed the vehement Chief with resigned weariness.

"You really have missed the bus O'Toole. Haven't you heard? Lying is merely a state of mind here in Washington D.C. these days," he calmly explained. "Why the Attorney-General himself has said as much."

The other officers at the table grew silent. It was Inspector Nick Cuffington that finally interrupted the awkward pause in dialogue.

"Chief Teasedale, it is quite apparent to me that Chief O'Toole is not going to consider my suggested approach to the impending Congressional murder investigations. And, as he so eloquently pointed out earlier, is in charge of this entire Congressional nightmare. Therefore, I respectively request I be allowed to excuse myself from any further involvement in this meeting."

Chief Teasedale quickly calculated the potential implications of further confrontation. She stared at Cuffington.

"Permission granted, Inspector."

With that, Nick Cuffington rose from the table. Immediately, Detective Maria Fuentes stood up and followed the Inspector. Before he opened the office door, Cuffington turned to face the officers still seated at the table.

"Happy hunting boys and girls"

And with that, Cuffington and Fuentes were gone.

Chapter Nineteen

Inspector Cuffington and Detective Fuentes entered Chief O'Toole's elevator. Once on the ground floor, they exited U.S .Capitol Police headquarters and traversed the restricted back parking lot to Fuentes' police cruiser. The Detective started the engine and proceeded to leave the grounds.

"Well that went well, Inspector," was Fuentes' terse summation.

"It could have been worse. O'Toole could have had me arrested on two counts; one for proposed obstruction of justice and the other for telling the truth," noted Cuffington, cynically.

Fuentes pulled to a stop at the security booth. Unexpectedly, two U.S. Capitol Police guards blocked their lane of exit.

"I may have spoken too hastily," laughed Cuffington.

The man in the security booth was not the same officer who had been on duty earlier. He lowered the Plexiglas window. Fuentes lowered the driver's side window.

"We've already been thrown out!" she hissed. "No need to check whether or not our weapons are loaded. Unfortunately, they still are!"

The officer ignored Fuentes' outburst.

"Photo I.D.," demanded the guard.

He examined the cards and compared them to the automobile's occupants.

"Inspector Cuffington, you have been requested to return to U.S. Capitol Police headquarters," stone faced the officer.

"For what reason?" inquired the Inspector of Metro Police.

"Orders"

Cuffington nodded at his Detective to comply with the directive.

Once again, they confronted the steel-plated non-entry door. This time, however, two taps were not required. The doorway opened and Captain Killingsworth ushered them inside. Lieutenant Ginger Snapp was conspicuously absent.

"Chief O'Toole wants a word with you Nick," was the Captain's only words.

His face was uncharacteristically grim.

"Alright Pat, let's go," complied the Inspector.

"I said *you*," admonished the Captain.

A clumsy silence resonated throughout the private corridor.

"Detective Fuentes will accompany me if I so choose," decided the Inspector.

Captain Killingsworth glanced nervously at Detective Fuentes and then cemented his attention on Cuffington.

"Listen to me Nick, don't take a chance on flushing her career down the crapper along with yours."

His tone of voice was sub-rosa, but urgent.

Cuffington hesitated, trying to assimilate the Captain's words and the situation facing them. With deliberation, he turned to confront Fuentes.

"Detective, why don't you wait for me outside in the car?" prodded the Inspector.

The emerald eyes of Maria Fuentes flared with vehemence more combustible than the circumstances currently engulfing Washington D.C.

"Inspector, I am your ranking Detective. I think I've earned the right to decide whether or not to remain part of this investigation," she insisted.

Cuffington stared long and hard into the young woman's eyes.

"Maria, in certain situations, sometimes the only way to assure oneself of a future role of meaningful significance here in Washington D.C. is to accept a temporary position of disinterested non-involvement," postulated the Inspector.

"Nick, if you leave me out of the loop on this one, I won't be waiting for you outside in the car," she vowed.

Again, the Inspector searched the face of his Detective.

At length, he turned towards Killingsworth.

"The lady has spoken, Pat."

The Captain shook his head with subdued dismay.

"It's your funeral little girl" he said resignedly.

"It's Detective Little Girl, Captain," corrected Fuentes with a grin.

Captain Patrick Killingsworth forced a humorless smile.

They emerged from Chief O'Toole's elevator.

Roland was still glued to his computer screen. He did not even bother to look up and acknowledge their arrival.

Captain Killingsworth knocked on Chief O'Toole's door and entered without waiting for consent. Chiefs O'Toole and Teasedale were standing in front of the office window, trying to comprehend the ever widening media highway being paved below them. O'Toole turned and directed his attention at Cuffington.

"Inspector, Chief Teasedale and I were just discussing your rather "unconventional" suggestion as to how best to proceed with the Congressional murder investigation. "Why don't we reseat ourselves at the conference table," he motioned.

The five law enforcement officers reclaimed their prior seats. Lieutenant Ginger Snapp was not present. Emma Teasedale studied Detective Fuentes for a long moment. At length, she addressed her with carefully selected words.

"Detective, I'm a little surprised at your presence," she candidly admitted.

"And why is that Chief Teasedale?" inquired Fuentes.

Teasedale glanced uncomfortably at Cuffington.

"Because, I mistakenly assumed that the Inspector would have a little more consideration for your future career at Metro Police," confessed the Chief.

"Oh that!" dismissed Fuentes. "Truth be known, I don't give a rat's ass about my future at Metro. Right now, my only concern is bringing to justice those responsible for these insidious crimes perpetrated inside our nation's capital," asserted the Detective.

This revelation clearly unsettled the always composed Emma Teasedale.

Chief Henry "Hammering Hank" O'Toole focused on Cuffington.

"Captain Killingsworth has explained your insistence for a prompt joint news conference to be held by U.S. Capitol Police and Metro," opened O'Toole. "We, he nodded in the direction of Chief Teasedale, "now agree with that course of action."

Chief O'Toole continued his carefully orchestrated delivery.

"Obviously, it is of paramount importance that U.S. Capitol Police and Metro present to both the public at large and the Media, in particular, a truly united front dedicated solely to the immediate apprehension of any and all involved in these despicable acts of transgression!"

Inspector Nick Cuffington sat impassively, waiting for the inevitable legally illegal Washington D.C. proviso.

Chief O'Toole paused. Once again, he glanced at Chief Emma Teasedale, as if tacitly re-confirming their already agreed upon course of action.

"It is for this reason that I have already instructed my aide, Roland to announce a press conference to be held at three o'clock this afternoon at the front entrance of U.S. Capitol Police headquarters."

O'Toole paused in an attempt to gauge Cuffington's initial reaction. None was forthcoming. The Chief of U.S. Capitol Police continued.

"At this press conference, Captain Killingsworth will explain to those Media present the unified commitment on the part of both U.S. Capitol Police and Metro Police in the pursuit of justice as it pertains to the recent Congressional slayings.

Chief Henry O'Toole paused before continuing his verdict.

"Captain Killingsworth will then introduce you as the newly appointed "Head of Investigation," in charge of apprehending those responsible for the two Congressional killings."

Chief Henry O'Toole was clearly at odds with himself and his next words.

"From that point forward, the ball will be in your court. Any questions, Inspector?" smiled the Chief of U.S. Capitol.

`"None at this time," he replied with indifference.

Cuffington, Killingsworth, and Fuentes rose from the table and began to exit the office.

"Oh Inspector," called out O'Toole. "Happy hunting," sneered the Chief of U.S. Capitol Police

Cuffington stood at the still closed door. He turned and smiled at O'Toole.

"I'm always happy when I'm hunting O'Toole. That's because I never know whose head I am ultimately going to be mounting on my trophy wall."

Cuffington opened the door to allow Fuentes and Killingsworth egress. Before he departed, he once again stared at O'Toole.

"It's my understanding that badger is in season," confirmed Cuffington.

With that, the Inspector closed the door behind him.

Chief Henry O'Toole swiveled uneasily in his seat of authority.

Chapter Twenty

Captain Killingsworth was seated behind his office desk at U.S. Capitol Police headquarters. Inspector Cuffington and Detective Fuentes were occupying the two front desk chairs. It was a little after two-thirty in the afternoon. The press conference was looming. Killingsworth silently rotated to and fro in his leather back. At last, he came to a stop and faced the Inspector.

"Listen to me Nick, if you think for a moment that I had anything to do with how this press conference was set up, you are dead wrong!" implored the Captain.

"I believe you Pat," soothed Cuffington with genuine conviction.

Cuffington's assuaging demeanor served only to further provoke the Captain of U.S. Capitol Police. He slammed a meaty fist angrily into the desktop. His eyes snapped at the Inspector.

"If you believe, even for an instant, that I'm proud of the position O'Toole cornered me into you're way off base!

Killingsworth stared defiantly at Cuffington.

"Can you possibly presume that I am going to get some sort of thrill playing emcee at your hanging in the public square?" he smoldered.

"No I don't, Pat" replied Cuffington a with calm assuredness.

The Inspector's placidity further stoked the ire of Killingsworth.

"Do you want to know what my option was?" ranted the Captain.

"Do I have a choice, Pat?"

"NO!" blasted the Captain.

Killingsworth took a deep breath and measured his words with muted venom.

"I could've taken an immediate medical leave of absence," he slowly exhaled.

"Would it have been a paid leave of absence, Pat?" smiled the Inspector.

Killingsworth strained facial expression relaxed.

"You truly are a son of a bitch aren't you, Cuffington?"

Both men laughed.

Suddenly, the door to Captain Killingsworth's office burst open. Lieutenant Ginger Snapp fluttered forth.

"Pat, I was just informed that you are still in the building!"

Ginger Snapp stopped short. The unexpected presence of Inspector Cuffington and Detective Fuentes immediately halted the walking wiggle. Her eyes had frozen in mid flutter.

"I didn't realize you had people in your office, Captain," she stammered.

"Obviously, I do Lieutenant," was the Captain's curt response.

Ginger Snapp stood awkwardly in the middle of the room.

"Have you anything else you would like to tell me?" inquired the Captain.

"No sir," was all she could manage.

"Then close the door as you leave," ordered Killingsworth.

The office door securely shut, the Captain continued the conversation.

"Nick, I've long understood that O'Toole is a self-serving dick. However, it was not until today, that I came to the full realization that he's just another Washington D.C. Dickless Tracy," confided Killingsworth.

Detective Maria Fuentes' Cuban blood, instantaneously, went to rapid boil. Instinctively, she wanted to claw the eyes of the sexist pig. Her sudden loathing for Captain Killingsworth was tempered only by an unapologetic respect for Inspector Nick Cuffington. She remained silent. Killingsworth continued his emotional catharsis.

"Nick, I was the one responsible for dragging you into U.S. Capitol Police's dirty laundry in the first place. I just couldn't find it within myself to toss you overboard, by yourself, for political chum at this stage of the game."

"And what stage of the game are we really at, Pat?" prodded Cuffington.

"Nick, for all I know, at this point you are privy to more information than I am."

The Captain drew a deep breath and continued.

"The only thing I can say with certainty is that you are about to come to the plate, behind in the score, in the bottom of the ninth, with two out and no one on base," affirmed the Captain.

With that, Killingsworth rose from his seat and sauntered to the office's side bar. He chose a glass and poured a fortifying dram of Irish. He stooped and tugged at the door of the mini-fridge. He added ice into the glass and pulled a cold one for Cuffington.

"Beer, Detective?" he asked Detective Fuentes without glancing backwardly.

Fuentes turned to address Cuffington.

"Well, I don't know. Are we officially off duty, Inspector?" fluttered Maria.

Killingsworth ignored the obvious barb. He returned to his desk and placed the glass of Irish in front of his leather back. He handed Cuffington a can of Bud. He then placed an iced bottle of Hatuey in front of Fuentes.

"Sans glass, if my recon is accurate," offered the Captain of U.S. Capitol Police.

He winked at Fuentes and reseated himself.

Marias's outward appearance remained unperturbed. Inwardly, however, her heart was racing at the speed of surprise.

"Have I underestimated the talent of Captain Patrick Killingsworth? Is his obvious display of clumsiness an intended ruse? Is he, in fact, playing me the fool?"

Fuentes found the possibilities frustratingly unnerving.

Killingsworth opened a desk drawer. He retrieved a cigar and two ashtrays. He unwrapped the "Cuban" with care and struck a match.

90

"Inspector, I want you to be the first to know this is a smoke free environmental workplace," he asserted while carefully puffing to ensure an evenly lit cigar.

"I'll keep that in mind," acknowledged Cuffington.

"So Nick, have you decided how you are going to compromise your career this afternoon?" exhaled the Captain of U.S. Capitol Police.

Cuffington pulled at his beer with thoughtful deliberation. He paused, and then fixed his eyes on Killingsworth.

"Pat, you are going to adhere to the script O'Toole has conveniently written for you. Introduce me as the lead investigator and then step discreetly into the shadows of secondary involvement.

"You didn't answer my question Nick. What the hell are you going to say?" insisted Killingsworth.

"Pat, I'm going to stick to the facts as I have interpreted them. It's going to be short, sweet, and oblique."

"Maybe O'Toole was right. A judgeship very well might be your calling," smiled Killingsworth. "What about questions?" he pursued. "Are you going to open the flood gates of no return?"

"I rather doubt I'll have a choice in that matter," conjectured Cuffington.

"Good luck with that segment of the side show," sighed the Captain.

Killingsworth's desk phone buzzed. He hit the conference call button.

"Yes?"

"Sir, it's three o'clock and the natives are getting restless," reported a subordinate.

"We'll be down directly," confirmed Killingsworth.

The Captain sipped his cocktail and continued to smoke his cigar.

"I don't think Greeley's ghouls are going anywhere any time soon," he concluded.

"Patrick deep down inside you inhabit the soul of a renegade!" encouraged Cuffington.

"Yea, and look at where Geronimo ended up!" frowned Killingsworth.

"Yes, that's true. However, Geronimo sealed his own fate," lectured Cuffington.

"Really, and how's that Nick?"

"As a Native American, Geronimo repeatedly entered Mexico illegally, via the then evolving United States border. Furthermore, once in Mexico, Geronimo proceeded raid and plunder the spoils that were rightfully the loot of the Mexican banditos.

Cuffington paused to light a cigarette. He resumed.

"To add insult to injury, after being banished to an Apache Reservation, in the United States, Geronimo escaped and once again re-entered Mexico and illegally settled there. He then continued to persistently re-enter the United States Illegally to ravage the spoils of American outlaws," explained the Inspector.

"Well, that does explain things, Nick," agreed Killingsworth.

"I thought it might," concurred Cuffington.

Killingsworth drained his drink and snuffed his cigar. He rose from his desk. He looked both Inspector Cuffington and Detective Fuentes squarely in the eyes.

"It's face time," he uttered with resolve.

Chapter Twenty-One

Killingsworth, Cuffington, and Fuentes entered "Chief O'Toole's" elevator and descended to the first floor of U.S. Capitol Police headquarters. Exiting the vestibule, they made their way through the main lobby and stopped in front of the main doors and their impending destiny. The usual complement of U.S. Capitol Police officers were stationed at their customary positions of assignment. Captain Killingsworth sensed a palpable change in the manner in which his fellow officers were now regarding him; the heretofore, warmth and respect had suddenly evaporated into an intentional disregard. Killingsworth's suspicions were confirmed when Lieutenant Ginger Snapp confronted the now ostracized trio.

"Captain Killingsworth, I have been instructed to remind you of your previous orders," she delivered with self-conscious awkwardness.

"And what exactly are those orders Lieutenant?" demanded the Captain of U.S. Capitol Police.

"To ah, to ah, introduce Captain Cuffington, I mean Inspector Cuffington as your, I mean as the lead investigator in the situation, I mean, the situations on the hand," she stuttered with flutter.

"Order delivered and understood," acknowledged Killingsworth. "Now Lieutenant, you are dismissed!' ordered the Captain.

Killingsworth stood stoically reticent. He calmly surveyed the lobby of the headquarters that until that very moment had been his domain. He sighed with a quiet resolve and awaited his cue to take the "stage."

"Pat, what the hell was that all about?" asked the Inspector.

"They call it consorting with the enemy," answered Killingsworth.

"They?" pursued the Inspector.

"U.S. Capitol Police," responded Killingsworth with preoccupied detachment.

"What the hell are you saying to me Pat!" demanded Cuffington.

"C'mon Nick, you've been in this town long enough to know that if they ain't us, then they are the enemy!" explained a now exasperated Captain of U.S. Capitol Police.

"Pat, I was under the presumption that those inane Mickey Mouse turf wars between the myriad of Washington D.C. law enforcement agencies had been pretty much put out to pasture by the current regime," defended Cuffington.

"Nick, quite frankly, you are beginning to disappoint me," admitted Killingsworth, with impatience.

Captain Patrick Killingsworth surveyed Inspector Nick Cuffington with malaise.

"Nick please don't tell me that you actually bought into the rhetoric that the petty political infighting that infects all of Washington D.C., on all levels of governmental authority was going to magically disappear with a stroke of Tinker Bell's wand," he scolded. "Only in Disney Land do the denizens listen with big ears to big ears!"

"Patrick, your point is well founded and completely correct," confessed Cuffington. "I made the mistake of placing hope in front of common sense. "I shall never that make that error in judgment again," vowed the Inspector of Metro Police.

Cuffington paused in front of the securely guarded front doors of U.S. Capitol Police headquarters. He turned to face Maria Fuentes.

"Detective, what time is it?" he inquired.

"Three-thirty p.m.," she responded.

"Maria, I want you to wait inside. At three-forty-five, I want you to come outside and whisper into my ear," instructed the Inspector.

"And what do you want me to whisper, Inspector?"

"Sweet little nothings," confided the Inspector. "At that point, I'll step away from the live mics and assume the look of deep contemplation," informed Cuffington. "After that, you and I shall be out into the afternoon."

"Do you think fifteen minutes is going to give you enough time to satisfy the appetite of the hungry?" questioned the Detective.

"If fifteen minutes was long enough for Warhol, it should be more than adequate for me," mused the Inspector.

Cuffington smiled wryly at his Detective. With that, he thrust opened the doors of no retreat.

"You first Captain. After all, you are the emcee of this political roast," reminded the Inspector.

The Medusa like Media bared their brazen claws in the form of flashing lights. The entire atmosphere was more carnival than conference. U.S. Capitol Police had sealed off the top steps of the front entrance with red, white, and blue sawhorses to preclude physical contact with the microphone laden podium. Behind the crush of news trunk cables, a secondary line of defense had been erected to dissuade the growing mass of gawkers from interfering with the official proceedings about to take place.

Killingsworth stood in front of the podium. He was flanked by Inspector Cuffington to his right. The Captain paused, collecting his thoughts and trying to keep his emotions in check. He launched head-long into the frenzy of the moment.

"As most you know, I am Captain Patrick Killingsworth of U.S. Capitol Police. The gentleman standing next to me is Inspector Nick Cuffington of Metro Police."

"We have convened this press conference to update you on the circumstances surrounding the deaths of Congressman Barry Sooner and Senator William Ryder," began Killingsworth.

Pandemonium erupted. The instantaneous commotion of lights, camera, and action rendered any further explanation a virtual impossibility. Killingsworth stepped away from the microphones. He glanced at Cuffington and shrugged in wordless exasperation.

Inspector Nick Cuffington assumed center stage. He surveyed the chaos taking place before him with an eerie equanimity. With intent of purpose, he squelched the microphones, sending an ear piercing cacophony throughout the gathering.

"It was poison," he revealed in a stage-like whisper.

There was a momentary hush to the media madness.

"What did you say?" a lone voice from the gallery shouted.

"It was poison!" shouted the Inspector into the microphones. "Both Congressman Sooner and Senator Ryder were poisoned," affirmed Cuffington.

A somber pall fell upon the gathering.

The Inspector now had everyone's undivided attention.

"Now, if you journalists of the Media will start acting as such, I will continue. If not, I'm out of here," threatened Cuffington.

With a semblance of order restored, the Inspector continued.

"First and foremost, it is vital for you all to know that U.S. Capitol Police and D.C. Metro are working both Congressional deaths in tandem. We are investigating as a united force of one," explained the Inspector.

"Secondly, we are treating both deaths as homicides. Simply put boys and girls, we have a killer of members of the United States Congress on the loose here in Washington D.C.."

Immediately, the assembly transformed itself into an incoherent wave of hysteria. And once again, Inspector Cuffington tempered the flames of their thirst with an ear-piercing squelch of the microphones.

"If I can't hear your questions, you will not get any answers," he stated with unyielding finality.

The Media melee momentarily paused to reload.

"With that, I will answer some of the inquiries you undoubtedly have," volunteered the Inspector.

He pointed arbitrarily to a reporter standing in the forefront of the crowd.

"Inspector Cuffington, what kinds of poisons were used?" asked the first questioner.

"The samples are still being evaluated by our labs for definitive identification. However, I can say with certainty that the same toxin was used in both deaths," detailed Cuffington.

"Inspector, how are the two murders connected?" inquired a different reporter.

"At this point in time, only by the fact that both victims were members of the United States Congress and both were poisoned with the same substance."

"Inspector Cuffington," continued yet another reporter, "the fact that both men were killed on the same night, was that by design or rather some quirky coincidence?"

"Coincidence is a word of semantics. Given the circumstances surrounding these two homicides, it would be logical to assume that there existed a common thread of intent," concluded the Inspector.

"Does that mean whoever killed them wanted them dead at the same time and for the same reason?" barked another inquisitor.

"It's far too early to speculate on the motives of this particular murderer," insisted Cuffington.

At precisely three forty-five p.m., Detective Maria Fuentes burst through the front doors of U.S. Capitol Police headquarters and approached Inspector Cuffington with an apparent sense of urgency. Immediately noticing her presence, the Inspector stepped away from the podium and turned to face the Detective. She whispered into his ear and then stood back awaiting his response.

Cuffington stood silently for a moment, ostensibly weighing the newly dispatched information. In an unhurried manner, he nodded at Fuentes and then returned to the podium. He addressed the now almost noiseless crowd.

"Unfortunately, I find it necessary to inform you that I must conclude this press conference immediately," he announced with practiced deliberation. "Certain developments have just materialized that require Captain Killingsworth's and my prompt review," ended Cuffington.

With that, Inspector Cuffington, Captain Killingsworth, and Detective Fuentes hurriedly disappeared inside the secured front doors of U.S. Capitol Police headquarters.

The outrage and indignation of a slighted news corps made its sentiments known immediately. The din of the gathering was now louder than prior to the press conference. The front guards of U.S. Capitol Police tightened ranks and observed the chaos with subdued resolve.

Once inside the lobby, the threesome made their way to the center of the room, affording them more privacy.

"Why don't we go upstairs to my office and figure out our next move?" suggested Killingsworth.

"I don't think your office is a good idea Pat. Why don't we reconvene at a more neutral site? I, once again, suggest Brewster's Bistro."

"Should I bring anyone from U.S. Capitol Police along for the ride? You know, just to maintain a balance of authority?" asked the Captain.

"Pat, bring anyone you trust," encouraged Cuffington.

Killingsworth thought for a moment. He slowly shook his head in dismay.

"I'll be coming alone."

Chapter Twenty-Two

Inspector Cuffington and Detective Fuentes descended to the lower level of U.S. Capitol headquarters in Chief O'Toole's elevator. Once outside, they walked across the fortified back parking lot to Fuentes' obviously unmarked cruiser. They exited the premises through the guard booth checkpoint. This time, however, no officers attempted to impede their departure.

"How do you think it went Nick?" asked the Detective as they began the short drive across town to Brewster's Bistro.

"I guess as well as could be expected, given the circumstances," was the Inspector's assessment of the truncated press conference.

"Nick, I hope you realize that you have put us in a position that that doesn't afford a lot of latitude, she cautioned. "

Inspector Cuffington sat silently staring somberly through the passenger side window. Fuentes continued.

"Not only that, the initial list of possible persons of interest starts at five hundred and thirty-five, every member of the United States Congress! Then, when we include their friends, family, business associates, political donors, disgruntled constituents, drug dealers, and extra-marital love interests, that number becomes exponentially staggering!" theorized the Detective.

"Well, on the positive side Maria, you're wrong. The initial list of potential persons of interest in Congress is only five hundred and thirty-three," reasoned the Inspector.

"That's the best news I've heard in two days!" agreed Fuentes.

The Detective pulled to a stop in front of Brewster's.

As they entered the bistro, the same cosmopolitan waiter accosted them with the warm smile of social-networking recognition.

"Why Inspector Cuffington, how gracious of you to join us this afternoon," beamed the young man. "You know, I haven't been able to escape you for one second today. You are, quite frankly, everywhere!" he exclaimed.

"I'm an on the move kind of guy," responded the Inspector glibly.

"Captain Killingsworth is already here and expecting you!" he giggled. "Right this way!"

The Captain was seated in the same booth they had occupied during the first meeting at Brewster's Bistro. He sat alone, save for the tall glass providing him companionship.

"Glad you two decided to show up," was his maudlin greeting.

"Pat, how long have you been waiting?" Cuffington wanted to know.

"Not long enough," as he drained the remainder of his adult beverage.

Cuffington and Fuentes seated themselves facing the Captain of U.S. Capitol Police. Their waiter returned with two beers and a re-enforcement for Killingsworth.

"I took the liberty," explained the Captain.

"Always appreciated," confirmed Cuffington as he raised his beer in salutation.

Fuentes also hoisted her drink, following the precedent established by her Inspector. The three toasted to their newly forged friendship and the foreboding future that very bond had created.

"To tell you the truth Nick, I couldn't wait to get out of U.S. Capitol Police headquarters," admitted Killingsworth. "Too many political shenanigans going on for my liking" he confided in a barely audible whisper.

"What are you suggesting, Pat?" pushed Cuffington.

"I'm not suggesting, I'm saying! O'Toole has been waiting for the right moment to discredit me in the minds and hearts of the men and women of U.S. Capitol Police," revealed Killingsworth.

"And why the hell would he want to do that?" continued Cuffington.

100

"Why, you ask? I'll tell you why. Resentment!" erupted Killingsworth.

"Go on, Pat," prodded the Inspector.

"When I transferred from the Secret Service to U.S. Capitol Police, it was with the sanction that I retain the rank of Captain. That would allow me to remain in the field. However, it was also stipulated that once in place at Capitol Police, I would answer directly to the Chief ," explained Killingsworth.

"So, what's the issue?" puzzled Nick.

"So, the issue is, and always has been, that this arrangement has ruffled some feathers," continued Killingsworth

"Make your point, Captain," insisted Cuffington.

"In the structured hierarchy of U.S. Capitol Police, a Captain traditionally, first reports to the Inspector; no offense intended, Nick."

"None taken, Captain"

"Then, the Inspector is to report to the Deputy Chief, who in turn, is supposed to report to the Assistant Chief who, at that point, is permitted to knock on the door of the Chief of Police, only if he or she isn't too busy," finished Killingsworth.

"So your presence there, as currently configured, violates the good old boy network at U.S. Capitol Police," concluded Cuffington.

"Something like that," agreed the Captain

Killingsworth took a long draught from his drink.

He once again addressed the Inspector.

"Anyway, O'Toole has not only resented the disruption in his chain of command, he's also sick and tired of the belly aching coming from his immediate subordinates."

"But why is the fat in the fire at this particular moment?" searched Cuffington.

"Because I handed myself to O'Toole on a silver platter, that's why!" snapped the Captain.

"And how did you accomplish that feat, Pat?" shrugged Nick.

"By involving Metro Police, in general, and you, in particular before informing O'Toole of what actually went down regarding both Sooner and Ryder," finished Killingsworth. "I can only assume that today was not the first time you and O'Toole have met!"

"No it wasn't," confirmed the Inspector with no further elaboration.

The booth grew quiet, as the three officers wordlessly sat pondering how to proceed next. It was Detective Fuentes that jolted the table's silence.

"Captain Killingsworth, where is Lieutenant Ginger Snapp?"

"At this stage of the game, Maria, it's Pat, not Captain," corrected Killingsworth. "But, to answer your question, she is where you should be right now, trying to preserve and advance her career in law enforcement," admonished the Captain.

Detective Maria Fuentes did not react immediately to Killingsworth's well-intentioned advice. When she did, it was with measured but resolute words.

"Captain, I believe my presence at this meeting is advancing my career in law enforcement. As a police officer, my top priority must always be bringing to justice those who break the laws of the land. I think that is exactly what we are attempting to do here this afternoon."

"Maria, you are obviously a well-intentioned young woman. However, you have a lot to learn about how Washington D.C. interprets the law of the land," chided Killingsworth.

"You're mistaken, Pat. Washington D.C. has a lot to learn about how I interpret the law," refuted Fuentes.

Killingsworth was about to retort. He was cut off by the unexpected appearance of a woman. She approached their booth and stood imposingly in front of Cuffington .

"Inspector, we have to talk."

Chapter Twenty-Three

Inspector Cuffington rose from his seat to politely acknowledge the presence of the young lady. He recognized her because she had been in attendance at several press conferences he had conducted over the previous several years. Oddly, he did not recall seeing her at the media circus held earlier that afternoon.

Talia Teller was in her early thirties. She was rather tall, sleekly slender, and a strikingly handsome woman. Teller was African-American. Her intellect was keen and her wit even more honed. As a general rule, Talia intimidated most women and, down-right unnerved most men. Always one to speak her mind, she inevitably placed herself in the eye of the storm of resentment when in pursuit of her two ultimate goals; the truth, and the facts that preceded that truth. Teller was a beat reporter working for a local D.C. newspaper. *The Washington Rumor* did not enjoy the world-wide circulation and readership of the more prestigious Washington D.C. publications. However, in recent years, its popularity had been steadily increasing with the citizens of Washington D.C. Apparently, there was a growing number of people becoming dissatisfied with the always predictable and slanted biases of the more established tabloids. It was further evidence that individuals had become weary of the same hackneyed, mundanely arcane rhetoric spewing forth from the self-appointed important "reporters of the news," who were, for the most part, still pedantically mired in the dogma of the twentieth century. For readers, both young and old, *The Washington Rumor* offered a refreshingly unique alternative. Its manner of actually reporting the news was, indeed, a novelty for most of them. By challenging its readers with journalism, *The Washington Rumor* was winning the day. In ever increasing numbers, those seeking "the truth, and the facts behind that truth," were realizing that in order to achieve that goal, they had to follow *The Rumor*!

"It's Talia, if I recall properly," smiled Cuffington, extending his hand in welcome.

"You have an impressive memory, Inspector, she said accepting his hand and returning the smile.

"Please join us," insisted Cuffington with requisite social grace.

Teller glanced at Killingsworth and Fuentes with intuitive hesitation.

"I think I'd rather chat with you privately," she concluded. "I'll wait for another more discreet opportunity," she demurred.

"You very well may never get another opportunity," promised the Inspector.

Talia Teller weighed her options. Reluctantly, she took a seat next to Captain Killingsworth.

"Talia, the gentleman seated to your left is Captain Patrick Killingsworth of U.S. Capitol Police, introduced Cuffington.

"I already know who he is," dismissed the Reporter.

Killingsworth smiled with professionally polite skepticism.

"And this is Detective Maria Fuentes of Metro," continued the Inspector.

"That, I didn't know," replied Teller.

The two women immediately evaluated one another. Not surprisingly, they both came to the same conclusion at the very same time. Each smiled politely, adhering to professional etiquette. However, their rivalry was, already well under way.

Once the reporter was seated, their waiter assaulted the booth with unbridled enthusiasm.

"I know who you are!" he exclaimed with unabashed admiration. "You're Talia Teller from *The Washington Rumor!*" gushed the young man. "I'm simply all over your blog every day!"

"I do so much appreciate that," she grinned with her first display of genuine emotion.

"What can I get for you Ms. Teller?" he asked excitedly.

Teller surveyed what her fellow booth occupants were imbibing and then focused her eyes on the waiter.

"I'll have a Bud, no glass," she instructed.

"One Bud it is!" he cheerfully complied. "You know, I can't honestly believe that Brewster' Bistro is becoming a celebrity Mecca!"

The young waiter bustled towards his appointed duty.

"So Ms. Teller, is Brewster's one of your regular watering holes?" smiled Cuffington.

"Actually Inspector, this is the first time I've had the pleasure of experiencing the ambience of Brewster's," admitted the Reporter.

"So then what did bring you here this afternoon Talia," pursued the Inspector.

"You're presence," was her succinct explanation.

"And how did you know I'd be here today?" continued Cuffington.

"Her," responded Teller, nodding emphatically in the direction of Detective Fuentes. "I simply followed your car after you left the securely guarded back parking lot of U.S. Capitol Police headquarters," divulged *The Washington Rumor* reporter.

Talia Teller passed an almost imperceptible smirk in the direction of Maria Fuentes.

"Well that does, indeed, explain your coincidental appearance here at Brewster's," concluded Cuffington with unemotional acknowledgement.

Their waiter returned with Teller's beer. He placed it gracefully in front of the reporter.

"Is there anything else I can do for you for you at this time, Ms. Teller?" he asked, obsequiously.

"No thank you. I'm fine," answered the reporter.

"Well I'm not!" interrupted Killingworth. "Another round for law and order!" demanded the Captain.

"Of course Captain Killingsworth, how foolish of me not to have asked" fumbled the waiter.

Once more, he ducked out of sight.

The Inspector had been quite careful not to alter his facial expression. If Teller's revelation about how she had managed to track them was bothering him, Cuffington was not tipping his hand.

Fuentes, although maintaining a veneer of outward equanimity, was absolutely roiling beneath her skin.

"How could I have been so damn careless?" she thought to herself. "How did I fail to pick up the tail of an amateur?" "What the hell is Cuffington going to say or do about my professional lapse?"

Her head was spinning and her stomach churning. And as for any possible rivalry between the two young women, clearly round one had been awarded to Teller.

"So Talia, now that you have secured my undivided attention, just what is it you want to discuss," continued the Inspector without missing a beat.

Once again, the reporter looked at Killingsworth and Fuentes with hesitant wariness. In spite of her reservations, Teller proceeded.

"Well, what I wanted to discuss with you Inspector. . ."

She was interrupted by the return of their waiter. After carrying out the Captain's orders, the young man left without saying a word.

"You were saying Talia?" resumed the Inspector.

"I wanted to meet you and discuss the deaths of Congressman Sooner and Senator Ryder," continued the reporter.

"Well shiver me timbers!" guffawed the Captain. "Who would ever in their lifetime have guessed such a surprising motive!"

Cuffington shot Killingsworth a short scowl of disapproval.

The Captain quietly re-focused his attention upon the cocktail on deck.

"Go on Talia," encouraged the Inspector.

Teller sipped her beer as she gathered her thoughts. She appeared to be conflicted by what she was about to say.

"When it became apparent to me that Senator William Ryder was going to become the youngest member of the United States Senate to qualify for induction into the prestigious club known as

106

the Gang of 20/20, I thought it would be appropriate to do a comprehensive feature highlighting the Senator's legislative accomplishments," explained Teller.

She stopped to take an earnest pull from her beer.

"Anyway, during the course of routine background research and various interviews with people who were friendly with Senator Ryder, it quickly became apparent to me that the Senator was living a, how should I put it, a rather alternative life-style," disclosed the reporter from *The Washington Rumor*.

She, again, paused for the moment that refreshes.

Teller continued.

"No, alternative isn't the proper word, bizarre is far more applicable in his particular situation," she amended.

"Talia, if you're alluding to Terry Frailey, we're already aware of the late Senator's predispositions," assured the Inspector.

"Inspector Cuffington, Terrence Frailey is not even the tip of the iceberg!" declared Teller.

"Tell me about that iceberg Talia," persisted the Inspector.

"That I cannot do Inspector," exhorted the reporter.

"And why is that Talia?" pressed Cuffington.

"Because I don't know exactly what that iceberg actually is!" lamented Teller.

Cuffington paused to evaluate the young reporter's countenance.

"You don't strike me as the type not to follow through on a work in progress," he noted with a tone of skepticism.

"You are absolutely correct. I was warned that you have a knack for reading people rather quickly," commented Teller.

"So then why did you call off the dogs?" demanded Cuffington.

Talia took another sip of her beer. She stared at Cuffington. She was trying, in her own mind, to accurately evaluate the man seated across from her; a man she had met for the first time just moments before.

"Cuz, dem dang dawgs, they be muzzled Mr. Rhett."

The Inspector nodded with empathy.

"Well, I am now beginning to understand the full scope of your plight, Prissy," consoled Cuffington.

Although not an iceberg, the ice of unfamiliarity between the Inspector from Metro and the Reporter from *The Washington Rumor* had been broken. They smiled at one another, conveying the acceptance of mutual trust and respect.

Captain Patrick Killingsworth and Detective Maria Fuentes stared blankly at one another, trying to decipher what had just taken place before their very eyes.

"Talia, can you at least tell me what you do know about that iceberg?" urged the Inspector.

"No."

Cuffington sat quietly, carefully choosing his next question.

"Can you tell me who pulled the plug on your background research endeavors?"

"Management," was her one-worded answer.

'Why?" continued Cuffington.

"Too much heat, I suspect," was her contention.

"Are you saying that *The Washington Rumor* was effectively shut down when it came to your investigation of Senator Ryder?" demanded the Inspector.

"No. What I am suggesting is that even The Rumor can be persuaded to take a seat in the back of the bus when it comes to facts. Don't forget Inspector, we are living in Washington D.C.," she scolded.

Although frustrated, Cuffington remained congenial. He was determined to come away with something that might further his investigation.

"Talia, what are you at liberty to tell me about your background check on Senator Ryder?"

The young journalist studied the face of Inspector Nick Cuffington. When she finally responded, it was with the conviction of commitment to her chosen profession.

"I can tell you that I am a proud graduate of the Tim Russert School of Journalism. That said, if I don't have command of all the facts, I have absolutely no story to report," affirmed Teller.

Cuffington smiled affectionately at the young reporter from *The Washington Rumor*.

"I can appreciate that Talia. In point of fact, you probably have no idea just how sorely I miss that lost journalistic tenet when it comes to today's reporting of the news," admitted the Inspector.

Talia Teller rose from her seat, dutifully performed the obligatory polite farewells, and headed for the front door of Brewster's Bistro. Suddenly she stopped. Without a blink of hesitation she turned to, once again, engage Cuffington.

"Oh Inspector, there is one more thing I can tell you and still reside comfortably within the parameters of my interpretation of journalistic ethics.

"And what might that be Talia?" was the Inspector's half-hearted response.

"The heat was turned up when I informed The Rumor's editorial staff of recurring links between Senator Ryder and Congressman Sooner; none of which was in any way connected to the business of the United States Congress, if such an animal still exists in Washington D.C."

With that, the reporter for *The Washington Rumor* was gone.

Chapter Twenty-Four

Cuffington, Killingsworth, and Fuentes remained seated in their booth at Brewster's Bistro.

Each was mentally trying to digest and then make some sense of what Talia Teller had conveyed to them. Captain Killingsworth was the first to speak.

"I for one don't buy any of it!" he concluded, vehemently.

"Buy any of what, Pat?" asked the Inspector.

"Any of whatever it is Teller's trying to sell us, Nick."

"And what makes you think she's trying to sell us anything?" rebutted Cuffington.

"Ah come on Nick! She strolls in here and conveniently drops a beautifully wrapped package right in our laps; a box full of nothing, if you ask me."

Cuffington sat motionlessly. He said nothing. He was busily trying to thread the eye of an extremely elusive needle.

"Okay Pat, let's assume Teller isn't what she purports to be, what the hell was her purpose in seeking us out in the first place?" challenged the Inspector.

Killingsworth sipped at his cocktail.

"If you want my opinion, she was sent here with the directed intent of dragging us into the kinky little after hours world of the late Senator Ryder," dismissed the Captain.

Cuffington gave no initial reaction.

Killingsworth continued with his theory.

"She can't get too specific, so how better to keep things murky than by creating a shroud of moral and professional ethical standards! But she's not done. The empty box needs a nice pretty ribbon. That's when she baits her present with some crap about possible ties between the late Congressman Sooner and the sordid socio-pathetic underworld that Ryder called home!"

110

The Captain had completed his hypothetical masterpiece.

Cuffington gave Killingsworth's contention some thought.

"And why is Teller doing all of this in the first place, Pat?" demanded the Inspector.

"She or they are trying impede our investigation, to throw us off track," conveyed Killingsworth with confidence.

"Yes, but Pat, as of right now, we don't have a track to be thrown off!"

"True, but they don't know that!" reasoned the Captain.

Cuffington sighed and shook his head. He turned to face Detective Fuentes.

"What's your take on Talia Teller, Maria?"

"I think she's a bitch," replied Fuentes.

Cuffington eyed his Detective with quiet exasperation.

"Can you please put away the claws for a moment, Cat Girl? Right now, I need what I have long considered to be your valuable input," he instructed with patience.

Fuentes sipped her beer. She sat back and looked upwardly at the ceiling. Shortly, she exhaled a long, slow breath of decision. She squared to face the Inspector.

"For the most part, I tend to agree with Pat's assessment of the woman and her motives for the impromptu meeting. I think it a safe assumption that her presence here this afternoon was designed to hinder rather than help," she finished with reasonable certainty.

Cuffington carefully parsed her words.

"What exactly guided you to that destination?" stalked the Inspector.

"Common sense," asserted the Detective.

"Enlighten me."

Detective Fuentes sipped at her beer.

"Because, it makes perfect sense to me that if whoever or whatever is in a position to "muzzle" *The Washington Rumor*, it stands to reason the same whoever or whatever is more than capable of transforming one of the Rumor's reporters into a pawn of its own bidding," surmised the Detective.

This time it was Cuffington who leaned back and gazed up at the ceiling.

"Of course, both of them are probably right," he thought to himself. "Killingsworth's conclusion, albeit somewhat emotional, is, nonetheless fundamentally plausible. And Fuentes' premise is, as always bed-rocked in sound logic. But if not someone involved in the twisted underworld of Washington D.C., then who or what is responsible for the deaths of the two members of Congress?"

The Inspector first looked at Detective Fuentes and then to Captain Killingsworth.

"Okay, let's assume you two are right and Talia Teller is nothing more than a decoy of distraction sent to throw us on a pointless chase. The question then becomes, why the hell would anyone connected with the two Congressional murders knowingly introduce us to someone that might prove useful to us in our investigations?" Cuffington threw out for grist.

Both Killingsworth and Fuentes began to ponder what the Inspector had introduced for conjecture.

The Captain shifted restlessly in his seat.

"Listen Nick, it's been a long day. I for one need some rest. Tomorrow, I'll start touching bases with some my contacts over at The Service" he promised.

Killingsworth rose to leave. As he did, he motioned their waiter for the check. Cuffington and Fuentes followed suit and also stood to depart. Their server returned with what appeared to be the tab.

"I'll take that," insisted the Captain.

Killingsworth looked at Cuffington.

"Nick, it's my turn. You paid last time."

The waiter, undeterred, proceeded towards the Inspector and handed him the slip of paper. He then turned to Killingsworth.

"Captain the bill has already been taken care of by Ms. Teller," explained the young man as he bowed and turned to go.

Cuffington slipped the piece of paper into his pocket.

The three officers left the building and said their goodbyes on the street.

"Pat, I'll be waiting to hear if your friends over at The Service have anything of interest," confirmed the Inspector.

The ride across town towards Foggy Bottom began with a strained silence between Inspector Cuffington and Detective Fuentes It was Fuentes who spoke first.

"Inspector," she began.

"It's Nick," remonstrated Cuffington

Fuentes fell back into nonspeak mode.

Cuffington turned from the passenger side window and stared at his Detective. His tone of speech was calmly measured and yet decisive. Fuentes eyes remained riveted on the road before her.

"Maria, if you are going to dwell on the fact Teller got the jump on you this afternoon, you're not only wasting your time, but mine, as well," entreated the Inspector.

The Detective remained distantly inattentive.

"Listen to me Maria, there's absolutely nothing I can say or do to punish you any more than what you are already doing to yourself," assuaged Cuffington. "Besides, if you are going to let me down by continuing to feel sorry for yourself, you'll prove to be of no further use to me during the duration of these investigations."

"It's one to nothing," brooded the Detective.

"I don't get your meaning, Maria," admitted Cuffington.

"It's Talia Teller one Maria Fuentes zippo!" she explained in disgust.

Cuffington once again turned his attention to the passenger side window, feigning disinterest. He was smiling to himself.

"If you want to get technical, it's actually Teller dos and Fuentes nada," revealed the Inspector. "But then again, who's keeping score, anyway?"

"And how did you arrive at that those numbers," she challenged.

"It's really quite simple, Watson. Not only did she beat you to the draw this afternoon, she also managed to uncover ties between Congressman Sooner and Senator Ryder that apparently escaped your in depth research."

Detective Maria Fuentes hit the brakes of the vehicle.

Her obviously unmarked cruiser came to an abrupt halt in front of the Cuffington residence.

She rammed the transmission into park.

She turned and faced Cuffington with bellicose resentment.

"Your instructions to me were to turn up political connections between Sooner and Ryder!" she snarled.

Not finished with her tirade, the Detective continued.

"If you wanted me to get down their shorts, you should have said so, Inspector! Besides, how much time did Teller have to do her background check? I for one had a couple of hours after a full day's duty!"

Cuffington climbed out of the car.

He turned to address Fuentes.

"You know, you're right Detective, my instructions were a bit restrictive. Next time, I shall try to give you more room to roam."

He shut the car door and walked away.

Detective Fuentes re-engaged the cruiser's transmission and peeled off in a squeal of rubber.

As he approached the side door of his home, Nick Cuffington paused and laughed aloud.

"She's back!"

Chapter Twenty-Five

Cuffington entered his house through the kitchen door. Leigh was perched on a stool at the center aisle, quietly absorbing the ongoing media hysteria perpetuated by the twenty-four hour a day news cycle of cable television. Nick walked up to his wife, kissed her on the back of the neck, and momentarily paused to witness the ever unfolding melodrama as it was being construed by the T.V. media's reporting of the facts.

"Darling, I never realized how totally non-photogenic you are in front of the camera," she critiqued without taking her eyes off the screen.

"That's exactly why I had Fuentes give me the hook as soon as I did, cherub," he responded playfully.

Mrs. Cuffington beckoned her husband hither. She planted a kiss on his lips, and then promptly returned to the rapture of Washington D.C.'s Most Wanted.

"I bet you didn't know that two members of the United States Congress were murdered right here in Washington D.C.," he kidded.

"Why no, I hadn't heard that!" responded Leigh, answering the call of jest with emoted surprise. "Please, do tell me all about it!"

"I wish I could," was Nick's humorless come-back.

Cuffington started towards the refrigerator.

Leigh muted the volume on the flat screen.

"Nick, while you're up, would you mind getting me a glass of wine?"

"At your service," he complied.

Cuffington reached into a kitchen cabinet for a wine glass. He opened the door to the fridge and selected a bottle of white. He also surveyed the contents of the kitchen's cooler.

"Are you hungry, Nick?"

"No, not really," he replied with indifference.

He returned to Leigh with her request.

"Given the current set of circumstances you're dealing with, I had absolutely no idea what time you were going to be home. So, I took the liberty of a very late lunch with several friends from The Fiction Revue," confessed Mrs. Cuffington.

"Guilty as charged then," smiled Nick. "Actually, I'm glad you did."

He handed her the glass of white.

"I thought there might be some pizza left," he frowned.

"Oh, today was garbage pick-up, dear," she explained impishly.

"I was kind of hoping you might have at least waited until the recyclables," he grumbled.

"No such luck, Inspector!" as she sipped her wine.

"Well, in that case, you leave me little alternative for sustenance," he concluded.

Nick walked back to the refrigerator, claimed a cold one, and ambled towards the kitchen door.

"Meet me on the patio, at your leisure, of course," summoned the now dethroned Prince of Pizza.

Cuffington stepped outside into the stillness of his backyard. He found comfort in the warm darkness that immediately enveloped him. The absence of both public and professional scrutiny was a welcomed respite.

The outside kitchen light snapped on, emitting a harsh glare of illumination. Leigh Cuffington emerged from the house and sat down next to her already seated husband. She studied his face, trying to determine the true mood of her husband before speaking.

"Nick, honestly, how are you holding up under all this?" she asked with heart-felt concern.

Cuffington shifted his attention from the shadows of introspection and focused on the one true flame of his life. Although his smile was strained, the humor in his eyes remained intact.

"Well considering the fact that Chiefs Teasedale and O'Toole have seen fit to appoint me lead investigator in the most heinous, not to mention most controversial murder case to plague Washington D.C. since the Lincoln assassination ; one I might add, that has absolutely no solid leads, I'm feeling rather feisty, if not photogenic," he summarized with a grin.

Again, Leigh Cuffington stared at her husband.

"Knowing you, Inspector, I can only assume you engineered that appointment!" as she shook her head, dubiously.

"Guilty as charged," corroborated the Inspector.

"Nick, how the hell are you managing to concentrate, whatsoever, under the microscope of these obsessively over-stepping media?" wondered Leigh.

"By avoiding them as best I can," conceded Nick.

It was then that the Inspector remembered the slip of paper handed to him by the young waiter at Brewster's Bistro. Cuffington reached into his pocket and retrieved the note. It read:

"Inspector, here is my private number. I urge you to keep our lines of communication fluid." T.T.

Nick handed the piece of paper to his wife. Leigh read the succinct note.

"Who's it from Nick?"

"One Talia Teller," briefed the Inspector.

"I know who she is!" exclaimed Mrs. Cuffington. "She writes for *The Washington Rumor*. Now that's the one publication here in Washington D.C. whose words you can take to the bank!" exalted Leigh.

"Be very careful where you're making those deposits in this town these days," cautioned the Inspector.

Leigh Cuffington frowned at her husband.

"I'll have you know that *The Washington Rumor* represents the last bastion of legitimate journalism we have sounding the trumpet of truth here in Washington D.C.!" she proclaimed.

Cuffington listened to his wife's impassioned words with a simultaneous mixture of sardonic and genuine remorse. He shook his head with slow deliberation.

"The reality, Leigh, is that the truth here in Washington D.C. is a commodity packaged by and sold to the public by the politicians and bureaucrats. It is then reinforced by the media that so devoutly serve those very same politicians and bureaucrats."

Leigh Cuffington fell silent. She thoughtfully sipped her wine and then calmly questioned her husband.

"So, Nick, what do you think the truth really is in trying to explain the murders of Congressman Sooner and Senator Ryder?" she asked with resolve.

Cuffington reached for his pack and lit a cigarette.

"I don't know for sure. But what I do know is that it's something none of us here in Washington D.C. has ever encountered before!" he stated with commitment.

Leigh Cuffington was valiantly trying to accept what she considered to be her husband's growing state of paranoia as a symptom of work related stress.

"Nick, you're making absolutely no sense. Listen to me. You've had along and exceptionally hard several days. Why don't you go upstairs and try to get some rest."

"I won't fight you on that front," yawned the Inspector.

"Honey, after some sleep, these abstract notions of yours regarding unseen forces and bogeymen will suddenly crystallize into cogent thoughts about those truly responsible for these unforgiveable acts of terrorism," reassured the Inspector's wife.

Cuffington killed his beer and snuffed his smoke. He rose to leave the patio. He kissed Leigh goodnight.

"Are you going to bed, Nick?"

"Yes, after I make a phone call."

"And who the hell are you going to annoy at this hour of the night?" she demanded.

"The Bogeyman"

Chapter Twenty-Six

Cuffington awoke at seven a.m.. His sleep had been sound and undisturbed. Nick shaved, showered, and dressed. He descended the second floor flight of stairs and entered the kitchen.

Leigh was standing in front of the small flat screen holding a mug of coffee. Cuffington came up behind her, wrapped his arms around her waist, and kissed her good morning.

"I left you for dead," she smiled, warmly.

"Merely an undressed rehearsal, dear," reassured the Inspector.

"Nick, I hope the sleep did you some good. Quite frankly, your nonsense last night about unseen forces lurking about Washington D.C. had me a little concerned," she admitted with a shudder.

"Not to worry Mrs. Cuffington, I'm refreshed and ready to do what I've always done best. I am prepared to crystallize into thought those responsible for these unforgivable acts of terrorism!" he announced with unbridled enthusiasm.

"Nick, never condescend to me," she growled.

The Inspector retreated into banality.

"Changing the subject, what are you watching?" he asked with disinterest.

"What everyone who is anyone in Washington D.C. watches in the earlier hours of the day, *Morning Joe*," she explained.

"Oh, I've seen that show," asserted Nick. "That's the one where the husband and wife argue over politics."

"You're wrong on both counts, Inspector," contended Mrs. Cuffington. "To start with, Joe and Mika are not married," she explained.

"Well they sure as hell fight like they are," insisted the Inspector.

"Point number two is that Joe and Mika never argue over politics. They politely and professionally discuss the geo-political events of the day. That is, of course, until Joe starts injecting his convoluted concepts of the conservative movement in this country," concluded Leigh.

"I'll take you at your word, dear," relented the Inspector.

Cuffington crossed the floor of the kitchen to retrieve two glasses for his usual water and juice combo.

"Nick, today, *Morning Joe* is going to have on a prominent, former F.B.I. profiler to help sort out and explain the two Congressional murders," Leigh revealed with excited anticipation.

"Now that is breaking news. When he reveals the names and the motives of the killers, I trust you will bring me up to speed so I can make the appropriate arrests and then oversee their politically correct releases," implored the Inspector with unmasked disdain.

Leigh stood enraptured, hanging on every word pouring forth from the formally prominent ex-F.B.I. profiler.

Nick started across the kitchen, heading for his office.

He paused behind Leigh to momentarily observe the object of her enthrallment.

"I know that guy! That's Burnt Von Sleuth," acknowledged the Inspector.

"Nick, hush! I do so want to hear what this man has to say," scolded Leigh Cuffington.

"Do you want to know why he is a formally prominent ex-F.B.I. profiler? Because he couldn't catch a STD or a DSK in a Parisian whorehouse, that's why!"

"Nick, I'm trying to listen to his analysis. So please, be quiet!"

"You're absolutely right sweetheart. I'm going to trundle off to my office, update my resume, and send it off to *Morning Joe*. At the very least, they'll have a possible replacement on file should Burnt Von Sleuth ever decide to return to the field."

Cuffington entered his office.

He sat down in front of his desk top.

Before checking his E-mails, he reactivated his cell phone for messages.

There were none.

That was not a surprise.

Of the five people that had access to his cell phone number, two were currently not overly anxious to speak with him, two disliked conversing on the phone under any circumstances, and Leigh was at home with him.

He swept through his e-mails.

Other than the opportunity save on products and services of utterly no use to him, there was no news.

"There is an upside to contracting professional leprosy," he smiled to himself.

He picked up his phone and pushed speed dial.

"You're up early this morning Nick," noted Detective Fuentes.

"The early bird always manages to catch something," laughed Cuffington.

"I won't even bother to ask what you mean by that Inspector"

"You disappoint me, Maria."

"Nick, are you okay?" she asked with concern.

"Never better," boasted the Inspector. "Foggy Bottom at eleven-thirty," instructed Cuffington.

"And what is our destination Inspector?"

"Gatsby's place," as he severed the connection.

Leigh Cuffington knocked on the door of her husband's office and entered.

She stood in front of his desk, clasping the same ceramic coffee mug.

"May I have a word with you Nick?"

"Of course, since when have you ever felt the obligation to ask?"

His question went unanswered.

"Nick, do you want to know what I have just learned by listening to that formally prominent ex-F.B.I. profiler?"

"Enlighten me, Leigh."

"Burnt Von Sleuth is quite certain that the killer's motive was completely a personal matter and had absolutely nothing to do with any political machinations surrounding Washington D.C."

"Killer?" asked the Inspector, incredulously.

"Yes killer. And to my way of thinking, that shoots all your recent meanderings about unseen forces, multiple assassins, and political chicanery all to hell!"

"Well, I'm heartened that your fears have been alleviated," accepted the Inspector.

"Furthermore, Nick, I'm saddened to say that I believe the former F.B.I. profiler's assessment of the current situation is far more in tune with the reality of the circumstances surrounding the Congressional murders than your inexplicable witch hunt."

She paused before rendering her final decision.

"Quite frankly, I believe a far more rational approach than yours will be required to ultimately bring this scoundrel to justice!"

"Fear not fair maiden, I have little doubt that the Powers to Be here in Washington D.C. will share your sentiments regarding the two Congressional killings and react swiftly and rationally to protect their own safety and self-interests," concurred the now exiled Inspector.

Chapter Twenty-Seven

It was eleven-thirty a.m.

Detective Maria Fuentes coasted to a stop in front of the Cuffington home. Uncharacteristically, the Inspector was standing in the driveway anticipating her arrival. He got into the passenger seat and buckled up for safety. The Inspector turned to face Fuentes.

"Let's go," he ordered.

"What's our destination?" she asked with weathered indifference.

"Uptown.," instructed Cuffington.

"Nick, in case you haven't noticed, these days, most of Washington D.C. and its surrounding suburbs are "Uptown." Which slice of the People's Pie are you specifically referring to?" she insisted with obvious scorn.

"The North West Quadrant," barked the Inspector.

"Now that is "Uptown," agreed Fuentes as she pointed her car in the direction of their now announced port of call.

"And which opulent neighborhood do you have in mind this morning, Inspector?" smiled the Detective in an unsuccessful attempt to thaw Cuffington's frigid mood.

"Sheridan Kalorama," pin pointed the Inspector.

As was his custom, Cuffington stared out through the passenger side window in silence, pondering the passing scenery.

"Why Nick, Sheridan Kalorama isn't "Uptown," it's "Toptown!" marveled Fuentes.

The Inspector did not respond.

Unexpectedly, their ride was interrupted by a sudden slow-down in the traffic flow. For only the second time during their cross town trek, Cuffington diverted his attention from the window.

"What's the holdup?" he demanded.

"Most likely, the ever increasing number of protestors making their presence felt here in Washington D.C.," speculated the Detective.

Their cruiser inched closer to an intersection that would enable them to turn off, and thus, hopefully circumvent any further delay. The inevitable red, white, and blue lights of authority began to make themselves, visible in the distance. Cuffington checked his wrist watch.

"We're expected at twelve, are we going to be on time, or should I call ahead?" demanded Cuffington.

"Your guess is as good as mine, Nick," concluded Maria.

As their vehicle continued to creep towards the cross street, the first demonstrators came into view.

Cuffington returned his attention to the passenger side window. The Inspector began to analyze the people who were exercising their right to freedom of assembly. The anger in the faces of the people who had taken to the streets was palpable; but, peaceful, nonetheless. The first thing he noted was the utter absence of commonality. Their ages, genders, colors, and styles of dress were diverse. Even the signs, placards, and slogans were motley. As they neared their intersection, Cuffington glanced at Fuentes.

"I'm assuming this is the Squatting on Whore Street Movement," he conjectured.

"No way Nick," dismissed the Detective.

"How can you be so certain?" his interest now piqued.

"Because these people are day trippers," she explained with patience.

"Day trippers?" questioned Cuffington.

"Yes, this group comes to protest for the day. At the end of that day they leave. However, inevitably, they always return."

"And the Squatting on Whore Street Movement aren't day trippers?" asked the Inspector.

"No, when the Squatting on Whore Street Movement sets up camp, it's generally for the duration," elaborated Maria.

"Unfortunately, more times than not, it's without a change of clothing or proper hygienic facilities."

"I would imagine that such a combination might make for a rather bold bouillabaisse after several days of non-stop squatting," postulated the Inspector, smiling for the first time that morning.

"And then some Nick, from what I've heard," winced Maria.

"Well, if not the Squatting on Whore Street Movement, who exactly are these people?" challenged Cuffington.

"The Herbal Brigade," replied Fuentes without hesitation.

"And what the hell have they come to Washington D.C. to demonstrate against?" implored the Inspector.

"Essentially Nick, they are here to protest against what they feel is too much Federal Government. In particular, too many taxes, too much regulation, too much Federal spending and, above all else, an out of control National Debt," abridged the Detective.

Cuffington brooded over her words. He found himself wrestling with the one question that had formulated itself in the forefront of his thought process.

"Quite frankly, I don't know who has the bigger fight on their hands; the Herbal Brigade taking on the Establishment of Washington D.C. or the Squatting on Whore Street Movement doing battle with the bankers on Wall Street," admitted the Inspector.

"Actually Nick, your question is somewhat moot," decided the Detective.

"And how do you figure that Maria?" questioned Cuffington.

"Because, in the final analysis, Washington D.C. and Wall Street are an inextricably interwoven extension of one another," chided Fuentes.

Inspector Nick Cuffington chose not to hazard a comment.

Slowly, they made their way to the intersection. Fuentes turned left. No longer encumbered by the gnarl of American protestors, she quickly accelerated to compensate for the time lost by the public display of outrage and indignation.

Cuffington once again glanced at his watch.

"Are you going to phone ahead Nick?"

"No. We'll just be fashionably late," decided the Inspector.

"You couldn't have chosen a more appropriate neighborhood to be tony," observed the Detective. "Do you have a particular address that I can GPS," gawked Fuentes.

"Belmont Road N.W.," he replied curtly.

"So, you've been here before?" she asked with mounting curiosity.

"Yes."

"Do you mind telling me when and why?" persisted, the Detective.

"Yes."

"Will you at least inform me when we have arrived?"

"You'll know it when you see it," was Cuffington's cryptic answer.

Fuentes turned onto Belmont Road N.W. She drove without speaking, taking in the impressive homes that dominated the "Private Road." Maria continued to drive until she instinctively stopped in front of a majestic beau arts mansion.

"I get the feeling that this is the place," she guessed.

"You're right, Detective. I've always maintained the utmost respect for your professional sixth sense," nodded the Inspector.

Maria Fuentes ventured into the driveway and was immediately greeted by a closed wrought iron security gate.

The Detective looked at Cuffington.

"So now what Nick, she asked." I can only assume that you must be privy to the "open sesame" pass code."

Before the Inspector could answer, the security gate's speaker squawked to life.

"Yes?" was the haughty, singularly worded question of indifference.

Fuentes peered at Cuffington, apprehensively.

"Sanzio," edified the Inspector.

"Sanzio," repeated the Detective, fully expecting the imminent arrival of snarling guard dogs.

With that, the heavy gates slowly opened, affording them access to the imperial grounds.

"Nick, are we really supposed to be going into this place?" flustered Fuentes.

"When in doubt, always follow the yellow brick road, Detective," advised the Inspector.

Chapter Twenty-Eight

Maria proceeded to drive slowly up the long, lushly treed, undulating cobbled lane. She came to a stop on a semi-circular driveway directly facing the imposing front door of the impressive home. Maria shifted the car into park. Before she had a chance to turn off the ignition, a valet parking attendant accosted the driver's side door and opened it.

"I'll take it from here ma'am," he offered, deferentially.

Fuentes flashed her badge.

"No you won't! Regulations," she stressed.

The young man jumped back, as if the car's door handle was electrified.

"Of course, Detective," he acquiesced apologetically. "Just follow this road," he pointed. "It's about one hundred yards."

"Nick, why don't you get out here, and I'll meet you inside," she suggested.

"Hell no," decreed Cuffington. "You very well might get lost. Besides, I'm just along for the ride anyway," smiled the Inspector.

After parking in the designated location, Cuffington and Fuentes made their way back to the front of the mansion. Prior to given the opportunity of ringing the chimes, the front door opened. Standing in front of them was a tall, gray haired aristocratic looking man. He appeared to be in his latter sixties. Although not dressed in the traditional attire, his taste in clothing was impeccable. He left little doubt as to who he was and what his responsibilities were.

"Your arrival is a bit on the tardy side this afternoon, Inspector," chastised the Gentleman.

"Ran into a bit of Democracy ," explained Cuffington

"Ah, that can be so intrusive at times," smiled the Gentleman with an immediate understanding for the reason of their delay.

The Gentleman led them into an expansive foyer.

The vaulted ceilings were over-shadowed only by a magnificent bridal staircase. The foyer furnished three distinctive hallways. The Gentleman chose door number three.

"Master Sinclair is awaiting your arrival on the first floor sunning room. Please follow me," was his dictate.

After walking down an elaborately furnished hallway, their guide stopped, solicitously opened a glass-paneled door, and beckoned Cuffington and Fuentes to enter. Once inside the exquisitely decorated "sunning room," the man anticipating their arrival rose to greet them.

"Nick, how good to see you!" he beamed.

He turned to address their tour guide.

"That will be all," he commanded.

"Sir"

The Gentleman sealed the door behind him.

"So Nick, what special occasion brings you to my humble abode?" he gleamed knowingly.

"Why Nelson, no one even bothered to tell me that you had entered the legal profession. You must realize, of course, that asking questions one already knows the answers to is almost always the certain reek of an attorney."

"Moi, a mal-practitioner of our land's laws, perish the thought," he disavowed with the wave of a hand.

Nelson Lloyd Sinclair was rich. His father was richer, and his grandfather, at the age of ninety-eight, even richer. Nelson was in his early forties. He was of medium height and weight. All in all, Nelson Lloyd Sinclair was considered to be quite attractive by most women and men, alike.

Cuffington had first met Sinclair while they were both living in New York City. It had been at a book signing reception Leigh had asked the Inspector to attend. Although the two men had very little in common, for whatever inexplicable reason, they had immediately formed a bond of mutual congeniality. They had remained friendly ever since.

Sinclair's world revolved around the Universe of the Arts. His passions were paintings and sculptures. However, his patronage extended into most fields of artistic endeavor. He was highly respected, not to mention greatly appreciated, by Washington's cultural community, en masse. Sinclair had relocated to Washington D.C. several years after the Cuffington's had departed New York City. The first time Cuffington and Sinclair had run into one another, after their respective relocations to Washington D.C., had been several years prior. The occasion had been a "Celebration of the Arts" dinner sponsored by one of Leigh's charitable organizations. Mrs. Cuffington had "requested" Inspector Cuffington's attendance. During the "courses" of that evening, Sinclair had explained his decision to relocate to Washington D.C.

"Nick, without variation, Art will always follow the money trail." He went on to point out that seven of the ten wealthiest counties in the United States were now located in and around Washington D.C..

"So you see old friend, I was left little choice. However, in my particular case, the equation was inverted; money followed art."

The opportunity for Cuffington to explain the reason for his relocation from New York to Washington D.C. never came up in conversation.

Sinclair stood appraising Fuentes with full appreciation.

"And who is this lovely accomplice of yours, Inspector?" he asked while extending his hand towards Maria.

"Nelson, this is Detective Maria Fuentes," introduced Cuffington.

"Nick has always had fine taste when it comes to women," he smiled while kissing her hand.

Sinclair immediately noticed Maria Fuentes' uncertainty about why she was where she was in the first place.

"To answer you're unasked question, Detective, you are here to inquire about the unfortunate passing of Senator William Ryder," he informed her.

Nelson Lloyd Sinclair disengaged and walked with purpose to the room's darkly-grained mahogany bar. There was an opened bottle of wine waiting to be tasted. He picked up the bottle and savored its bouquet. Placing it back on the bar, Sinclair went behind the counter and selected two wine glasses. He looked at Cuffington.

"And why have you concluded I might be of assistance in your investigation of the late Senator's murder, Inspector?"

"I thought that, perhaps, you might have some indirect familiarity with the late Senator's social circles," explained the Inspector.

"Billy Ryder was a socio-pathological deviant," affirmed Sinclair. "No more, no less!'

Nelson refocused his undivided attention upon Detective Fuentes.

"Maria, won't you graciously indulge me by enjoying a glass of wine?" he entreated. "After all, it is a bottle of Petrus 68', which, coincidently, happens to be my year of birth," revealed their host.

"Is it your birthday, Mr. Sinclair?" inquired Fuentes.

"No. But why should that inhibit us?" he asked without expecting an answer.

The Detective looked at her Inspector for a directive.

Cuffington, in spite of the dire situation currently swirling around them, simply could not help himself.

"Why I don't know, Detective, are we officially off duty?" he fluttered.

Fuentes successfully masked her immediately ignited anger.

"Yes, I think I shall join you in a glass, Mr. Sinclair," agreed Maria.

"My friends call me Nelson."

"Nick, I'm guessing you will have your usual?" assumed their host.

"Nelson, I never deviate!"

Sinclair emerged from behind the bar with two wildly expensive glasses of wine and one can of domestic beer whose company was then currently owned by an internationally controlled corporate conglomerate.

"Please, do be seated ," as he motioned to a plush cocktail table and chair ensemble located in front of the twelve foot high floor to ceiling windows that afforded a grand view of the vast expanse of wealth.

Maria sipped her wine.

"Mmm, this is exquisite, Nelson, and the view is simply breathtaking!" gushed the now awe struck young Detective.

"As a matter of fact Maria, Kalorama is the Greek for "fine view," enlightened their host.

"Well, it's that and more!" exclaimed a now overly impressed Fuentes.

Cuffington impatiently tugged on his can of beer.

"Nelson, Senator William Ryder," he interloped.

Sinclair idly twirled his glass, carefully examining its contents. At length, he once again absorbed its bouquet and sipped with refined contentment. With reluctance, he turned his attention to the Inspector.

"Silly Billy could be a very naughty boy," cringed Sinclair.

"Naughty enough to enrage someone to murder him?" posed the Inspector.

"Obviously"

"So, you do believe that it was his socio-pathological deviant life-style that contributed to his death," baited Cuffington.

"Maybe yes, maybe no," was Nelson's non-committal response.

Sinclair slowly relished his wine and then addressed Cuffington with unsolicited candor.

"You know, Nick, you're not the first to come here recently to sniff Silly Billy's dirty laundry," revealed Nelson Lloyd Sinclair.

"Really, and who beat me to the Laundromat?" demanded the Inspector.

"A young female reporter," he answered with aplomb. "In hindsight, it now strikes me as somewhat ironic."

"And why's that Nelson?" pressed Cuffington.

"Because, she approached me before his unseemly demise," conceded Sinclair.

"Do you recall her name, Nelson?"

"I can't say that I do. However, I do remember the name of the publication she purported to represent. It was *The Washington Rumor*."

Sinclair relished the remainder of his wine and rose. He picked up Cuffington's empty beer can.

"Maria, may I entice into one more glass of bliss?"

"Oh, thank you Nelson, but no. I'm driving. Besides, I'm already light-headed as it is," she smiled at her host and then fluttered daggers at Cuffington.

"Nick?"

"Need you ask?"

"It's merely the decorum of decadence, Inspector"

Sinclair returned with a replenished Petrus 68' and a fresh beer.

Smiling, he handed the can to Nick and raised his glass.

"To the seekers of the truth, no matter how Byzantine the current stewards of Washington D.C. have chosen to cloak it"

The two men toasted.

Sinclair's countenance quietly turned somber. He studied Cuffington with an ambience of resolve.

"Nick, why don't you come out and simply ask me the questions you came here to have answered?"

The Inspector minced no words.

"Nelson, who might you know that was so intimately involved in the personal lives of both Senator Ryder and Congressman Sooner that he, she, or it would see fit to kill them both, on the same night?"

Sinclair pondered the question in unhurried silence. When at last, he spoke, it was with unwavering resolve.

"I can think of absolutely no one!"

"Nelson, how can you be so certain of that?" persisted the Inspector.

"Because, Billy Ryder was a born miscreant; he understood no other way of life. Although I really did not know Congressman Sooner all that well, it is my understanding that he simply had no clear idea of who he really was. In any event, there were no sparks flying in the direction of either one of them."

Cuffington stared at Sinclair, attempting to assess the sagacity of his conclusion. Nelson Lloyd Sinclair observed the Inspector's assessment with patient indifference.

"Listen to me Nick. If your game plan, in the pursuit of the Congressional killer, is to stalk the darkness of Washington D.C.'s after-hours circus, you'll only be spinning the wheels of this lovely young lady's car."

Sinclair took a slow, deliberate sip of Petrus 68'. He looked at Cuffington and shook his head with the utmost certainty.

"On that, you have my word, old friend."

Chapter Twenty-Nine

"So, what do you think?" asked an anxious Detective Fuentes.

"What do I think about what?" sighed the Inspector.

"Do you believe a word that came out of Sinclair's mouth?" impugned a skeptical Fuentes.

"I have little reason to think Nelson has any plausible motive to lie," reflected Cuffington.

"Then, that shoots Little Ms. Smarty Pants' theory straight to hell doesn't it now?" gloated Fuentes with relieved, self-satisfaction.

"Teller's postulation was not the only one just banished to Dante's Inferno," added the Inspector.

After leaving the estate of Nelson Lloyd Sinclair, Cuffington and Fuentes were in her obviously unmarked patrol car en route to the Tangerine Oriental Hotel. Their objective was to re-examine the front desk's guest log, review security video tape, and question any personnel on duty the night of Senator's Ryder's murder.

"Is he?' titillated the Detective.

"Is who what?" responded the Inspector.

"Is Nelson gay?" pried Maria.

"To tell you the truth, I don't know," admitted Cuffington.

"Oh c'mon Nick, you've obviously known him long enough to draw your own conclusions," pestered Fuentes.

"Maria, I'm from a very old school. I don't ask, and, more importantly, I don't care. "Besides, he's never been my type anyway," dismissed the Inspector, with a wink.

"Nick how did you, of all people, ever become friendly with Nelson?" pursued Fuentes.

"It was pure happenstance. I met Sinclair while we were both living in New York City."

"And how the hell did that ever happen?" wondered the Detective, more audibly musing to herself than directing a question.

"I met Nelson at a charity dinner party Leigh had been asked to attend. Sinclair and I were waiting for refreshments at the open bar, and happened to strike a chord. We've been friends, of sorts, ever since," explained Nick.

"So Nelson is a wealthy ghost writer?" conjectured Maria.

"No, Sinclair is a wealthy patron of the arts," clarified the Inspector.

The Detective took in and processed the Inspector's answers.

"What prompted you to contact Sinclair at this particular point in time?" hounded the Detective.

"That's really quite simple Maria. I've known for some time that the late Senator Ryder and Nelson knew each other socially. The purpose of today's visit was to reduce the possible areas of investigation," he explained with patience.

"Why did Nelson Sinclair relocate from New York City to Washington D.C.?" she continued with determination.

Mercifully, the Detective's dogged background interrogation was thwarted by the intrusion of her cell phone's ring tone. She scanned the caller I.D.

"It's Killingsworth"

"So, pick it up," suggested the Inspector.

"Why the hell doesn't he call you directly?" she carped irritably.

"Most likely because he doesn't have my number," admitted Cuffington.

"And why's that?"

"Because *I* don't know it," grinned the Inspector.

"Then why do you have a cell phone in the first, Nick?"

"So I can perpetuate the pretense of social mobility here in Twenty-First Century America, why else?"

The Inspector returned to his passenger side window.

Detective Fuentes angrily stabbed at the cell.

"Yes, Captain?"

"Do you know Inspector Cuffington's whereabouts?" he demanded.

Fuentes looked at Cuffington. He nodded affirmatively.

"As a matter of fact I do; he's seated next to me."

"Put him on!" ordered the Captain.

Maria handed her phone to Cuffington.

"Yes, Patrick"

"We've got problems, Nick," related Killingsworth

"Where would you like to begin Pat," chuckled Cuffington.

"No, I'm serious Nick. We have to talk and we have to talk now! I want you meet me at headquarters," implored the Captain.

Nick turned his head to face Fuentes.

"How long will it take us to get to U.S. Capitol Police headquarters, Detective?"

"Barring traffic—assuming that to be a still reasonable assumption—here in Washington D.C., twenty minutes," she confirmed.

"No, no, not U.S. Capitol Police headquarters, our headquarters!" he directed. "Brewsters man, Brewsters!"

Again, the Inspector looked to Fuentes for calculation.

"About the same ETA," she shrugged.

"Alright Pat, we'll try to be there within twenty. . ."

Killingsworth's line had already gone dead. Cuffington returned to Fuentes, her Link to Life.

"Nick, what do you think that's all about?" hazarded the Detective.

"What does it matter?" was the Inspector's resigned conclusion. "We can only play the cards we're being dealt, and unfortunately, it's not our turn to deal."

As they neared their downtown D.C. destination the traffic, once again, began to bog.

"I'd rather fancy a good old fashioned car wreck," mused the Inspector.

"Not likely, Nick. This is probably just another geo-political, socio-economic Washington D.C. gridlocked stand-still," wagered Fuentes.

The Detective was proven to be correct. As they slowly advanced downtown, throngs of demonstrators started to come into view. It appeared to be two distinct groupings of protestors.

"Maria, fill me in on today's line-up cards," insisted the Inspector.

Fuentes quickly surveyed the crowded melee and reported back, as ordered.

"The demonstrators on the left side of the street are the Squatting on Whore Street Movement. The protestors on the right side of the street are the Herbal Brigade," briefed the Detective.

"And the uniformed officers in the middle of the street, where do you think they stand in all of this, Maria?" queried Cuffington.

"Getting paid over-time for their trouble!" grumbled the Detective.

With absolutely no parking spaces available, Maria opted to pull into the No Parking Fire Zone directly in front of Brewster's Bistro.

As they climbed out of the obviously unmarked cruiser, two uniformed officers from Metro quickly descended upon them. Immediately, both of them recognized Inspector Cuffington and Detective Fuentes.

"Don't worry, Inspector, we'll keep a close eye on the vehicle," assured one of the men.

"Yea Maria, don't give it a second thought, we're not going to let anyone squat on your trunk!" laughed the other young patrolman.

"Dream on, Tampon!"

Before Fuentes had time for further social discourse, Nick grabbed her arm and gracefully guided the Detective to the front entrance of Brewster's. The late afternoon luncheon crowd was

138

literally out the door and queued nearly half a block. Cuffington looked dubiously at the long waiting line.

"You know, I don't mind getting bad news, so much. However, I do mind waiting in line to get it.

C'mon, we're out of here Detective," decided Nick.

They turned to leave.

Suddenly, through the crowded front of Brewster's Bistro burst forth their waiter.

"Inspector Cuffington don't leave! Your table awaits you!" proclaimed the young man.

With practiced agility, the waiter eased Cuffington and Fuentes through the crush of people and glided them towards their pre-arranged seating.

"My name is Toby, by the way," he offered, cheerfully.

Cuffington seriously studied the young man for the first time.

"Toby, do you ever take a day off?" smiled the Inspector, congenially.

"You know, it's funny you should ask that question, Inspector. I've been wondering the very same thing about you and Captain Killingsworth."

Chapter Thirty

Toby ushered them to what he had recently christened "Cuff-Kill Corner." Killingsworth was already seated at their booth. A woman sat beside him.

The Captain rose to greet Cuffington and Fuentes as they approached.

"Nick, Maria, I hope you guys didn't hit too much traffic," he smiled as he extended his hand towards the Inspector. "Nick, I want to introduce you to Special Technician Miriam Hightower. Miriam, this is Inspector. . ."

"I already know who he is, I've seen him on the television," related the Special Technician.

Killingsworth reseated himself. Fuentes and Cuffington sat down in the seat facing the two officers from U.S. Capitol Police. Hightower studied the Inspector with careful deliberation before arriving at her final determination.

"You're not quite as unattractive, in person, as you appear to be in front of the camera," was her curt evaluation.

"Why, thank you, Miriam. Truth, be told, you're not the first to bestow such a gracious compliment," confided Cuffington with instant disinterest for the woman seated across the table.

"And Miriam, this is Detective Maria Fuentes," introduced Killingsworth.

"I've never seen her on the television," she dismissed.

Special Technician Miriam Hightower was a mirthless woman of middle-age. Her facial features were, at best, benignly unremarkable; and her frame quite reminiscent of Sponge Bob Square Pants.

Toby the Waiter returned to their booth. He placed a filled glass in front of Killingsworth, cold ones in front of Fuentes and Cuffington, and presented "Bob" with a diet soda.

"Will there be anything else?" he asked, deferentially

"We're fine for the moment," acknowledged the Captain. "Here's to professional co-operation," as he lifted his glass.

Killingsworth addressed the Inspector.

"Nick, Miriam heads up technical security and support for U.S. Capitol Police," explained the Captain.

Cuffington fixed his gaze upon the Special Technician.

"Miriam, please enlighten me as to what technical support and security specifically entails." lured the Inspector.

"Computers Inspector Cuffington, pure and simple. I presume you have heard of that form of communication," condescended the U.S Capitol Police's guru of technology.

"Yes, I have heard that such machines do, indeed, exist," admitted the Inspector.

Nick sipped at his beer and continued his conversation with Hightower.

"So, you are the cyber gatekeeper when it comes to U.S. Capitol Police's internet security?" he gaped in the guise of surprise.

"As a matter of record, I am, Inspector. You seem a bit disquieted by that revelation," she flouted.

"Simply put, I am," admitted Cuffington.

"And why is that Inspector?"

"Because, I've been under, the now obvious misconception, that today's true heavyweights in that particular area of expertise are of a younger generation than yours, Miriam."

Killingsworth and Fuentes simultaneously exchanged silent glances of apprehension.

Special Technician Hightower sipped her diet soda. She choked her disapproval. Miriam Hightower put her glass down and motioned to Toby the Waiter.

"Yes ma'am?"

"This beverage is flat," complained the nabob of U.S. Capitol Police technology.

"I'll replace straightaway, ma'am," assured the young man.

"You will replace it with a double Absolut on the rocks with one twist of lemon and one wedge of lime!" she requested.

"I'll be back in a blink," assured the now steward of Cuff-Kill Corner.

Miriam Hightower stared at Cuffington in a moment of introspection.

"Selecting my fruits has always proven to be a conundrum for me, Inspector," she smiled for the first time. "As for my age, in relationship to computers, putting me at some sort disadvantage in today's internet world, I believe just the opposite to be true," insisted the troll of cyber patrol.

Special Technician Hightower shifted her seated position to better directly face Cuffington.

"You see, Inspector, the little communication saviors have been the mainstay of my existence since middle-school. Indeed, they were my life during years at M.I.T and Cal. Tech.

Hightower leaned over the table as if protecting secrecy.

"In fact, I helped promote the concept of computer science as a post-graduate field of endeavor. So when it comes to computers, don't ever try to introduce the age card to this old broad!"

"It's Nick, Miriam," nodded Cuffington with newly found respect.

Toby returned with the Special Technician's drink and departed. She took a long drain from her glass and then placed in front of her.

`"Let's get down to business, shall we?" suggested Hightower.

Miriam concentrated her attention on Inspector Cuffington.

"Nick, U.S. Capitol Police's computer data base was breached within the last twelve hours," exposed Hightower.

"Breached?" questioned Cuffington.

"Unauthorized entry into our main warehouse," elucidated the Special Technician.

"So, U.S. Capitol Police's computer system was hacked by persons unknown," concluded the Inspector.

142

"Not exactly, Nick," corrected Hightower. "There are identifiable distinctions between hackings, break-ins, and invasions. Would you like me to walk you through their nuances?" offered the Special Technician.

"Absolutely not, just give me the bottom line, Miriam." requested the Inspector.

"The bottom line is that two, and let me emphasize, only two files were tainted by what I deem to have been an invasion of our information domain," asserted Miriam Hightower.

Cuffington finished his beer and motioned to Toby the Waiter. He then focused in on Captain Patrick Killingsworth.

"Let me just take a wild guess at the identity of those two files Pat; one Congressman Barry Sooner and one Senator William Ryder," he recited.

"Give that man a cigar!" acknowledged Killingsworth, with unenthusiastic corroboration.

Cuffington began rapidly flipping the pages of possibilities over in his mind.

He finally settled his undivided attention upon Special Technician Hightower.

"Miriam, besides the four of us seated at this table, what other parties are privy to this information," he asked while still attempting to absorb its full implications.

"Just the members of my unit," she answered sipping her vodka.

Special Technician Miriam Hightower then answered Cuffington's yet to be asked question.

"Inspector, the players on my team are far more concerned with how this invasion of our domain occurred, rather than the 'who and the why.' As for myself, I have complied with my mandated responsibility and dutifully reported the incident to Captain Killingsworth. I am now going to return to -my battlefield."

Miriam Hightower finished her drink and rose to leave.

"Nick, it has truly been a pleasure meeting you. Detective Fuentes, I also enjoyed the pleasure of your company, although you don't say too much."

"Miriam, please!" warned the Inspector, with a smile.

Heading towards the front door of Brewster's, Special Technician Miriam Hightower stopped and turned to address Inspector Cuffington.

"Nick, I'm not privy to the implications this cyber theft has upon your investigation, but I do know this, Inspector; whoever engineered this particular invasion is good; they're real good."

Chapter Thirty-One

Cuffington, Killingsworth, and Fuentes lingered at their booth in Brewster's Bistro. As the late luncheon crowd began to thin out, people gearing up for Happy Hour began to make their presence felt. Special Technician Miriam Hightower's revelation about the cyber trespass at U.S. Capitol Police headquarters was just another unwelcomed kink added to an already seedy affair. The three officers sat in silence. Each was attempting to come up with a reasonable course of action under the new glare of the information theft. It was Captain Killingsworth who opened the discussion.

"Miriam said the heist occurred within the last twelve hours. It jumps out at me, that we should start to feel its effects at any time now," reflected the Captain.

"So Pat, you are suggesting that we should take a wait and see position," confirmed Detective Fuentes.

"And what exactly are the other alternatives, Maria?" contested Killingsworth.

"Well for starters, we could at least make an attempt to find whoever ripped off U.S. Capitol Police headquarters data base," offered Fuentes.

"And are you volunteering to lead our little cyber posse, Detective?"

Fuentes thought for a moment and quietly shook her head.

"You've made your point, Captain," acknowledged the Detective.

"Actually, this turn of events could prove to be our first real break in these murders," proffered the Inspector, speaking for the first time since Hightower's departure.

Both Killingsworth and Fuentes stared at Cuffington with blank expressions.

"Would you mind explaining just how you figure that, Nick?" urged the Captain.

"By the nature of the crime itself," clarified Cuffington.

"Go on!" pressed Killingsworth.

"Stealing classified Federal documents is not exactly a petty larceny offense," maintained the Inspector.

"Your more than right on that front," concurred the Captain. "In fact, depending upon the specific circumstances, it could actually be construed as treason!" emphasized Killingsworth.

"Exactly," confirmed Cuffington.

"Okay, so explain to me how the seriousness of the cyber robbery as a crime is going to provide us with any tangible leads as it pertains to the Sooner and Ryder murders?"

"So, who but someone with skin in the game would even consider undertaking such an enormous risk?" posited Cuffington.

Killingsworth did not respond immediately. He sat pondering the fresh perspective the Inspector had introduced.

"Alright Nick, allow me to play devil's advocate," ventured the Captain. "If those responsible for the two Congressional murders had anything material to do with what went down at U.S. Capitol Police headquarters why in the world would they assume such an additional risk in the first place?"

"Possibly to get a handle on what we actually know," suggested Cuffington.

"Which happens to be absolutely nothing!" reminded Killingsworth.

"Pat, as you've already pointed out, they don't know that!" stated Cuffington, echoing the Captain's earlier contention.

Detective Fuentes had been patiently following the back and forth of her two colleagues. She decided it was time for her voice to be heard.

"It simply doesn't matter if the "invaders" of U.S. Capitol Police headquarters are in any way connected to the Congressional deaths. Either way, the break-in is a win-win for our team," she concluded.

"Continue Detective," smiled the Inspector.

"Whether these people were in any way involved in the Congressional killings or not is moot. Once apprehended, they will provide us with a very plausible temporary public scapegoat; a scapegoat that will take some of the heat of our asses and buy us some more time," she ended.

"That's a very good point, Maria," nodded Cuffington, approvingly.

Nick's cell phone sounded its annoying ringtone. It was Leigh Cuffington. Fuentes, noticing the caller I.D., tapped Nick on the shoulder.

"I have to powder my nose," she whispered.

The Inspector rose to allow her exit.

Killingsworth, picking up on Marie's cue, stood up and motioned in the general direction of the men's room. Cuffington flipped a mental coin. He decided to answer the call.

"Yes, Leigh?"

"Nick, where the hell are you?" she asked in an exasperated tone of voice.

"Frolicking in quicksand, dear, what are you up to?"

"Nick, I'm being serious!"

"So am I"

"Listen, about this morning." . .

Cuffington cut her short.

"We'll discuss that next time our paths happen to cross," he dismissed.

"Nick, please don't tell me you've forgotten about the Hounderson's book-signing dinner party," she pined.

"Leigh, I haven't had the time to remember to forget the Hounderson's literary soiree," confessed the Inspector. "What time are Washington's literary luminaries supposed to appear?"

"Cocktails are at six," she confirmed.

Nick glanced at his watch. The time was well after five p.m.

"Leigh, there's no way I can make it. Besides, if I have to discuss Washington D.C.'s current state of chaos, I will be better served by doing so with people that might actually help in unraveling this labyrinth."

"I completely understand," she empathized. "I just thought it might have proven to be a welcomed respite for you. Let me know what time you are going to be home and I shall make a gracious exit from the festivities."

"Will do," he verified.

"I love you, honey. Oh Nick, before I forget, Talia Teller has called here twice in the last two hours. She says it is urgent that she speak with you. Do you have her number?"

Cuffington trawled his pockets and pulled the piece of paper Teller had handed him at the end of their first meeting.

"Yes, I have her number."

"Nick, do you know what she wants?"

"Most likely, an exclusive"

"All right then, I'll wait to hear from you."

Mrs. Cuffington rang off.

Nick Cuffington left his seat at the booth, and headed for the front door of Brewster's Bistro. Toby the Waiter accosted him.

"Is there anything I can do for you, Inspector?" he asked with attentiveness.

"Yes Toby, as a matter of fact there is. Please let Captain Killingsworth and Detective Fuentes know, I went outside to make a phone call."

"Yes sir!"

Nick walked through the front hallway and onto the street. He lit a cigarette. Before the venomous second-hand smoke had the opportunity to slither its way into the lungs of the yet born, a Johnny Blue Suit was on the job.

"Hey buddy, put out the butt; this is a no-smoking zone," informed the officer.

Cuffington turned to face the Regulator of the Rules. In a flash, the policeman from Metro identified the perpetrator.

"Inspector Cuffington, I didn't realize it was you! Please forgive my intrusion. I mistakenly assumed you were just Joe Citizen," he explained, awkwardly.

"Just don't let it happen again," warned the fire-breathing dragon.

And with that, the enforcer of the 'Law for the People' disappeared in a puff of smoke.

Cuffington retrieved Teller's slip of paper. He reached for his cell phone and placed the call.

"Hello?" answered a woman whose voice resonated with trepidation.

"Talia Teller, please"

"Who is calling?" the woman asked warily.

"Inspector Nick Cuffington"

"Oh, Inspector it's you! I do recognize your voice. I just didn't know your number from caller I.D.," she explained.

"Don't give it a second thought, I wouldn't have been able to identify it myself," admitted the Inspector. "What's so urgent, Talia?"

"Inspector, I must see you as soon as possible," implored the young reporter.

"Okay, where are you now, Talia?"

"In my office at *The Rumor's* headquarters"

"I'm just about to go into Brewster's Bistro, can you meet me there?"

"Yes"

"How long will it take you to get here?"

"About fifteen minutes," she estimated.

"I'll be waiting for you Talia," committed the Inspector.

"I'll be there!"

Chapter Thirty-Two

Cuffington re-entered the restaurant and made his way to Cuff-Kill Corner. Killingsworth and Fuentes were already re-seated. The Inspector sat down next to Maria.

"I just got off the phone with Talia Teller," he informed his comrades.

"And what did that little-ms.-know-it-all want?" hissed Fuentes.

"She didn't say," related the Inspector. "Although, Talia didn't sound like a person in total command of her situation when I got off the phone with her," observed Cuffington.

"So, how did you leave it with her?" demanded Killingsworth.

"She will be joining us in about fifteen minutes."

"Nick, I for one do not trust that one," warned Detective Fuentes. "She's just a little too silky smooth for my comfort zone."

"She didn't sound all that composed when I was speaking with her," countered the Inspector.

Fifteen minutes elapsed into over a half-hour.

"Maybe she can't figure out how to find the place again without direction," smirked Fuentes.

It was Cuffington that first spotted Teller entering the front door of Brewster's. The Inspector was startled by the noticeable change in the reporter's demeanor. Gone was the self-assured swagger he had encountered at their first meeting. That confidence had been seemingly supplanted with self-doubt. Twice, she looked behind her, as if making certain she was not being followed. As Talia Teller approached their booth, she clutched a manila envelope in both arms. She was quite clearly at odds with demons both real and illusionary. As she approached Cuff-Kill Corner, the Inspector stood up to greet her.

"Talia, we were getting a little concerned," greeted Cuffington.

"Sorry I'm so late," Talia apologized, as she sat down next to Captain Killingsworth. "The traffic in this town is becoming murder to drive in. I've never seen Washington D.C. so besieged with demonstrators."

"Would you care for something to drink Ms. Teller?" offered Killingsworth.

"Yes, I would. That will be rather refreshing," she smiled,wanly.

The Captain motioned to their waiter. Toby was there before the Captain had lowered his hand.

"Can I get you a cold beer Ms. Teller?" he asked with deference.

"No. I think I'd prefer Pinch on the rocks. Actually, why don't you Pinch me twice, Toby?"

"With pleasure, Ms. Teller" Their waiter was off to the races.

Talia Teller did not take her eyes off Inspector Cuffington. She tossed the once clasped manila envelope onto the center of the table.

"I found this on my office desk when I returned from lunch this afternoon," she shuddered.

Cuffington remained motionless, engaging the young reporter's stare.

It was Captain Killingsworth that broke the eerie silence of their stand-off. "What the hell is it Teller?" demanded "The Killer."

"Nothing you haven't seen before Captain," was her jagged response.

The Steward of Cuff-Kill Corner returned with Teller's drink. He placed it before her and then stepped away from the booth. Toby sensed danger.

Cuffington and Teller continued their uninterrupted stare down. It was the reporter who spoke first.

"I have no idea who left that for me or why," she pledged, nodding to the package on the table.

She sipped her cocktail, bracing for the Inspector's first question. Inspector Cuffington picked up his beer and drained its contents. He then motioned to Toby. He then re-engaged Teller.

"Do you routinely abandon your desk during normal lunch hours?" he asked.

Talia Teller rolled her eyes in disbelief. Some of the lost confidence was beginning to rear its defiant head.

"Inspector, the contents inside that package are far more important than my dining habits," she frowned with disdain.

Toby returned with Cuffington's beer. Once again, the young man vamoosed.

"Inspector, aren't you curious about what's inside that envelope?" exhorted the reporter.

"I think I may already know, Talia. My only question is what is your assessment of its contents? "he asked with calm resolve.

With that, Captain Patrick Killingsworth smashed a ham-handed fist on the table, momentarily disturbing the loud din of Brewster's Bistro.

"Will one of you please take the time to enlighten the less fortunate of us as to what the hell is in the damn envelope!" he bellowed.

Cuffington nodded to Talia Teller. She squared to face the Captain of U.S. Capitol Police.

"The complete autopsies of both Congressman Sooner and Senator William Ryder," as she nodded towards the envelope.

Killingsworth maintained a composed outward appearance. However, inwardly, both his mind and senses were racing at breakneck speed with absolutely no definitive destination.

"So what are your interpretations and conclusions of the autopsies' findings after reviewing them?" questioned the Captain

Talia Teller carefully measured her words before speaking.

"If Doctor Savage's approximations of how long it took the toxins to induce death after ingested and ,his approximations of the times of those deaths are accurate, I come away with only one plausible conclusion."

"And what might that be?" pursued Killingsworth.

"That Inspector Cuffington has been less than forthcoming with his assessment of the circumstances surrounding the two Congressional deaths," was her accusation.

"In what manner have I been less than candid Talia?" confronted the Inspector.

The reporter bit her lower lip. Talia was obviously wrestling with what she should say next. With a short sigh of resolve, she took the plunge.

"That you've known all along there were more than one killer involved in the deaths of Congressman Sooner and Senator William Ryder," alleged Teller.

Cuffington sat silently. He searched Talia's face trying to determine what she intended to do with her newly acquired information. The Inspector, atypically, did not have a clue.

"So what are your plans for that?" as he gestured to the manila envelope resting on the center of the booth's table, impatiently waiting to consternate all of Washington D.C.

"Truthfully, I haven't decided, Inspector," revealed Talia Teller.

"Oh Talia, where is that 'Hypocritical Oath of Journalism' when I could honestly put it to good use?" smiled Cuffington, sarcastically.

The reporter frowned at him.

"Inspector, I told you the first time we met that I am from the Tim Russert School of Journalism," reconfirmed Teller.

"Where is the man when all of us, here in Washington D.C. really need him?" mused the Inspector.

Talia Teller looked at Inspector Nick Cuffington through genuinely compassionate eyes.

"Inspector, believe it or not, I completely understand why you assumed the position you did, as it relates to the circumstances surrounding the murders of Congressman Sooner and Senator Ryder," she empathized.

"And what exactly do you understand Talia?" cornered Cuffington.

"I fully recognize the fact that all of Washington D.C. is going to go Neddy in the Woods, when it becomes public knowledge that their town has at least two murderers on the loose and lurking," she grimaced.

"With a Penis hanging low!" emphasized Detective Maria Fuentes.

"Well, where are you going from here with it Talia?" invoked the Inspector.

Talia Teller finished her drink and rose to leave.

"Technically, as of now, I don't have the complete story.

The writer for *The Washington Rumor* paused to formulate her next words.

" Therefore, I am going to give it forty-eight hours from the time I received that little present from hell, before I take any course of action," she promised.

Talia Teller hesitated before departing. She stared at Nick Cuffington with ambivalence.

"And I'll have you know Inspector, forty-eight hours is pushing both my professionalism and my journalistic Code of Ethics!"

"Until this very moment, I hadn't realized such a code of journalistic ethics was still in existence here in Washington D.C.," commented Cuffington with admiration and respect.

Without further comment, the reporter for *The Washington Rumor* turned heel and walked unknowingly towards her own awaiting crossroads of further dilemma.

Chapter Thirty-Three

The long majestic black limousine with tinted windows gracefully exited a private air strip located adjacently to Dulles International.

The two VIPs seated in the back of the stretch were none too happy that their well-earned vacation had been so rudely interrupted by a hastily scheduled meeting ordered by the President of the United States. Both dignitaries loathed being summoned back to Washington D.C. prior to the conclusion of the No Labor Day Weekend.

"Would you care for a glass of wine Fanny?" enticed Frank Bentklin, Vice-President of the United States.

"Have you ever known me to say no, Frank?" giggled Fanny NoGosi, Minority leader of the United States House of Representatives.

Vice-President Bentklin poured two glasses and handed one to NoGosi.

"To Parrot Cay," toasted the Vice-President.

"As ephemeral as it was," lamented NoGosi.

They clinked goblets and savored the richly expensive grapes.

"Frank, what's on His agenda?" demanded the disgruntled Minority Leader.

"He wants to start pushing his American Gangrene No Jobs Action Bill," informed the Vice-President.

"And that's why he's seen fit to intrude upon our most deserved R&R?" she shook her head, incredulously.

"That's not all, Fanny. The Big Guy is planning to place condoms on his docket at this meeting!"

"Really, now that does re-arouse my appetite for public service!" she smiled, anxiously.

The Vice-President sipped his wine and then spoke to Fanny NoGosi with a somber tone.

"Fanny, you of all people here in our Washington D.C. should know better than most, just how important it is that each and every one of us preserve the façade of representing them, the People," admonished Bentklin. "I say this with the full understanding of what an inconvenience that can be!" he commiserated.

"Yes, but Frank, even you have to admit, this ongoing encroachment by the People on the privileges, perks, and private lives of public officials is starting to get out of hand!" complained the Minority Leader. "After all, just how much time do they expect us to spend complicating their already overly regulated miserable, inconsequential existences?" bemoaned NoGosi. "Haven't we done enough to them already?"

"The Show must always go on here in Washington D.C.!" heralded Frank Bentklin, with political fervor.

As their limousine approached its appointed destination, traffic gridlocked.

Vice-President Bentklin grabbed the inter-auto phone and began to rail at the driver.

"What the Betty Boop is the hold-up, Jeeves!"

Their driver patiently hit the conference call button.

"Protestors Mr. Vice-President," explained the chauffeur.

Bentklin slammed the phone back into its cradle. He glanced at his wrist watch. It was three-forty five p.m.

"I slated this meeting to commence promptly at four p.m. At this pace, I'm going to be tardy for my own call to order! This is simply outrageous!"

"Frank, what did I just finish telling you?" reconfirmed the House Minority Leader.

She dangled her now emptied wine glass. Bentklin replenished the chalice. He was careful not to neglect his own.

"You know Fanny, thinking about what you just said, maybe it is time we started to consider the monitoring of the People's free access to our town," affirmed the Vice-President.

He sipped from the crystal stemmed trough.

"I mean, all kidding aside, this unrestricted presence they claim to be their right to Washington D.C. has become more than bothersome; it is now becoming an actual infringement upon our duly elected responsibility to legislate and oversee their daily activities!" complained the Vice-President.

"Frank, you're preaching to the choir!" was the Minority Leader's exasperated response. "In fact, I might go as far as to suggest a total make-over of Washington D.C.," pursued NoGosi.

"What do you have in mind Fanny?" spurred Bentklin.

"A complete face lift for our town!" urged NoGosi.

"You've stolen my ear Ms. Minority Leader," sipped the Vice-President.

"I envision a theme park motif. The great unwashed will be fully capable of understanding and appreciative of such a familiar venue."

"Go on!" urged a now excited Vice-President.

"We shall construct toll booths and charge a daily POP admittance fee plus tax to gain admission into the Kingdom of Smoke and Mirrors," suggested NoGosi.

"You're whetting my whistle Fanny!" exclaimed Bentklin

"Once inside our dominion, they shall only be allowed to visit those sites that we have deemed to be opened to the public on that particular day. Furthermore, while touring our bastion of authority, the People shall only be permitted to purchase food and beverages sanctioned as eatable and drinkable by the Food and Drug Administration," continued a now inspired NoGosi.

"I'm luvin it!" salivated the Vice-President.

"More importantly, public sexual activity on the streets of Washington D.C. shall only be condoned and embraced if the proper contraceptive devices, duly authorized and issued by The Department of Health and Human Services, are legally in place at the time of fornication!" she climaxed.

"I just came to the very same conclusion!" panted Bentklin. "I'm going to run it by the Big Guy once we stall his American

Gangrene No Jobs Act Bill in committee," promised the Vice-President.

Their elegant, long black limousine had now grounded to an unacceptable stand-still. Vice-President Bentklin again, checked his watch. It was now after four p.m. His brief spurt of impassioned euphoria had been supplanted by outraged indignation. The vast number of street demonstrators had rendered access to the U.S. Capitol Rotunda impassable. Bentklin observed the huge throng with utter contempt.

"Don't these people ever work!" yelled the Vice-President. "This obstruction by demonstration is beyond the boundaries of toleration!" he screamed.

Bentklin angrily slapped a button to lower his tinted-glassed window. The Vice-President craned his torso outside the vehicle and gestured a digital vulgarity at the crowd.

"Why don't you losers spend more time working at the jobs we have created for you?" he ranted. "Can't you no bodies get it through your primitive skulls that you are impeding our progress?" he railed.

Up until the Vice-President's outburst, the multitude of protestors, on both sides of the street, had been peacefully exercising their freedom of assembly. However, after witnessing the wrinkled old man's exhibition of uncouth loathing, the mood of the masses swiftly became vengeful.

"That's BENTKLIN!" yelled a lone voice from the Right side of the street.

"Yea, that's FRANK BENTKLIN! in that big fancy car!" hollered another voice from the Left side of the street.

The House Minority Leader began to panic.

"Frank, for God's sake, get your ass back in this car and shut the window!" she shrilled.

A low, impassioned wail of pent up resentment growled into an ear piercing roar of marching, charging feet. The target of their ire was the long, black, luxuriously appointed limousine. Four motorcycle police officers had been assigned to escort the Vice-President's limousine. Three of the four peeled off from the front of the vehicle to man both flanks and the rear. The lead motorcycle officer hit the button to his phone.

"Veep-Jeep is under siege. I am requesting back-up."

Fanny NoGosi awkwardly fumbled for the automobile's rear seat intercom. She spilled the expensive wine over her more expensive designer suit in the process.

"Is this piece of crap equipped with the mandatory shatter-proof tinted window glass mandated by the Federal Transit Authority for high-level governmental personages such as myself?" she screamed.

The driver lowered the limo's partitioning glass window. He looked into his rear view mirror and stared at the Minority Leader of the United States House of Representatives.

"Lady, I think we're about to find out."

Chapter Thirty-Four

Captain Patrick Killingsworth stared across the table at Inspector Nick Cuffington and Detective Maria Fuentes.

"Will one of you please be kind enough to explain to me what the hell it is I'm supposed to make of Ms. Talia Teller?" he brooded, shaking his head.

The reporter for *The Washington Rumor* had just left their booth at Brewster's Bistro. It was Cuffington who first opined his sentiments.

"I think we can safely conclude that Talia Teller is a dedicated journalist, Pat," committed Cuffington.

"Yea, but dedicated to what, Nick?" challenged Killingsworth.

"Dedicated to her chosen profession of reporting the news," narrowed the Inspector.

"Then I suppose my real questions are how and why did she manage to end up with the two autopsy reports?" pondered the Captain.

"Let's step back a moment shall we?" interceded Detective Fuentes.

She drew the unequivocal attention of both men.

"Teller originally sought an audience with Nick because she felt that she might have knowledge pertinent to the murder investigations of Congressman Sooner and Senator Ryder," began Fuentes.

The Detective paused to organize her thoughts.

"She obtained this information while researching a story about the late Senator Ryder. Teller claims that the story was deep-sixed by some higher-ups at *The Washington Rumor* after she uncovered some "indiscretions" involving the Congressman and Senator."

"You mean the very same "indiscretions" intended to send us on safari into the late Senator Ryder's twisted nocturnal activities?" sneered, Killingsworth.

"Exactly" confirmed Fuentes. "However, quite possibly, it wasn't Teller trying to set us up after all!" speculated the Detective. "Maybe, just maybe, it was the reporter herself that was the intended mark," conjectured Fuentes.

Killingsworth rolled his eyes and raised his hand to summon their waiter.

"Toby, I'll take another in the pursuit of truth and justice here in Washington D.C., clamored Killingsworth.

"You are in for a long evening Captain," commented the Steward of Cuff-Kill Corner.

Cuffington sorted his thoughts and then addressed Killingsworth candidly.

"Pat, there is strong reason to believe Maria's theory that Talia Teller may, in fact, be an unwitting pawn in this unfolding Arcanum has validity," vouched Cuffington.

"And why is it you feel so confident with the Detective's supposition, Nick?" asked the Captain.

"Because of information I received at a meeting earlier today," answered the Inspector.

"And what meeting might that be?" pursued Killingsworth.

"A chat with an old friend who seems quite certain the late Senator Ryder's midnight ramblings had nothing to do with his death," revealed Cuffington.

"May I, be so bold as to ask you the identity of your "old friend?" pried the Captain.

Toby the Waiter returned from yet another successful mission.

"Anything else?" he inquired before taking his leave.

"To answer your question, Pat, Nelson Lloyd Sinclair"

Killingsworth did a double take.

"The Nelson Lloyd Sinclair?" he asked in disbelief.

"The very one," confirmed Cuffington with lack of any pretense.

"Nick, how the hell do you know him?" urged the Captain.

"I met him when we were both living in New York City," explained Cuffington.

"And what makes you so certain that Mr. Sinclair is in any sort of position to know exactly who or what may or may not have killed the late Senator Ryder?" persisted Killingsworth.

"Nelson runs in a wide array of social circles and networks. If there was the slightest whisper that Senator Ryder's death could be traced to his bizarre life-style, Sinclair would have heard about it," contended the Inspector.

"Nick, has the possibility crossed your mind that Mr. Sinclair might have, indeed, heard something and simply chose not to tell you?" he rebuffed, candidly.

"No, it has not," declared Cuffington, resolutely.

"And why not?" pressed the Captain.

"Because Nelson Lloyd Sinclair would never allow himself to be put in a situation that would require him to be less than truthful with me," asserted Cuffington.

"Meaning?" probed Killingsworth.

"Meaning, that if Nelson had something he felt he couldn't tell me, he would never have agreed to meet with me in the first place," concluded the Inspector.

Killingsworth shifted his attention to Fuentes.

"Maria, were you present at the meeting?" asked the Killingsworth.

"Yes, I was Captain"

"And do you concur with the Inspector's contention of Mr. Sinclair's veracity?"

"Pat, I came away from today's meeting with no reason to suspect Mr. Sinclair was in anyway trying to be deceptive or elusive," was her careful response. "After all, what does he have to gain or lose?"

162

"Billions!" declared an increasingly frustrated Killingsworth. "This whole damn thing just keeps getting murkier!"

Cuffington, recognizing the Captain's growing angst, attempted to steer their dialogue in a more positive direction.

"Pat, let's assume for a second that Maria's right about Teller being the dupe, that means. . ."

Killingsworth cut the Inspector short.

"It means that whoever initially set Talia Teller up is the same person or persons who broke into U.S Capitol Police headquarters data base," he concluded with chagrin.

With that, the Captain slumped back in his seat and stared into his self-perceived impending career oblivion.

Cuffington thoughtfully sipped his beer. "You know Pat, there is a bright side here," declared the Inspector.

"Yea, and what's that Nick?" grumbled Killingsworth.

"Well, just several minutes ago we were facing four unanswered questions; one, who killed Congressman Sooner, two, who killed Senator Ryder, three, who broke into U.S. Capitol Police headquarters data base, and four, who conned Talia Teller."

"So what Nick?" shrugged Killingsworth.

"Well, if your supposition is valid, questions three and four are one in the same, thereby leaving us now with only three unanswered questions," reasoned Cuffington with a smile.

Captain Killingsworth sat stirring the ice in his drink as he reflected upon the Inspector's words.

"You know something Nick, viewing this entire ordeal through that particular prism of kaleidoscopic perspective, it does suggest that we are, indeed, making some progress!" confirmed the Captain. Both men were now laughing.

Chapter Thirty-Five

After finishing their dinner, Inspector Cuffington, Captain Killingsworth, and Detective Fuentes departed Brewster's Bistro.

The streets outside the restaurant were no longer teeming with either patrons or protestors. Killingsworth had decided to return to U.S. Capitol Police headquarters to receive an update on the progress being made to determine who or what had been responsible for the cyber "invasion." Cuffington and Fuentes were in her obviously unmarked cruiser motoring towards Foggy Bottom. As usual, the Inspector sat in the passenger seat quietly pondering the day's events through the side window.

"It's been a fun filled day hasn't Nick?" jested the Detective, trying to provoke Cuffington into conversation.

"Maria, I'm afraid the fun is just getting underway," responded the Inspector.

"What the hell is that supposed to mean?" she asked while quickly trying to extrapolate his cryptic assessment.

"Truthfully, I don't really know what I mean Maria; a feeling, a hunch, maybe male intuition, I can't put my finger on it. But I am certain of one thing; whatever it is that has descended upon Washington D.C has not yet made its full impact felt," concluded the Inspector.

Detective Maria Fuentes momentarily averted her eyes from the road before her to confront Cuffington. She was visibly troubled.

"Nick, you're starting to talk in abstractions," she chastised.

She took a deep breath and continued.

"Listen to me. Let's forget, for a moment, the fact that the two guys whacked were members of the United States Congress. When you break it down and analyze the whole damn thing, they're nothing more than two homicide investigations."

Detective Fuentes rolled to a stop in front of Cuffington's home.

"So, what's on our schedule for tomorrow?" she asked, expectantly.

"Assuming Miriam Hightower hasn't figured out who is responsible for the breach at U.S. Capitol Police headquarters, the Tangerine Oriental," declared the Inspector.

"It sounds to me like you're not placing too much faith in the Special Technician's capabilities," observed the Detective.

"She's too old," dismissed the Inspector.

"And what does that make you, Nick?" she smiled, kiddingly.

"Way too old"

The Inspector was not smiling.

"Nick, Hightower struck me as more than competent. Besides, experience does count for something in today's world of cyber communication."

"You listen to me, Maria. In today's cyber world, always put your money on the kid who grew up knowing no other kind of world," warned Cuffington.

"So, you are convinced that whoever hacked into U.S. Capitol Police's computer network is on the younger side?" she concluded.

"I'd bet Killingsworth's pension and life-time medical benefits on it," grinned the Inspector.

Nick Cuffington got out of the car.

"Ten a.m. unless you hear from me otherwise," he smiled and closed the car's door.

As he approached his house, Nick noticed that Leigh's car was parked in the driveway. He glanced at his watch. It was seven-thirty p.m. Cuffington entered the house through the kitchen door. He walked down the hallway to Leigh's library. Its door was open but the room was empty. He returned to the kitchen. Looking out a window, he saw Leigh seated at the patio table enjoying the evening's final rays of sunshine. Nick stepped out onto the patio and moved towards his wife. He affectionately kissed the top of her head and drew a chair to sit beside her.

"Why did you decide not to attend the Hounderson's dinner party?" he asked, with surprise.

"The more accurate question is, why did I not stay at the Hounderson's book event," she corrected, humorlessly.

"Because they ran out of books?" was his factitious best guess.

"You really can be so insensitive, at times. There are moments when I really wonder how I allowed myself to fall in love with you," she sighed.

Sensing the urgency of the moment, Inspector Nick Cuffington regrouped and charged head-long into the unfamiliar terrain of sensitivity.

"Leigh, what really does have you so upset? Please, tell me what happened at the Hounderson's that made you want to leave so early?" he asked, gently.

Leigh Cuffington sternly studied her husband's face, searching for a genuine countenance of concern. Finally, convinced of his sincerity, she continued.

"Nick, no sooner did I arrive at the Hounderson's front portico, whereupon, I was literally besieged by a horde of guests dogging me for information about those ghastly Congressional murders!" she shuddered.

Leigh Cuffington paused and then continued.

"They frenetically kept pressuring me with questions, to which, I obviously have no answers. At one point, I thought I was going to faint!"

"I'm truly sorry you had such an unpleasant experience," he iterated with genuine empathy.

"That's why I had no choice but to leave" she explained, shaking her head in dismay.

Leigh Cuffington stared into the face of her husband.

"Nick, these Congressional murders have really rocked the Washington D.C. establishment. Do you have any idea as to what is really going on?" she beseeched.

The Inspector returned his wife's gaze.

"Unfortunately, I don't have a clue," he admitted with total candor.

Cuffington rose from his chair to go back into the kitchen.

"Nick?"

Leigh Cuffington pointed to her empty wine glass. Cuffington returned from the kitchen with a refurbished glass of wine for his wife and a cold frosty for team Metro.

"You know Nick, the only positive I can come away with this evening is the fact that your somewhat surreal ideas of murderous goblins were pretty much debunked by those in attendance at the Hounderson's this evening," she revealed.

"That is the first bit of good news I've heard all day," asserted Nick Cuffington.

"In fact, if I may give you some guidance, Inspector, it has been pretty much established by over-all consensus that the murderer is, in reality, the third cog in a perverse love triangle involving Congressman Sooner and Senator Ryder," divulged Leigh Cuffington.

"Well, it sounds to me as if this whole unsavory affair is about to be tied up and delivered in a neatly wrapped package to the Attorney-General's office fast and furiously," commended the Inspector.

"As well it should be," agreed Mrs. Cuffington. "Let the people, here in Washington D.C., see to it that the atrocities committed in Washington D.C. are atoned for in Washington D.C.!"

"Leigh, I do believe your wish is about to be granted," acknowledged the Inspector.

Chapter Thirty-Six

The Vice-President of the United States convened the high-level meeting several hours after it's originally scheduled starting time. The proceedings were taking place in a secluded conference room tucked away inside the U.S. Capitol Building. Seated to Vice-President Bentklin's left were Senate Majority Leader Morey Drainer and Minority Leader of the House, Fanny NoGosi. Positioned to Bentklin's right were House Speaker Jim Spendforth and Senate Minority Leader Steve "Pitch" Middleton.

The "Second in Command" immediately established the gravity of the situation at hand.

"Before we officially get under way, I want you all to know, that due to the unfortunate delay in the commencement of this afternoon's meeting, I am determined to keep this thing as short as possible to reduce the possibility of interfering with any evening plans you may have already made," promised the Vice-President.

"Hear, hear!" was the unanimous, bi-partisan voice of approval.

"Okay, now that we're officially off the record, allow me to kick off by apologizing to everyone in this room for this late start," opened Vice-President Frank Bentklin. "As Fanny will attest, while on our way to this VIP summit, our convoy was ambushed by some of the primitives that now roam so freely the streets of our city," explained the Vice-President.

"Don't give it a second thought, Frank," reassured Jim Spendforth, Speaker of the House. "After hearing the local traffic reports, Steve and I decided to leave one of our limos behind. "We actually car-pooled!" related the House Speaker.

Not to be outdone by the obvious partisan pandering, Minority Leader NoGosi let her shrill be heard.

"What the hell do you think Frank and I did this afternoon, Mr. Speaker!" whined the Minority Leader. "In fact, we took the initiative to car pool even before we had learned of the Mongrel Invasion!"

The Senate Majority Leader shifted uneasily in his chair. "You know, something really has to be done about this notion of unrestricted public access to the streets of Washington D.C.," insisted Morey Drainer.

"Oh, you need not worry about that, Morey. Such plans are already in the works!" avowed Fanny NoGosi.

"Alright then," continued Bentklin. "Oh, lest I forget, let me mention, in passing, the sudden and shocking deaths of Barry Sooner and Bill Ryder," recited the Vice-President.

"Sudden yes, shocking no!" commented the Senate Majority Leader, Morey Drainer.

"Unfortunately, I tend to agree with you, Morey," sighed Steve "Pitch" Middleton, Minority Leader of the Senate. "After all, Billy's social proclivities were not exactly tucked away neatly in some dark closet! Actually, in retrospect, I suppose something like this was only a matter of time."

Fanny NoGosi felt an obligation to weigh in on the Congressional deaths. "The only aspect of these horrific incidents that caught me with my pants down. . ."

"Was your husband, Fanny?" snickered House Speaker, Jim Spendforth.

"That's very funny, Jim. Actually, at his age, the only thing my husband catches these days is his own zipper. Anyway, I had heard the ongoing swell of rumor regarding Barry Sooner for years, but I was never able to come up with anything I could firmly get both hands around," admitted Fanny NoGosi.

"I'll second Fanny's notion," offered Jim Spendforth. "I always found Barry to be a difficult person to pin to the mat when it came to matters of total reconciliation."

Vice-President Bentklin slapped his hand soundly on the conference table.

"I shall remind each and every one of you seated at this table that it has never been, nor will it ever be, the business of members of the United States Congress to question the conduct of one of our own!" he sternly reprimanded.

"Hear, Hear!" was the, once again, bi-partisan agreement from both sides of the table.

With a semblance of purpose restored, Vice-President Bentklin carried forth.

"It is with great disappointment that I must inform those present today, that The Big Guy will be unable to attend this afternoon's VIP summit meeting. However, he does send his regrets and regards," announced the Vice-President.

The atmosphere of the room was momentarily hushed by the news. It was the Speaker of the House that raised the first question about the President's absence.

"And why the hell can't he be here, Frank?" he demanded.

Vice-President Frank Bentklin sat stoically at his seat of authority. He carefully crafted his choice of words before making The Announcement.

"Because, The Big Guy has just embarked upon his Billion or Bust Canadian Built Bus Re-election Extravaganza Tour!" heralded the Vice-President with excitement.

A palpable thrill ran up the leg of every person present in the room.

"Frank, you should have just come clean and told us!" apologized Jim Spendforth. "Of course, I now understand why he couldn't possibly have spared the time to join us today!"

"Besides, he didn't get his re-election campaign underway a day too early," noted Fanny NoGosi. "After all, the election is just a little over a year and a half away!"

"Well, he does seem to have his priorities in good order," concluded the Senate Majority Leader, Morey Drainer.

"And how extensive is this fund raising excursion going to be?" inquired Steve Middleton.

"It is my understanding that this particular phase of the operation, promo code "Raising Dollars and Change for Hope," will

170

be concentrating primarily on the key battleground states," affirmed Vice-President Bentklin.

"All fifty-seven of them, Frank?" marveled Middleton.

"Mind you, I only perused a preliminary itinerary," skirted Bentklin. "Nonetheless, whether we find ourselves meeting here in Washington D.C. or crisscrossing the vast looted plain of our country, the show must go on! The show must always go on here in Washington D.C.!" shouted the Vice-president.

Speaker of the House Jim Spendforth refocused the group's discussion. "Frank, you called today's meeting to review the Big Guy's proposed No Jobs Inaction Bill legislation," reminded Spendforth. "More specifically, how he intends to provide the funding for such an undertaking."

Vice-President Bentklin looked at Spendforth and smiled with confidence.

"Mr. Speaker, I fully anticipated your demands for the specifics outlining how we intend to pay for the No Jobs Inaction Bill legislation. That is why I took the liberty of inviting an unscheduled, scheduled guest . . . ."

Before the Vice-President could complete his sentence, there was a knock on the conference room's door.

"Enter!" boomed the baritone voice of Frank Bentklin.

The door opened and a man cautiously slipped inside the room and then quickly closed the door behind him. Standing in front of those seated around the large rectangular table was none other than the United States Secretary of the Treasury, Skim Lighter.

Lighter was a diminutive, ferret-like looking fellow. His eyes were beady and his smile crooked. He seated himself at the end of the large table directly facing the Vice-President. Lighter was afflicted with the unconscious habit of perpetually rubbing his hands together; very much like a squirrel hungrily anticipating its next acorn. The Treasury Secretary required no introductions.

"I have asked Secretary Lighter to sit in on our meeting this afternoon, with the hope that he will be able to answer any and all questions as they pertain to the source of funding for the Big Guy's No Jobs Inaction Bill," briefed Vice-President Bentklin.

Jim Spendforth observed the Secretary of the Treasury with the wary eye of political suspicion.

"So then, let's cut right to the chase, shall we, Mr. Secretary?" confronted the Speaker of the House.

"But of course Jim, that's the only reason I'm here today," was his unctuous response.

"Where the hell is another half a trillion dollars coming from to finance the Big Guy's No Jobs Inaction Bill?" demanded the Speaker of the House.

The Treasury Secretary listened to the objective question with patient indifference and then responded.

"By Treasury officials utilizing revenue and accounting measures and techniques that will maintain the nation's solvency," he dismissed, condescendingly.

"The same sort of accounting measures you apply when completing and filing your personal income taxes Mr. Secretary?" challenged the Speaker of the House.

The Secretary of the United States Treasury snidely appraised Jim Spendforth. "I can always conveniently arrange to have your personal income tax returns scrutinized," was Skim Lighter's not so veiled threat.

The House Speaker's eyes began to mist. The Vice-President of the United States quickly intervened.

"This line of questioning is strictly prohibited, Jim. You of all people should know that!" snapped Frank Bentklin.

Always the consummate Washington D.C. political intermediary, Senate Minority Leader Steve "Pitch" Middleton, once again, exited the bull pen and strolled to the mound.

"So, in essence, what you are proposing, Mr. Secretary, is that we borrow more money now to provide the funding for the Big Guy's No Jobs Inaction Bill and leave it to a bi-partisan Congressional committee, to be formed at a later date, to discuss the possibility of future spending cuts, at some time in the future," summarized the Senate Minority Leader.

The United States Secretary of the Treasury smiled with genuine admiration and respect.

"You know Steve, I never realized until this very moment that your area of expertise was the complex world of finance," complimented Skim Lighter.

"Yes, but what is your long-term solution to our country's insatiable thirst for National Debt?" beseeched a now weeping House Speaker Spendforth.

"Quite candidly, Jim, I don't have an answer to this country's growing National Debt," replied the Treasury Secretary.

"But let's not forget that a growing National Debt is now the way America does business!" emphasized Morey Drainer, Senate Majority Leader.

"Not only that, the enactment of the Big Guy's No Jobs Inaction Bill will legislatively mandate us to increase and extend unemployment benefits to those who may lose these future jobs when the funding for the No Jobs Inaction Bill runs out!" trilled Fanny NoGosi with gleeful enthusiasm.

The Secretary of the Treasury nodded his head in knowing approval.

"And add to that the ephemeral stimulation it very well might infuse into our nation's unacceptably weak economy, and I think we've got a no brainer," concluded Skim Lighter.

Vice-President Frank Bentklin looked at his wrist watch and shook his head.

"This whole thing is starting to cut into my cocktail hour," he complained. "Therefore, I move to bring the Big Guy's No Jobs Inaction Bill and our adjournment to a vote!" he summoned and stood up.

"All in favor of the Bill's funding and us getting the hell out of here, let your voices be heard!" urged the Vice-President of the United States.

"Hear, Here!" was the unanimous bi-partisan call for adjournment.

Chapter-Thirty-Seven

The two women had just completed a leisurely round of golf on the Gold Course at Congressional Country Club. In their environmentally friendly golf cart, they tooled back to the women's locker room. Duly showered, dressed, and primped, they emerged from the Club's conveniences and found themselves in an elegant foyer.

"I'm famished!" announced Mindy Muckler, a United States Congresswoman. "Would you consider joining me for a bite to eat?" she asked her golfing partner.

"Oh that would be a delicious treat!" admitted Rose Hedgegrowth. "But Mindy, do you have reservations?" she asked with trepidation.

"I am a member of the United States House of Representatives! As such, I do not require a reservation, I already have my seat!" she arrogantly declared.

"Well, in that case, lead the way!" giggled Rose Hedgegrowth.

Both women were in their middle forties and fairly non-descript. Congresswoman Muckler had spent ten terms in the House of Representatives. She was a member of the National Blue Party. Her home state was located in the southern region of the United States. Having lived in Washington D.C. for over twenty years, Mindy had become overly accustomed to feeding at the trough of self-indulgence; a trough that was being paid for by the people she was busily misrepresenting.

Rose Hedgegrowth was the wife of a prominent Washington D.C. lobbyist. Rose did not comprehend, nor did she care to understand the intricacies of "K" Street. However, given the opulent life-style she was enjoying, whatever her husband was doing on "K" Street was "A" okay in her mind, especially when it came to the balances in the house checking account.

The two women approached the desk of the maître d'. Without looking up from his dais, the man muttered.

"I'm sorry, ladies, there is no seating available at this time."

"Excuse me?" hissed the Belle of the South.

The man behind the greeting station looked up and immediately recognized the Congresswoman and his inexcusable faux pas.

"Oh, Madam Congresswoman, a thousand pardons for my carelessness!" bowed the man. He did so more out of fear for his job, than respect for the member of Congress.

"Right this way, a cherished window table for two has just been made available!" he beckoned.

"That's more like it; otherwise, you know where my annoyance is going to get you, buster!" threatened the Congresswoman.

The abashed maître d' led the two women to the coveted window table over-looking the eighteenth green.

"Your servers shall attend to you in the wink of a donkey's eye lash!" he promised, obsequiously, and quickly vanished.

"Mindy, you certainly have some pull around here!" gushed Rose Hedgegrowth.

"It comes with the occupied territory!" gloated the Congresswoman, triumphantly.

A wine steward was immediately dispatched to their table.

"Would you ladies care to visit our wine list?" he indulged.

Congresswoman Mindy Muckler looked at Mrs. Rose Hedgegrowth, expectantly.

"Rose, would you care to share a bottle with me?" smiled the Congresswoman.

"Oh Mindy, I don't think so," hesitated the woman.

"In that case, I shall have a glass of burgundy," ordered Muckler.

"Are you quite certain you won't join me, Rose?" implored the Congresswoman.

"Well, I suppose a glass might be in order," decided Mrs. Hedgegrowth.

"Two glasses of burgundy!" demanded Mindy Muckler.

"Very good, Madam Congresswoman," obliged the wine steward as he excused himself.

"Mindy, I must confess, you're golf game has improved markedly over the last several years," complimented Mrs. Hedgegrowth.

"Rose, that's because my responsibilities as a member of the United States House of Representatives affords me the luxury of devoting the time requisite to improving one's golf game," demurred Congresswoman Muckler.

A young woman accosted their table.

"Hi, I'm Jen. I will be your waitress this afternoon," she smiled.

The waitress began to dispense menus.

"No need for those!" snapped the Congresswoman. "What's this afternoon's special?" she demanded.

"Imperial Crown Roast," informed the waitress.

Mindy Muckler stared at Mrs. Hedgegrowth.

"Do you happen to be a vegan?" she peered, skeptically.

"Why Heavens no!" replied the Washington D.C. lobbyist's wife with disbelief.

"All right then, it's settled. Two orders of Imperial Crown Roast!" directed the Congresswoman.

"And how would you like them cooked?" asked their waitress.

"I shall have my piece medium-rare," instructed Mindy Muckler.

"And for you ma'am?" prompted the young waitress.

"Medium will be just fine for me," answered Rose Hedgegrowth.

The wine steward returned to their table brandishing two glasses of burgundy. Having duly placed the wine glasses, he melted into the background.

"To my ever improving golf game!" toasted Congresswoman Muckler.

"I'll drink to that!" admitted a blushing Rose.

The two women savored the expensive wine and settled in to enjoy an afternoon of fine food and juicy gossip.

Emboldened by the enveloping warmth of her drink, Rose Hedgegrowth approached Congresswoman Mindy Muckler with a question that had been nagging at her for years.

"Mindy, given the amount of time you spend here in Washington D.C., don't you ever grow homesick for friends and family?" she asked, nervously.

The Congresswoman sipped her wine and reflected.

"You know Rose, there was a time when such a possibility concerned me," admitted Mindy Muckler. "That was when I first arrived here in Washington D.C., nearly twenty-one years ago.

The Congresswoman lapsed into quiet reflection.

"Goodness, that seems like only the day before yesterday," she mused. "Anyway, as time passed, and my years in office increased, I gradually came to the realization that the only thing that actually made me sick was the thought of having to return home."

The Congresswoman sipped her pricey wine and continued.

"To be truthful with you Rose, the only distasteful aspect of my career here in Washington D.C. is having to head south every two years and rub shoulders with the hometown hicks around election time." The Congresswoman's face contorted with contempt.

"I can't tell you just how tedious the required ritual of pretending to give a damn about their thoughts and concerns every two years has become, of late," complained Muckler.

"Then Mindy, why do you continue to compromise yourself?" asked Mrs. Hedgegrowth. "Why not simply leave Washington D.C. and return home for good?"

"And abandon my seat in the House of Representatives? The seat that I proudly consider my own after over twenty years of dedicated service to Washington D.C.? NEVER!" she hissed, defiantly.

Jen the waitress returned with their meals.

Congresswoman Muckler picked up a fork and knife and sliced the center of her meat for inspection.

"I ordered medium-rare, not medium!" she yelled

The young woman flustered.

"My sincerest apologies, Congresswoman Muckler I'll take it back to the kitchen at once," she promised.

"See that you do! And also see to it that the wine steward gets back here pronto!" demanded the annoyed Congresswoman.

Mindy Muckler looked across the table at Rose Hedgegrowth.

"I hope, at least, your beef is fit for consumption."

"Oh yes, it's just fine," placated the lobbyist's wife.

The wine steward returned with two fresh glasses of burgundy and placed one in front of each woman.

"Oh no, I can't possibly drink a second glass," objected Mrs. Hedgegrowth.

"Leave them both!" instructed Muckler. "I'll make certain that neither goes to waste."

Their waitress returned with another plateful of that afternoon's luncheon special.

Mindy Muckler sliced into the slab of beef for perusal. She threw her utensils down in disgust.

"I ordered medium-rare, not rare!" screamed the Congresswoman.

The other patrons of the Club's dining room paused in silence to observe the escalating furor. Immediately, the maître d' rushed to the scene of the crime.

"Madam Congresswoman is there anything I can do to make your dining experience more palatable?" he beseeched.

"Yea, you can get my damn order right!" screeched Muckler.

He seized the plate scuttled towards the kitchen.

The Congresswoman picked up her second glass of wine and drained it.

"You know Rose, if this kind of ineptitude begins to become a pattern here in Washington D.C., I might find it necessary to start taking a special interest in who can and who cannot work in this town illegally!" she threatened.

The maître d' returned personally with the Congresswoman's lunch. He dutifully placed it before her and waited for her approval.

Mindy Muckler eyed it, sliced it, and then tasted it.

"Now this is what I wanted!" she smiled.

The maître d' bowed and retreated.

Suddenly, Muckler's skin complexion turned to parchment. Her eyes bulged and with both hands she desperately clawed at her throat. As she lost consciousness, her face fell into the luncheon plate.

Madam Congresswoman Mindy Muckler was dead. However her Imperial Crown Roast was cooked to perfection.

Chapter Thirty-Eight

The prominent Washington D.C. politician pushed through the heavy front door of the prestigious athletic club with an arrogance reserved solely for its membership. As he made his way down the long corridor, the man gladly ignored the callings of squash courts and gym facilities. After all, his preferred room for recreation was the Parthenon Tap Room, located at the far end of the building.

United States Senator John "Black Jack" Bidwell, was a chieftain of "royal standing" at Washington D.C.'s exclusive, Mount Olympus Wealth and Racket Club. Bidwell was in his middle fifties. His complexion was flushed and his hairline was in recession. At five-ten and nearly three hundred pounds, he had spent the bulk of his twenty-six years in Washington D.C. hungrily growing into a formidable political power-broker. When he had arrived on the scene in Washington D.C. as a first term National Red Party Senator, it was with the best of intentions to represent the people from the mid-Western state that had sent him there. However, it did not take "Black Jack" long to become caught up in the culture of Washington D.C. that has lured so many elected officials over the years. He was seduced by the illusion of his own self-importance and the right of "passage" that almost inevitably accompanies the misperception of "political power" in Washington D.C. Bidwell quickly became one of the town's consummate political players; always knowing when to hold them and when to fold them, in order, to increase his personal stake in the game. Forsaking the home residence of his native state, "Black Jack" purchased a townhouse in D.C.'s swank Capitol neighborhood. He did, however, retain a local address in the form of a P.O. Box for the benefit of public perception.

"Hey Jack, come over here and sit down. There's always room for you at this poker table!" urged one of the seated card players.

"Not just yet boys," declined the big man, formally from Fly Over, U.S.A. "I've got a little catching up to do!" he laughed and ambulated towards the packed bar.

As he neared his destination, the crowd parted, affording the big fellow direct access to his holy grail.

"What will it be this afternoon, Senator?" asked the bartender with well-practiced deference.

"A double Jack on the rocks," smiled the Senator. "Oh, and Phil, a round for everyone at the bar!" bellowed Bidwell.

The members of the Mount Olympus Wealth and Racket Club responded with thunderous approvals of appreciation.

"Black Jack is back! Black Jack is back!"

Shoulders were slapped and the drinks flowed freely.

The Chieftain assumed his usual throne at the center of adulation. The bartender returned with the Senator's drink order and handed it to him personally. Bidwell raised his glass and the crowd fell silent.

"Here's to all of us, the very people that have made this town what it is today!"

The raucous cheer of approval was muted only by the thirsty slurping of overly zealous gullets.

"Will you be lunching today, Senator?" asked the bartender.

"What's the special of the day, Phil?" Bidwell inquired in earnest.

"Roasted Pork, sir," responded the man behind the bar.

"Pork has always been an item on the menu I find to be impossible to resist," assented the Senator.

"Very good, sir," complied the bartender.

"Oh Phil, if you can find the time," requested Bidwell dangling a now emptied cocktail glass.

"At once, Senator," obliged the mixologist.

A gentleman burst through the door of the Parthenon Tap Room. He walked slowly towards the bar as if seeking out someone in particular. He spotted the person he was searching for, and made a bee-line towards Senator John Bidwell.

Russell Hedgegrowth was a well-known Washington D.C. lobbyist. He was somewhere in his forties. Russell was of average height and weight. In fact, his over-all appearance could be best described as average if not for his manner of dress. Hedgegrowth's suit and accessories were stylish, impeccable, and expensive.

As Hedgegrowth approached, the Senator turned to greet him.

"Russell, how good to see you," he grinned. "What are you drinking, because I'm buying!" thundered the big man.

"Scotch on the rocks"

"Phil, you heard the man," ordered the Senator.

The bartender was back in a flash.

"Jack, we have to talk!" demanded Hedgegrowth, under his breath.

"Okay Russ, what's on your mind?" smiled the Senator.

"Does the Key Lime Pie Line ring a bell, Bidwell?" smoldered the lobbyist.

Hedgegrowth had obviously been drinking. Nonetheless, "Black Jack" Bidwell's mood suddenly darkened.

"Okay Russ, we'll talk, but not at the bar," agreed the Senator.

Bidwell motioned to the bartender.

"Phil, we'll be sitting at that table over in the corner," informed the big man.

"Very good, Senator, I'll see to it that your pork finds you," assured the man.

Bidwell and Hedgegrowth sat down at a table abutting the rear wall of the room.

"Jack, you assured me that the Key Lime Pie Line Amendment was going to flow through the Senate without any trouble what so ever , I believe were your words," fumed the lobbyist.

"I know I did, Russ. Personally, I'm quite disappointed. However, unforeseen factors came into play at the last moment!" lamented the Senator. "I'm really very sorry."

"Sorry? What the hell good is sorry going to do for me as far as my clients are concerned?" demanded the now irate lobbyist.

A waiter came to their table with Bidwell's lunch. The Senator looked at it with disapproval.

"This isn't what I ordered! This is goat, not pork!" yelled Bidwell.

"I'm so sorry Senator. I'll take it back and replace it right away!" assured the server.

"Replace it you say? Indeed, you most certainly will!"

With that, Bidwell shoved the plate off the table sending it crashing to the floor. The din of breaking china momentarily hushed the once boisterous saloon. The Tap Room's general-manger hurried to the table and accosted the situation.

"What is the problem here, Senator?" asked the man, nervously.

"Your waiter dropped my lunch," explained Bidwell.

"Yes I know. I *saw* him do it!" agreed the manager.

The waiter began to clean up the mess on the floor.

"I shall personally oversee the serving of your lunch, Senator," kowtowed the manager. "May I offer you a round of drinks on the house?" he suggested.

"That would be a good start," nodded "Black Jack."

The manager of the Parthenon Tap Room scampered off to the bar to place the drink orders and then to the kitchen to direct the Senator's lunch order. The raucous noise level of the Tap Room returned to normal.

Phil the bartender personally delivered the drinks to Bidwell and Hedgegrowth.

"Gentlemen, these are on me," he bowed and returned to his duties behind the bar.

Hedgegrowth, immediately, resumed his tirade.

"Senator, you are recompensed quite handsomely to anticipate and preclude such unforeseen factors!" blistered the lobbyist. "You assured me repeatedly, that the Key Lime Pie Line legislation was a done deal in the Senate!" lambasted Hedgegrowth.

"Listen to me Russell, Morey Drainer was personally squeezing the stones of every member in his Senate caucus to reject the amendment!" explained Senator Bidwell.

"And why the hell was that!" snapped Hedgegrowth.

"Because the Big Guy himself was all over Drainer, like stink on a pig to have the amendment rejected!" groaned Bidwell.

"And how the hell is that going to salvage my career here in Washington D.C.!" fumed the lobbyist.

"Better it be your career down the crapper than mine!" snorted the Senator, smugly.

A new waiter approached their table with Bidwell's lunch. The Senator inspected it and with tacit approval dismissed the server with a wave of his fork and knife.

Russell Hedgegrowth swilled his cocktail and stood, to take his leave.

"If I'm finished in this town, you can't be too far behind me Bidwell!"

"Me, "Black Jack" Bidwell finished here in Washington D.C? Hedgegrowth, you've had more to drink than I thought. No, my career in this town is just beginning! So, little man, get lost before I get mad!" banished the Senator.

Hedgegrowth unsteadily guided himself to the front door of the Parthenon Taproom and disappeared.

At long last, Senator John "Black Jack" Bidwell turned his undivided attention to his meal. Unexpectedly, a numbing sensation began to hinder his movements. Awkwardly, he dropped his utensils, and began clumsily grasping at his throat. Desperately gasping for air, he violently lurched backwardly in his chair. The full weight of his near three hundred pounds caused the chair to topple cascading him to the floor of the Parthenon Tap Room.

His body was motionless.

Senator John "Black Jack" Bidwell was dead.

Chapter Thirty-Nine

Inspector Nick Cuffington and Detective Maria Fuentes were traveling in her obviously unmarked police cruiser on their way to the Tangerine Oriental.

Once at the hotel, they planned to complete the long overdue viewing the surveillance tapes and arrange interviews with any of the staff who had been on duty the evening of Senator Ryder's murder. The detective's cell phone ringtone sounded. Fuentes scanned the caller I.D. and handed the phone to Cuffington.

"It's Captain Killingsworth," she informed him.

"Yes, Pat?"

"There's been two more!" screamed the Captain.

His voice was quite agitated.

"Two more what, Pat?" urged the Inspector in a measured tone of voice.

"Two more Congressional deaths!" yelled the Captain.

"When Pat?" continued the Inspector.

"Both within the last hour," related Killingsworth.

"Who were they?" pressed Cuffington.

"Congresswoman Mindy Muckler and Senator John Bidwell," identified the Captain.

"Were they together?" asked the Inspector.

"No! Muckler died at the Congressional Country Club and Bidwell at the Mount Olympus Wealth and Racket Club."

"What were the causes of each death?" pressed the Inspector.

"Too early to say with any certainty," informed the Captain.

"Pat, have you got both scenes secured?"

"Affirmative, Nick. What is your present location?"

"Sitting in traffic on our way to the Tangerine Oriental," relayed Cuffington.

"How long will it take you to get to the Mount Olympus Wealth and Racket Club?" implored the Captain.

"That's anyone's guess, but we're on our way!" confirmed the Inspector.

"Good" acknowledged Killingsworth.

"Listen Pat, who from U.S. Capitol Police is over-seeing the proceedings at the Mount Olympus Club?" the Inspector wanted to know.

"Lieutenant Ginger Snapp," was his curt reply and cut off.

Inspector Cuffington handed the phone back to the Detective.

Initially, he said nothing. Instead, Nick quietly stared through the passenger side window taking in both the information passed on to him by Killingsworth and the ever increasing numbers of demonstrators filling the streets of Washington D.C.

Maria gave him some space before interrupting his thoughts.

"Nick, am I to assume our destination is the Mount Olympus Wealth and Racket Club!" she demanded.

As if being rousted from a deep slumber, Cuffington turned his head to face Fuentes.

"Yes, we're going to the Olympus Club!" he stated emphatically.

"Do you plan to fill me in or should I switch on the news?" she smiled.

Inspector Nick Cuffington, for the moment, hit the automatic pilot button.

"One Congresswoman Mindy Muckler and one Senator John Bidwell died within the last hour at the Congressional Country Club and the aforementioned Olympus Club, respectively. Both causes of death are currently unknown," he summarized.

Detective Fuentes assimilated his words and dutifully tried to transform them into something mirroring sense.

They slowly threaded their way through the seemingly endless clusters of protestors towards the Mount Olympus Club.

"Nick, what's your preliminary read on the two latest Congressional deaths?" ventured Fuentes.

"That Terry Frailey didn't have a hand in either one of them," he smiled.

"Now that truly is humorous. You really can be one funny guy when you put your mind to it, can't you Nick," she said shaking her head with the pretense of derision.

Cuffington looked at the Detective.

"Maria, how the hell can I begin to form any opinions given what we know at this point?" he argued." We will get a better handle on things once we check out the scene of the death."

"That's if we ever get there," she complained restlessly.

The masses of demonstrators continued to impede their progress towards the Mount Olympus Wealth and Racket Club.

"Well, to keep things in an upbeat perspective, if members of the United States Congress continue dropping dead, maybe the gridlock here in Washington D.C. might finally start to abate," reasoned the Inspector.

"Amen to that brother," concurred Fuentes, wholeheartedly.

As they neared their point of destination, the usual activity that accompanies death in public places was in full swing. The menagerie of "official procedure" was, in essence, a patriotically colorful display of random authority and ad hoc decision making.

"Detective, park this baby in the eye of the storm," ordered the Inspector.

"Yes, sir!"

Following her Inspector's fiat, Maria Fuentes punched the car's accelerator and burst through the familiar yellow tape of emergency demarcation quickly bringing her obviously unmarked police cruiser to a graceful stop directly in front of the heavy front door of the Mount Olympus Wealth and Racket Club.

As Cuffington and Fuentes climbed out of their vehicle, there was little need for identification. The officers on the scene were an equal complement of U.S. Capitol Police and Metro Cops.

"Where's Lieutenant Ginger Snapp?" barked the Inspector.

"She's inside, sir. Please follow me," requested a young female officer from U.S. Capitol Police.

The entered the hallowed establishment and proceeded down an impressive hallway. At the end of the corridor was a large glass-paneled door adorned with a plaque bearing the inscription "Ides of the Parthenon Tap Room."

"This must be the place," reckoned Detective Fuentes.

There were two police sentries monitoring the entrance. One was from U.S. Capitol and the other from Metro.

"Lieutenant Snapp is inside, Sir. She's expecting you," informed the uniformed officer and she turned to leave.

The door to the Tap Room was opened by one of the sentries. No incident of identification accompanied their admittance. There were only five people present in the room; four living and one supinely, dead. Lieutenant Ginger Snapp sat at the bar busily pecking away at her omnipresent lap top. A second U.S. Capitol officer was intently observing the activities of the two Metro Morgue forensics specialists. The late Senator John "Black Jack" Bidwell was planted motionlessly on his back, eyes staring blankly into vacuity. Inspector Cuffington and Detective Fuentes approached the seated Lieutenant.

Without looking up, the woman briefly held up her index finger, wordlessly requesting another moment to complete imputing her hand written notes. Once finished, the Lieutenant closed her lap top and rose to greet the two new arrivals.

"Inspector Cuffington , it's nice to see you again," she fluttered.

And then, as a second thought, acknowledged the presence of Maria Fuentes.

"And you too, Detective"

"Likewise, Lieutenant," returned Cuffington.

"Oh, it's now First-Lieutenant, Inspector, just for the record," she smiled with the contempt that generally accompanies newly bestowed increased authority. "Chief O'Toole commissioned my promotion personally."

"There's nothing like good old-fashioned leg work to guarantee a rise in the ranks," smiled Fuentes.

Wishing to avoid any further unpleasantness between the two women, Cuffington quickly shifted the focus of conversation to the immediate matter, at hand.

"First-Lieutenant, what is the initial consensus as to the possible cause of death?" diverted the Inspector.

"Obviously, we won't know until the final autopsy results are completed," she stated.

Cuffington gestured towards the two specialists from Metro Morgue.

"What's their opinion?" quizzed the Inspector.

"Those two are members of Doctor Savage's elite forensic field unit. As such, they have not nor will say a word regarding any findings," explained Ginger Snapp.

"I can understand that," Cuffington rationalized.

"For what it's worth, I'd be very surprised if it weren't natural causes," continued Snapp. "Look at him! He most certainly wasn't shy around the punch bowl and cookies," she pointed out.

The young U.S. Capitol officer who had been watching the forensic activity walked towards the bar.

"First-Lieutenant, the boys from Metro Morgue are wrapping things up over there. So, unless you need me for anything else, I'll be on my way."

"Very good, officer," she dismissed with an extra lingering little flutter.

Fuentes rolled her eyes.

"Detective, please inform the Metro sentry his presence is no longer required." requested the inspector

"Yes, sir," complied Fuentes and walked to the room's entrance.

Cuffington waited for Maria to return before speaking.

"Ginger, do you have an accurate account of the events leading up to the Senator's death?" questioned the Inspector.

"I spoke to the bartender on duty at the time. . ."

The First-Lieutenant's cell phone interrupted her in mid-sentence. She picked up the call and listened carefully. Nodding her head with understanding, she ended the call.

"That was Captain Killingsworth. He's just finishing up at the Congressional Country Club. He wants us to meet him at Brewster's Bistro," she fluttered.

Chapter Forty

Inspector Nick Cuffington and Detective Maria Fuentes had left the Mount Olympus Wealth and Racket Club. They were traversing downtown Washington D.C. on their way to Brewster's Bistro to meet Captain Patrick Killingsworth and the recently promoted, First-Lieutenant Ginger Snapp.

"So Nick, tell me what are your first impressions coming away from our visit to the Parthenon Tap Room this afternoon?" nudged Detective Fuentes, as she focused on the road in front of her.

"Another dead member from the United States Congress," responded Inspector Cuffington, rather tersely.

"Do you honestly believe that the cause of Senator Bidwell's death can realistically be attributed to natural causes?" pressured Fuentes.

"I most certainly would like to believe that such is the case," he replied, noncommittally.

"Given the circumstances surrounding the murders of Congressman Sooner and Senator Ryder, what do you think the plausible odds are of natural causes in the death of Senator Bidwell?"

"Not very likely," he admitted, glumly.

I agree, so why, do you suppose First-Lieutenant Snapp is so reconciled to the notion that Bidwell's death was the result of natural causes," insisted Fuentes.

"Because heart attacks and strokes require less "leg work" than do poisonings," smiled the Inspector.

"I won't argue with that straight forward conclusion!" she laughed.

The ongoing presence of the round the clock protestors continued to stymie the flow of traffic in downtown Washington D.C..

Cuffington and Fuentes arrived in the front of Brewster's a little after five p.m.. As usual, there was no available legal parking. The Detective pulled to a stop in what she now considered her private space; the No Parking Fire Zone Lane.

Brewster's Bistro was crowded with its usual cadre of metropolitan merry-makers. Immediately spotting them, Toby the waiter waived enthusiastically and nimbly weaved his way towards the two officers.

"Captain Killingsworth is already seated," he said, as he guided them towards Cuff-Kill Corner. "And Detective Fuentes, I have a special surprise for you," he beamed.

"How is it that Captain Killingsworth always manages to arrive here before we do?" asked the puzzled Detective.

"An insatiable thirst for the proof and the truth," hazarded the Inspector.

Pat Killingsworth and Ginger Snapp were seated side by side in the booth of law and order. Maria Fuentes and Nick Cuffington slid into the cushioned seat facing them.

"I'll be right back!" pledged their server.

Killingsworth looked haggard but, nonetheless upbeat in his mood. First-Lieutenant Ginger Snapp simply fluttered. After the obligatory social graces were exchanged, Inspector Nick Cuffington got down to the serious business of trying to unravel and understand the current depravity now so pervasively plaguing Washington D.C..

"Pat, what has Special Technician Hightower uncovered in response to the breach at U.S. Capitol Police's headquarters data base?" inquired the Inspector.

"Her team of professional techies has successfully been able to narrow its search for the invaders to the Northern Hemisphere of the planet!" he reported with managerial pride.

"Well, that does, indeed, shrink the list of potential suspects," agreed the Inspector, with a dubious shake of the head.

"To, precisely half!" smiled the Captain triumphantly.

Toby the Waiter returned to their booth.

"This is especially for you Detective Fuentes."

He placed a chilled bottle of Hatuey in front of her, sans glass.

"Just the way you like it," he glowed.

"Why thank you, Toby, that's so kind," acknowledged the Detective.

He then bestowed Cuffington with a can of Bud.

"I had to pull some strings to keep these cans of domestic in Brewster's Bistro," he confided.

"I do appreciate your daring thoughtfulness, Toby," complimented the Inspector.

With a wave of nonchalance, the waiter disappeared into the din of the evening crowd.

Cuffington pulled at his can of domestic and then zeroed in on the Captain.

"So Pat, fill me in on the circumstances surrounding the death of Congresswoman Mindy Muckler."

Killingsworth thoughtfully sipped his drink before formulating a cohesive response.

"As it turns out Nick, Congresswoman Mindy Muckler was a high muck amuck within the ranks of her national political party," imparted the Captain.

"That makes complete alliterative sense to me," conceded the Inspector.

'What's more, Muckler had no prior adverse medical history that might suggest she was a candidate for a sudden, unforeseen heart attack or stroke," emphasized Killingsworth.

"And how can you be so certain, so soon, of that fact, Pat?" questioned Cuffington.

"Because, I ran a C.M.I.B on the late Congresswoman," explained the Captain.

"And what the hell is that," questioned the Inspector.

"It's a Congressional Medical Information Bureau report," enlightened the Captain. "Those guys know if and when you belch the wrong way. Anyway, according to that report, Muckler was clean as a whistle," advised Killingsworth.

"So based upon that report, you are presuming the possibility of foul play?" concluded Cuffington.

"Truthfully, I'm leaning in that direction," admitted the Captain.

Killingsworth sipped his cocktail and continued.

"Anyway, the woman seated with Muckler at the time of her death assured me that the Congresswoman was seemingly fine one moment, and then, in an instant, was face down in her Imperial Crown Roast, cooked medium rare," conveyed the Captain.

"And how exactly do you know that the Imperial Crown Roast was cooked medium rare, Pat?" persisted the Inspector.

"Because the woman dining with Muckler told me the Congresswoman repeatedly sent her luncheon order back to the kitchen until the Imperial Crown Roast arrived at the table medium rare," avowed Killingsworth.

"And with whom was Congresswoman Mindy Muckler dining with at the time her face took a free fall into the Imperial Crown Roast cooked medium rare?" furthered Cuffington

Killingsworth killed his cocktail and proceeded.

"One Mrs. Rose Hedgegrowth," detailed the Captain. "From what I gather, she is the wife of a very prominent Washington D.C. lobbyist."

"Hedgegrowth!" fluttered First-Lieutenant Ginger Snapp. "I know that I know that I know that name from someplace!" she insisted, knowingly.

"I, for one, am thoroughly convinced the First-Lieutenant knows that name," smiled Fuentes.

With that, Ginger Snapp bent over to open her carryall. She retrieved her lap top, placed it on the table, and began pecking away at its keypad. Within seconds, she pulled up the object of her pursuit.

"Russell Hedgegrowth!" she exclaimed. "Mr. Hedgegrowth was sitting at the table just prior to Senator Bidwell's death!"

194

"Then Mr. Hedgegrowth witnessed the death of Senator Bidwell," assumed the Inspector.

"No, not according to Phil. Mr. Hedgegrowth left the room several minutes before the Senator collapsed.

"And who is Phil?" demanded Cuffington.

"Phil is the bartender who was on duty at the time of Senator Bidwell's death.

"Did Phil happen to mention anything else that might prove pertinent to the circumstances surrounding the Senator's death?" prodded the Inspector

"No, there's nothing else I can think of," as she shook her head. "Oh wait, there is one thing that Phil mentioned that might be of some interest," remembered the First-Lieutenant.

"And what might that be, Ginger," pumped Cuffington.

"Phil told me that the manager of the Parthenon Tap Room replaced waiters at Senator Bidwell's table midway through the meal."

"And why was that?" asked Cuffington.

"Because the first waiter dropped the Senator's luncheon plate, sending it shattering to the floor," elaborated Ginger Snapp.

"The pieces to this jagged jig saw puzzle are finally starting to fall into place!" crowed Captain Patrick Killingsworth.

"And how's that, Pat?" queried the Inspector.

"As I've told you all along, my professional instincts do not permit me to accept coincidence when it comes to murder investigations," repeated the Captain.

Killingsworth motioned to the Waiter, and then continued.

"That said, am I really supposed to accept the premise that Mr. and Mrs. Hedgegrowth just *happened* to be dining with Senator Bidwell and Congresswoman Muckler, respectively, on the very same day and at approximately the same time those two members of the United States Congress were poisoned? My Irish arse!"

"Pat, I think you might be getting a little ahead of yourself," cautioned the Inspector.

He sipped at his beer and then proceeded.

"First, and foremost, we don't know definitively that either Congresswoman Muckler or Senator Bidwell were murdered, let alone poisoned. Secondly, even if they were both intentionally killed the mere presence of Mr. and Mrs. Hedgegrowth at both scenes of the crimes can only be construed as circumstantial," rebutted Cuffington.

"I tend to agree with the Inspector," echoed Detective Fuentes. "Captain, to my way of thinking, your conclusions appear, to me, to be just a little too conveniently, pat."

Killingsworth was disappointed by their initial doubts, but remained undeterred.

"I'm not going let this husband/wife team out of my sight!" he vowed.

"Patrick, I assume you've already arranged to have Doctor Savage handle, personally, the autopsies of Congresswoman Muckler and Senator Bidwell," checked Cuffington

"*He* wouldn't have it any other way."

Chapter Forty-One

After leaving Brewster's Bistro, Inspector Cuffington and Detective Fuentes were Foggy Bottom bound. The time was seven-thirty p.m.. Although there were pockets of protestors still present on the streets of Washington D.C., the lighter traffic was moving without impediment.

"Nick, weigh in for me, if you will, on Captain Killingsworth's judge, jury, and executioner style approach to Mr. and Mrs. Hedgegrowth's possible involvement in the deaths of Congresswoman Muckler and Senator Bidwell?" Fuentes tossed out for bait.

The Inspector mulled his Detective's lure before articulating a response.

"I think Pat is quite anxious to get this entire Congressional quagmire put behind him," confided Cuffington.

"Can you really blame him?" defended the Fuentes.

"Look Maria, as I said to Pat at Brewster's, we don't yet know if either Muckler or Bidwell were even murdered at this point!" emphasized the Inspector.

"But you'll be surprised if they weren't, you said as much," reminded Maria.

"True"

The law enforcement duo from Metro Police traveled in silence for several miles. As always, it was Detective Fuentes who initiated further conversation, as it pertained to the unfolding events of the day.

"So let's assume, for the moment, that both Muckler and Bidwell were, indeed, murdered. In your mind, how do Mr. and Mrs. Hedgegrowth fit into the picture, Nick?"

Cuffington turned his head and stared into the face of Detective Fuentes before answering her question.

"Maria, it's my opinion that the Hedgegrowth's don't fit in at all," declared the Inspector.

"Nick, how, can you be so certain so soon?" questioned Maria.

"Because I tend to agree with the rationale you put forth earlier."

"And to exactly which brilliant rationale are you alluding, Inspector?" she asked grinning.

"The one that theorizes that Mr. and Mrs. Hedgegrowth are simply far too "pat" to be considered viable suspects," concluded the Inspector.

"Nick, that was merely my initial bristling to Killingsworth's self-certitude, not a complete repudiation of his premise," she clarified.

"Well, I, for one, have completely erased the Hedgegrowths from this picture," he stated with unyielding certainty.

"And specifically, why is that, Inspector?" pressed Fuentes.

"Because any involvement on the part of the Hedgegrowths in the deaths of either Congresswoman Muckler or Senator Bidwell would break the pattern of the unfathomable," explained the Inspector.

Detective Maria Fuentes slowed her car to a stop at the side of the road. She craned her head to closely scrutinize the expression on the face of Inspector Nick Cuffington. Fuentes remained silent for a moment, carefully weighing her words.

"Nick, I know you're prone to abstractions, but you're starting to get just a little too deep, even for me," she laughed, nervously.

Cuffington stared at the Detective, devoid of emotional expression. His taciturn gaze actually began to make Fuentes uncomfortable. When, at last, he did speak, it was as if the real Nick had suddenly resurfaced from the depths of retrospection.

"Think about it, Maria. From the very outset, starting with the murders of Congressman Sooner and Senator Ryder, we've been in the dark here, Charlie!" he smiled. "Look, we haven't even been able to come up with a suspect or a motive in either of those cases."

The Inspector paused to study Fuentes' facial reaction. Maria remained impassive as she got back on the road. He continued.

"Hell, we can't even identify the toxin used in the murders of Sooner and Ryder! Furthermore, those responsible for those murders have demonstrated the impressive capability of invading the data base at U.S. Capitol Police headquarters with impunity!"

"So what are you driving at, Nick?" she asked with growing ambivalence.

"What I'm saying is that even if the autopsies reveal that Muckler and Bidwell were murdered, the Hedgegrowths had absolutely nothing to do with either death," finished the Inspector.

"And why are you so damn sure of that?" demanded the Detective.

"Because, right now we're all clueless here in Washington D.C.," reasoned Cuffington.

"Well, that's not exactly all the news that is fit to print," she sighed irritably.

"It never is!" lamented Cuffington. "Nonetheless, logic mandates that if Muckler and Bidwell were murdered, the crimes were undoubtedly perpetrated by persons linked in some way to those responsible for the killings of Sooner and Ryder," rationalized the Inspector.

"So?"

"So, given the circumstances, as I've outlined them, the real question becomes why out of the clear blue are Sacco and Vanzetti, in the personages of Mr. and Mrs. Hedgegrowth, conveniently dumped into our laps?"

"You tell me, Nick. You seem to have all the answers," she shrugged.

"Diversion"

Detective Fuentes rolled to a stop in front of the Cuffington home. The Inspector got out of the car, and turned to speak with the Detective.

"As soon as I've determined tomorrow's itinerary, I'll be in touch. Also, Maria, I'd like you to obtain a copy of the guest list of those present at the dinner party the night Congressman Sooner was murdered," requested Cuffington.

"Why, to find out whether or not the Hedgegrowths were there?"

"Precisely"

"Well, in light of what you were just saying, what would it matter one way or the other?" she asked with a hint of disdain.

"If the Hedgegrowths were in attendance that evening, my suspicions will be confirmed.

Inspector Cuffington closed the passenger side door. Detective Fuentes drove away.

Nick entered his house through the side door. Leigh was in the kitchen chatting on the phone. Cuffington went to her and without disturbing her conversation, gently kissed the side of her face. He then turned his undivided attention to the refrigerator. Scavenging, he pulled out a brown papered doggie bag and placed it on the center aisle. He returned equipped with utensils and napkins, prepared to devour whatever the doggie bag's contents. Leigh ended the telephone conversation and walked over to her husband and hugged him.

"It's seafood salad, darling, she divulged. It's the remnants of my lunch this afternoon."

"Is it any good?" he asked and dug in without waiting for a response.

"Quite," she assured him

"Not bad at all," he agreed through mouthfuls of scungilli. "Although, it could have a little bit more garlic," he vetted.

Leigh Cuffington patiently waited for her husband to devour the remainder of the doggie bag's contents.

"That was Mimi Hounderson I was speaking with on the phone just now," informed Mrs. Cuffington.

"And how is the queen of Washington D.C.'s literary obscene?" asked Nick with unmasked disinterest.

Mrs. Cuffington, with political correctness, chose to ignore her husband's social boorishness.

"Far better than Mindy Muckler, I'm afraid," she reported ruefully.

"And why is that, dear?" entreated the Inspector.

"Oh Nick, you haven't heard?" she gasped in horror. "Congresswoman Mindy Muckler died this very afternoon, at the Congressional Country Club while having lunch," she dispatched.

"Come to think of it, I did hear some rumors to that effect," admitted the Inspector.

"It's really quite tragic. Mindy was only in her mid-forties. Besides that, she had dedicated her life to serving the people she represented from her home state. I rather doubt she has a single personal friend, here in Washington D.C. to help oversee the final arrangements," lamented Leigh Cuffington.

"Dear, we can only console ourselves with the hope that Congresswoman Mindy Muckler possessed the foresight to get a dog," assuaged the Inspector.

Leigh Cuffington looked at her husband quizzically, but offered no further comment.

Nick picked up the remains of his doggie bag dinner and proceeded to the garbage can and then the sink. After washing and putting away the silverware, he ambled towards the refrigerator to requisition a beer.

"Leigh, I'll be out on the patio"

Nick Cuffington opened the kitchen's door and stepped out into the final twilight of the evening. He pulled a chair, sat down at the table, and lit a cigarette. He was solaced by the evening shade, and the stillness of the moment. The door to the kitchen opened, and Leigh emerged. She walked to the patio table and sat down next to her husband. She nestled her head against his shoulder.

"You look overly tired," she nuzzled.

"More drained than fatigued," admitted the Inspector.

Suddenly, Leigh Cuffington sat upright in her chair. She stared at her husband with a new found angst.

"Nick, do you suppose Mindy's death could in some way be related to the murders of Congressman Sooner and Senator Ryder?" she asked with disquieted trepidation.

"That will depend upon the findings of the two Congressional autopsies being conducted as we speak, introduced the Inspector.

"Two Congressional autopsies?" she gasped in numbed disbelief

"Yes Leigh, two Congressional autopsies; Congresswoman Muckler's and the late Senator John Bidwell's," confirmed her husband. "He also died this afternoon."

"I wasn't aware of Senator Bidwell's death," she stammered.

"I find it hard to believe that you, of all people, weren't privy to the late Senator's untimely demise," yawned Mr. Cuffington.

"Nick, I haven't been out of the house all day. In fact, I didn't even turn on the news," she offered in her defense.

"A likely story," he challenged. "If you never left the house, as you claim, how did the seafood salad fall into your possession Mrs. Cuffington," grilled a now laughing Inspector.

"Guido's delivers," she smiled, demurely.

"Well, if that alibi checks out, I suppose that will leave me no alternative other than to scratch you off my list of possible suspects; if such a list existed."

"Nick, do you suspect illegal activity?" she asked anxiously.

Cuffington extinguished his cigarette and studied the face of his wife.

"Leigh, what town do we live in?"

"Washington D.C.," she answered without hesitation.

Mrs. Cuffington thought for a moment.

"You've answered my question, dear."

Chapter Forty-Two

The following morning, Nick showered, dressed, and descended the hallway stairs. Leigh was in the kitchen, fixated on the television.

"I was up and out early this morning," she declared. "Bagels are on the counter and you'll find lox in the refrigerator."

Nick went over and kissed his wife before retrieving his ritualistic two water glasses.

"Nick, how did you sleep?"

"Like a babe in the woods awaiting perdition."

"Then I can only assume you slept quite soundly," grinned Leigh.

"Leigh, what's on the television that has so riveted your attention?" Nick asked with a grin.

"Oh, you'll never guess, Inspector. Were you aware that two more members of the United States Congress died unexpectedly yesterday afternoon?" she lampooned.

Nick looked at his wife with an expression of seriousness.

"What were the causes of death?" he asked with genuine interest.

"How would I know, Nick?"

"Haven't the findings of the Muckler and Bidwell autopsies been reported on the news this morning?" he questioned with surprise.

"Absolutely not, in fact, that's exactly what's been fueling this maniacal media speculation," informed Leigh as she motioned towards the flat screen.

"I find that very odd," admitted the Inspector.

"Why, Nick?"

"Because the bodies of Congresswoman Muckler and Senator Ryder were brought to Metro Morgue sometime yesterday afternoon," answered Cuffington. "That should have allowed ample time for Savage to complete his preliminary findings sometime yesterday, thereby, making those findings public domain after midnight this morning."

"Well, whatever the reason, I'm sure Doctor Savage has a good explanation," assured Leigh.

"I don't doubt that for a moment," Nick agreed.

The Inspector moved closer to the T.V. to take in the action.

"Leigh, what has the general demeanor of the media been like thus far this morning?" solicited the Inspector.

"Frenzied would be unjustly understating the pitch of their fervor," she related. "And, I haven't yet gotten to the computer nor done any social networking," added Leigh.

"So, I may safely assume that the recent events here in Washington D.C. would more than justify an expansion of the 24 hour a day cable news cycle," he conjectured with a smile.

"If they could've, they already would've!" attested Mrs. Cuffington

"And how is the gang on *Morning Joe* spinning the cyclone of circumstance swirling around the most recent Congressional deaths?" pursued the Inspector.

Leigh did not answer immediately. Mrs. Cuffington's brow furrowed while selecting her words of response.

"The reporters in the field are extremely agitated," observed Mrs. Cuffington.

"That's a given, dear," dismissed her husband.

"Yes, but Nick, this entire scenario is playing out a bit incongruously," she tried to explain.

"In what way, Leigh," prompted the Inspector, while sipping his iced water and grapefruit juice.

"Well, the agitated reporters in the field are fully expecting to agitate the people they interview with the news of the most recent Congressional deaths."

"That's pretty standard stuff, honey. So, I don't see quite where you're going with this one," admitted the Inspector.

"What I'm saying is that, it appears to me, the agitated reporters, who are expecting to agitate the people they interview about the latest Congressional deaths, are not getting those people agitated which, in turn, agitates the already agitated reporters into further agitation."

"That's quite an observation, Leigh" offered her husband.

The Inspector mulled his wife's words. "So from your perspective, when people are confronted with the news of the two latest Congressional deaths, they're not getting very upset," summarized Cuffington.

"That's the impression I've been getting all morning," she averred.

Nick fixed himself a bagel and retreated to his office in order to scan his mail. He sat down at his desk and was immediately met by the ring tone of his cell phone. It was a call he had been anticipating.

"Good morning, Emma," greeted Cuffington.

"Tell me what's good about it, Inspector?" Chief of Metro Police, Emma Teasedale, was not in a good mood.

"What do you have for me, Nick?" she growled.

"Actually, I'm awaiting the autopsy results on Congresswoman Muckler and Senator Bidwell," acknowledged Cuffington.

"And what do you suppose they are going to reveal?" demanded Teasedale.

"Let's just say I have my suspicions, Emma," conceded Cuffington.

"Well, I certainly hope those suspicions are pointed in a specific direction," she pressed.

"Captain Killingsworth feels that we may have several persons of interest," he stated.

"But Inspector Cuffington doesn't agree," surmised the Chief of Metro Police.

"Unfortunately, I do believe that the persons in question will, ultimately, prove to be dead ends," dismissed Cuffington.

There was a long silence on Teasedale's end of the phone.

"Well, if the findings of the autopsies determine that either Congresswoman Muckler or Senator Bidwell were murdered, you might want to consider feeding those dead ends to the sharks, to buy a little time," suggested the Chief of Metro Police.

"Now there's a compassionate recommendation," acknowledged the Inspector.

"Spare me the homily, choirboy. I know exactly what you're capable of, Cuffington!" sneered Teasedale.

There was a pause on Emma's end of the phone. "Who's performing the autopsies?" she demanded.

"Savage"

"When do expect to hear from him?" asked Teasedale.

"Quite frankly, I'm surprised we haven't heard from him already," admitted Cuffington.

"I'll expect to hear from you immediately after you've finished with the good doctor," she instructed and hung up.

Leigh was standing in the doorway to the office. Once Nick was off the phone, she walked to his desk.

"Who was on the phone, Nick?" she inquired.

"Teasedale"

"That must have been pleasant," commiserated Mrs. Cuffington.

"Actually, I was expecting worse," he grinned. "But Emma is starting to feel some heat. That I do know."

"Anyway, Nick, I'll be working at the Book Revue this afternoon, and then having dinner with some of the girls. So that leaves you on your own this evening as far as eating is concerned," she smiled.

"I'll survive," he shrugged.

"You always seem to, Mr. Cuffington.

Leigh kissed her husband and left his office.

Chapter Forty-Three

Inspector Cuffington's cell phone sounded at two p.m. that afternoon. It was Detective Fuentes.

"Nick, I just got off the phone with Captain Killingsworth."

"What's the deal, Maria?"

"He wants us to meet him at Metro Morgue at four p.m.," she relayed.

"Did he have any information regarding the results of the Muckler and Bidwell autopsies?" urged the Inspector.

"No," reported Fuentes." "He just said something about having words on the phone with Savage and that the Doctor had hung up on him," alerted Maria.

"Seymour has always been a bit quirky when it comes to speaking on the phone," Cuffington clarified.

"Nick, I hate to be the one to break the bad news to you, but Doctor Seymour Savage is just plain quirky, period!" chided the Detective.

"Pick me up at three-thirty p.m.," ordered the Inspector.

"I would suggest you make that three-fifteen p.m.," advised Fuentes. "Believe it or not, the number of demonstrators flooding into Washington D.C. is still on the rise!"

"Three-fifteen it is," confirmed Cuffington and disengaged.

Nick returned his attention to the desk top in front of him. He had spent the lion's share of his day seeking common threads between Congressman Sooner, Congresswoman Muckler, and Senators Ryder and Bidwell. Thus far, his cyber quest had been one of futility. He rose from his office desk and went upstairs to get ready for Fuentes' arrival.

At precisely three-fifteen, the Detective sat idling in front of the Cuffington home. The Inspector came out of the house and climbed into the passenger seat.

"How are you, Maria," he asked perfunctorily.

Fuentes looked at him.

"Like you're really caring," she observed.

"I apologize, Maria. It's just that I've spent the better part of the day unsuccessfully trying to come up with common links that might help explain the murders of Sooner and Ryder, and the deaths of Muckler and Bidwell."

"Maybe, you should enlist you're little pen-pal from *The Washington Rumor*," suggested the now smiling Detective.

"That reminds me, I imagine we will be hearing from Talia Teller any time now," rued the Inspector.

Fuentes remained silent for several moments trying to anticipate what Teller's course of action might be regarding the autopsy results of Congressman Sooner and Senator Ryder.

"Nick, how do you think the writer for *The Washington Rumor* is going to play it?" asked the Detective.

"By her conscience," was the Inspector's succinct response.

"You know, changing the subject Nick, I'm afraid your initial concern about Hightower's age, in terms of cyber years, is proving to be prophetic," admitted Fuentes.

"Believe it or not, Maria, you are going to live to see a day when being wrong is the most pleasant surprise of that day," warned Cuffington. They both burst into tension breaking laughter.

Maria Fuentes mood grew somber.

"They were both there," she stated categorically.

"To whom are you referring, Maria?" questioned the Inspector, shaking his head unknowingly.

"Both Russell and Rose Hedgegrowth were in attendance at the gala where Congressman Sooner took his red carpet dirt nap," explained the Detective.

Cuffington thought for a moment, sifting Maria's information. The Inspector shook his head, listlessly.

"Maybe Killingsworth is on to something, after all," yielded Cuffington.

"But Nick, you said last night that their presence would confirm your suspicions," reminded the Detective.

"Yes, I know. But after today's for naught activities, maybe this entire Congressional snafu really is as simple as the Hedgegrowths," considered Cuffington, wistfully.

"That would be mercifully convenient," agreed Fuentes.

As they neared downtown Washington D.C., the traffic began to grind.

"Just how many more protestors and demonstrations can this town possibly accommodate?" wondered the Inspector, aloud.

"Nick, it's not just their increasing numbers that is causing the longer traffic delays. It is the protesters' convergence," explained the Detective.

"Maria, you can call it convergence, or anything else you choose, the net result is longer traffic delays," complained Cuffington.

"Nick, you're missing the mark. When the protesters first began to make their presence felt here in Washington D.C., they were two distinct and separate factions."

The Detective paused to formulate her explanation.

"At first, the Squatting on Whore Street Movement stayed strictly on the left side of the street and the Herbal Brigade remained staunchly on the right side of the street.

Maria Fuentes hesitated before continuing, choosing to determine Cuffington's reaction to her initial words.

The Inspector remained placidly quiet awaiting further explanation.

The Detective resumed.

"With time, however, both groups have gradually shifted to the middle of the street. This has resulted in the additional congestion," lectured Maria Fuentes.

"And what exactly precipitated this peaceful alliance," asked the Inspector, his curiosity now stirred.

"A newly recognized common enemy is now bringing the two factions closer together," asserted the Detective.

"And what is this common enemy that has so successfully united such disparate warring tribes?" demanded the Inspector.

"The long term elected politicians and the long term non-elected bureaucrats who habitually reside in and now claim as their own, Washington D.C.!" decried Fuentes.

"The long term politicians and the self-absorbed bureaucrats most certainly do seem to enjoy the climate here in Washington D.C.," reflected Cuffington.

As Metro Morgue loomed into sight, the throngs thickened. However, it was not demonstrators that crowded the front entrance of the building, but rather an "agitated" horde of media, thirsting for more bloody laundry.

"Maria, pull around to the back of the facility. We'll use the "personnel only" entrance. It's fenced for security," advised the Inspector.

After flashing her badge, Fuentes was guided to the "guests only" section of the parking lot. Walking towards the rear entrance of Metro Morgue, they spotted Captain Patrick Killingsworth standing outside, anticipating their arrival. Cuffington glanced at his watch. It was just touching four p.m. He nodded approvingly at Fuentes.

"You were certainly right about the three-fifteen starting time," noted the Inspector.

Killingsworth greeted them warmly.

"You guys are right on-time. I thought for sure you'd be running late, given these damn demonstrations," he smiled.

"Thanks to Maria, we happened to get off to an early start," explained the Inspector.

"Pat, where's First-Lieutenant Ginger Snapp?" inquired Cuffington.

"She's back at U.S. Capitol Police headquarters overseeing the data base break-in investigation," replied Killingsworth.

"I was under the impression that was Special Technician Hightower's bailiwick," questioned the Inspector.

Killingsworth looked around him to make certain no one was within earshot.

"Actually it is. However, after Ginger met Doctor Savage for the first time, she'd just assume it be her last," divulged the Captain. "I can't say that I really blame her. Anyway, she'll catch up with us later," assured the Captain.

They entered Metro Morgue and walked to the service elevator. Once inside the cab, Cuffington pushed the button for the top floor; the residence of the Office of Chief Medical Examiner.

During the ascent upward, Captain Killingsworth broke the ritual of staring blankly at the changing illuminated floor numbers displayed inside the elevator.

"I have some new details regarding Mr. and Mrs. Hedgegrowth and how these newly unearthed facts are pertinent to the deaths of Congresswoman Muckler and Senator Bidwell," he offered.

Inspector Cuffington stared sternly at Killingsworth.

"Pat, we'll discuss that and all other matters pertaining to the deaths of Congresswoman Muckler and Senator Bidwell after our meeting with Doctor Savage," insisted the Inspector.

"Whatever you say Nick, but I'm telling you that. . ."

The elevator door opened onto the designated floor.

Cuffington, Killingsworth, and Fuentes got off and proceeded down the long, dimly lit hallway until they reached the door of the O.M.E.C.. It was Cuffington who volunteered to venture forth, first. Seated at the front desk was none other than receptionist and laboratory assistant, Betty Ann Norge.

"Inspector Cuffington, Doc is expecting you!" she smiled, benignly.

Ostensibly, she did not remember Detective Fuentes. However, Betty Ann glowered at Captain Patrick Killingsworth. The Captain shifted uneasily on his feet, clearly uncomfortable in his current surroundings.

"Doc is in his office," informed the receptionist. "If you remember, Inspector, the last time you visited us he was in his man grave! Get it? Grave, cave! HAA HEE, HAA HEE!"

"Now stop that, Betty Ann, you're slaying me!" grinned the Inspector.

Captain Killingsworth and Detective Maria Fuentes exchanged uneasy glances. Betty Ann Norge's eyes welled with tears of naïf amusement. A pudgy finger pushed her tortoise-rimmed glasses back upon the bridge of an overly flattened nose. Once composed, she spoke again.

"Doc is on the phone, Inspector. But once this light goes out, she pointed to the telephone console, I'm supposed to take you into his office," she obediently explained.

"That would be very nice of you, Betty Ann," thanked the Inspector.

"The light just went off!" she exclaimed. "C'mon, I'll lead the way!"

Betty Ann rousted her ample frame from the chair and dutifully led the three officers to the office door of Doctor Seymour Savage. She knocked and without waiting for a response, opened it and beckoned the officers into the darkened room.

"They're here, Doc."

"I can see that, Betty Ann. Now, please close the door behind you," was the Doctor's request.

"Grave, cave," she muttered approvingly to herself and closed the door behind her.

Savage sat behind his desk and did not bother to stand up. Instead, he pushed a button that activated the ceiling lights and highlighted his collection of glass canisters that sat perched behind him.

"There, does that make you feel more comfortable?" he asked, baring his teeth for a smile. "Please, do sit down. Make yourselves feel right at home"

"Thanks Doc, but we prefer to stand," decided Cuffington." Besides, I don't think this should take too long."

"As you wish, Inspector," dismissed Savage with a wave of his skeletal hand.

He closed the file previously under his review and focused on the new arrivals.

"Oh, before I forget. Allow me to apologize, Captain, for being a bit testy on the phone with you earlier," pardoned the Doctor. "After all, it is our busy season."

"Please don't give it a second thought!" beseeched a clearly discomforted Killingsworth.

Cuffington cut short any potential protocol and zeroed in on his target.

"What are the results of the Muckler and Bidwell autopsies?" enjoined the Inspector.

Doctor Seymour Savage riveted his dark eyes upon Nick Cuffington.

"Quite clearly, they're both dead!" he chortled.

"That was a good one, Doc!" sounded Betty Ann Norge's HAA HEE from the front desk's intercom.

Inspector Nick Cuffington glared at Seymour Savage in silent disdain. For the first time, it was Savage who seemed somewhat out of sorts in his own home called Metro Morgue.

"Alright, alright, just my stab at a little post-mortem, inside the ice box humor," excused the Doctor of Death.

He then got down to business.

"Both Congresswoman Muckler's and Senator Bidwell's central nervous systems were ravaged by a lethal toxin. In fact, it was the identical little bugger that killed Congressman Sooner and Senator Ryder."

Doctor Savage paused to appraise the effect this revelation had upon Nick Cuffington. None was forthcoming.

Cuffington stared at Doctor Savage.

"Have you been able to identify the specific poison?" grilled the Inspector.

"Unfortunately, no; the substance is still an enigma and remains, at large, to usurp a bit of your jargon, Inspector," confessed the Doctor. "Any way, you know the drill, these results will stay with me until midnight this evening, and then it is face time!"

Nick quietly surveyed Seymour Savage before speaking.

"I was rather surprised that this information didn't hit the wires yesterday at midnight," questioned Cuffington .

"And not have the eminent Inspector from Metro be the first to know their ghoulish implications? Perish the thought!"

Doctor Seymour Savage lasered his attention solely upon Nick Cuffington, at the exclusion of everyone else in the office.

"As I said earlier, this is our busy season and I just couldn't quite manage to polish off Congresswoman Muckler and Senator Bidwell until a little after midnight, this morning," explained Savage."

The Doctor looked at Cuffington, as if tacitly seeking his approval. None was forthcoming. Savage continued his explanation.

"Besides, I rather enjoy watching the media frothing at the mouth; from a distance, of course!"

Cuffington turned to leave.

"Oh, Inspector, there is one more thing you may find of interest," enticed the Doctor.

Cuffington did an about face to confront Savage.

"And what is that, Doc?"

"To the best of my calculations, the interval time between the deaths of Muckler and Bidwell coincide precisely with the time that elapsed between the deaths of Sooner and Ryder," he added.

"And what does that signify," queried Cuffington.

"How should I know? After all, you're the one being paid to think outside the box!" he grinned.

"That's a good one too, Doc!" "HAA HEE HAA HEE"

Chapter Forty-Four

Cuffington, Killingsworth and Fuentes stood outside the rear entrance of Metro Morgue.

"Nick, I have to bring you up to speed on what I've turned up as it pertains to Mr. and Mrs. Hedgegrowth and the poisonings of Congresswoman Muckler and Senator Bidwell," exhorted the Captain.

"Alright, let's meet back at U.S. Capitol Police headquarters," suggested the Inspector.

"No can do, Nick," rebuked Killingsworth.

"And why not, Pat?"

"For two reasons; one, we might run into Chief O'Toole, and two, I told Ginger we'd meet her at Brewster's Bistro," explained the Captain.

Cuffington thought it over for a very brief moment.

"You've twisted my arm, Killingsworth," relented the Inspector. "We'll meet you there."

Cuffington and Fuentes were en route to hook up with Killingsworth at Brewster's Bistro. Although traffic was still moving very slowly, it was no longer the intolerable crawl of the earlier afternoon.

"Nick, don't you think you may have been a little brusque with Doctor Savage this afternoon?" questioned the Detective.

"We were at Savage's office today to ascertain the answers to three questions," brushed aside the Inspector. "He failed to do that!"

Maria paused before responding.

"Doctor Savage informed us that both Congresswoman Muckler and Senator Bidwell were, in fact, murdered. Furthermore, he concluded that the cause of death in both cases was by poisoning," continued Fuentes.

She hesitated momentarily to mentally double check herself before continuing.

"The only thing he couldn't come up with was the exact type of toxin used in their killings," summed up Maria. "Hey Nick, two out of three ain't bad," she encouraged, lamely.

The Inspector stared at his lead Detective with professional disappointment.

"Maria, we walked into Savage's office today pretty much expecting those very findings," reminded the Inspector. "Therefore, the only new piece of information that might have proven useful in our investigation was the type of toxin used. Savage was unable to accomplish that, thereby, rendering today's little get together pretty much a waste of time," lamented the Inspector.

Cuffington frowned and turned his attention to the passenger door window. At first, Fuentes said nothing, allowing him to settle into his self-imposed exile of frustration.

"Nick, why do you suppose Savage placed so much emphasis on the time intervals in the murders of the four Members of Congress?" lured Maria.

Cuffington remained silent. However, the Detective's "intrusive" question had managed to roust the Inspector from his languid state of malaise.

"I don't know exactly what the cynical, little purveyor of the perverse was gnawing at," admitted Cuffington. "But, I can tell you one thing beyond a shadow of a doubt, Maria," offered the Inspector.

"And what's that, Nick?"

"If Seymour Savage isn't playing with your organs, it's a sure bet he's playing with your head," winked Nick Cuffington.

Detective Fuentes shuddered at the mere thought of either horrid possibility.

They arrived in front of Brewster's around five-thirty p.m. Surprisingly, Fuentes managed to secure a legal parking space within half a block of the bistro. As they walked into the establishment's entrance, Toby the Waiter accosted them with his usual smile.

"The Captain and First-Lieutenant are already seated," he advised them.

"Why, Toby, when did you learn of the First-Lieutenant's promotion," inquired the Inspector.

"When, I made the mistake of calling her Lieutenant. Boy was she mad!" confided the waiter.

As Toby led them to Cuff-Kill Corner, Cuffington immediately noticed that Brewster's was doing an unusually brisk business that late afternoon. Killingsworth and Snapp were seated side by side at command post "headquarters." Fuentes and Cuffington sat down facing the two officers from U.S. Capitol Police.

"What did I tell you, Nick!" gushed the Captain.

Cuffington raised his hand in a gesture asking for silence.

"First things first," admonished the Inspector from Metro. "Exactly, where do we stand with the investigation in the data base breach at U.S. Capitol Police headquarters?" he began, as a point of reference.

Although Captain Killingsworth appeared startled by the Inspector's impromptu question, he recovered quickly.

"Yes, First-Lieutenant, where exactly do we stand on the matter of the data base break-in?" he demanded, with authority.

Ginger Snapp fluttered nervously. She, too, had been caught off guard by Cuffington's logical point of entry into the afternoon's discussion of the over-all investigation efforts.

"Well, I can say with confidence that Miriam, I mean Special Technician Hightower has successfully managed to pinpoint the origin of the cyber breach to the western sector of the Northern Hemisphere," she reported, optimistically.

"Now that is progress!" smiled Cuffington, wryly.

"I think so!" reinforced Killingsworth.

Toby the Waiter returned with two beers for the Inspector and the Detective and then disappeared.

"So, let's get down to brass tacks!" commandeered the Captain. "Upon further investigation, I was able to unearth the fact that both Mr. and Mrs. Hedgegrowth were, indeed, present at the dinner party where Congressman Barry Sooner was murdered," he unveiled, triumphantly.

Cuffington and Fuentes glanced at one another, knowingly.

"All right Pat, were both Mr. and Mrs. Hedgegrowth in attendance at the Tangerine Oriental the night of Senator William Ryder's murder?" challenged the Inspector.

"That doesn't really matter now, Nick," dismissed Killingsworth with an air of condescension.

"And why is that, Pat," pestered the Inspector.

"Because the Hedgegrowths had probable cause and, therefore, motive in the murder of Senator John "Black Jack" Bidwell," enlightened the Captain.

"I'm all ears, Patrick. Explain the Hedgegrowth's motive in the murder of Senator Bidwell," urged Cuffington.

Killingsworth settled back in his seat to enjoy the ride.

"It's really quite simple, Nick; especially after one does one's proper homework," lectured the Captain.

"Get on with it!" strained the Inspector.

"Simply put, the Honorable Senator John "Black Jack" Bidwell screwed Mr. and Mrs. Hedgegrowth on the Key Lime Pie Line deal!" crowed Killingsworth.

"Explain to me exactly what you are saying, Pat," demanded Cuffington.

"Nick, it went down like this: Russell Hedgegrowth's organization paid Senator Bidwell a barrel full of money to make certain that the Key Lime Pie Line amendment would pass through the Senate. At the twelfth hour, "Black Jack" got cold feet and voted against the Key Lime Pie Line resolution.

Killingsworth paused momentarily, to refuel.

"This, in turn, destroyed Russell Hedgegrowth's career in Washington D.C. as a lobbyist. Bottom line, no pun intended, the lobbyist frosted Senator Bidwell as retribution for his change of vote," concluded the Captain of U.S. Capitol Police."

Cuffington rationalized the Captain's words before responding.

"But Pat, that doesn't explain the murder of Congresswoman Muckler," he objected. "Bidwell was a member of the United States Senate. Muckler was a member of the United States House of Representatives, which to my understanding was not voting on the Key Lime Pie Line resolution at the time of the Congresswoman's death. Furthermore, Bidwell and Muckler were members of different national political parties," countered Cuffington.

Captain Killingsworth stared at the Inspector. He smiled and then chided his colleague and now friend with warmth and understanding.

"Nick, the once distinct responsibilities that separated the duties of the United States Senate and the United States House of Representatives have been, over recent years, adumbrated."

The Captain drained his drink and continued.

"And as for Bidwell and Muckler representing different caucuses; there no longer exists two major independent political parties here in Washington D.C. You, of all people, should have been shrewd enough to pick up on that reality several election cycles ago."

He then motioned Toby the Waiter for a well-deserved night cap.

After their server had come and gone, Killingsworth continued his lesson in the nuances of Washington D.C. politics.

"No, today, here in Washington D.C., we are left with only one big Fraternity House! And, it's glorified membership has only two objectives in mind; to be permanently re-elected and then to permanently slurp at the public trough!" he declared.

Cuffington carefully considered the Captain's contentions.

He very much yearned to have Killingsworth's "Hedgegrowth" explanation be the ribbon that would opportunely tie together the perplexing package he was so desperately trying to wrap up.

"Pat, how do the murders of Congressman Sooner and Senator Ryder fit into your Key Lime Pie Line supposition?" posed the Inspector.

Captain Killingsworth leisurely sipped his cocktail before answering.

"To be truthful Nick, I haven't had the time to thread those particular needles," admitted the Captain. "However, I rather doubt it will take too much of an effort to sew Congressman Sooner and Senator Ryder into the quilt of the Key Lime Pie Line scandal," he convinced himself.

The Inspector motioned Toby the Waiter for the check. The young man appeared, armed with bar tab, in hand.

"I'll take that, kid," ordered the Captain.

"Yes sir, Captain, sir," obliged the waiter with deference.

Cuffington made a play for his wallet, in an attempt to defray the evening's cost. Captain Patrick Killingsworth repelled the Inspector's foray.

"Tonight is on me and my U.S. Capitol expense account!" he announced with bravado. "After all, I've earned it today!"

The four officers of the law rose to leave Brewster's Bistro. As they filed out of the establishment, a young woman of purpose impeded their departure. Talia Teller, the beat reporter for *The Washington Rumor*, was no stranger.

Chapter Forty-Five

"Inspector Cuffington, I was hoping to find you at Brewster's. We really have to talk," insisted Talia Teller.

"According to my watch, forty-eight hours has not yet elapsed," responded the Inspector without emotion.

"My presence here this evening has nothing to do with the forty-eight hour deadline," explained the reporter for *The Washington Rumor*.

"Why didn't you call me first Talia?" questioned Cuffington.

"Quite simply, because I don't have your cell phone number," justified Teller.

"That makes two of us," grumbled Captain Killingsworth.

Teller resumed.

"I phoned your house several times, but kept getting the machine. So I took a chance, and here I am!"

"Well now that you've found me, what's so terribly urgent?" demanded the Inspector.

Teller surveyed the outside street surroundings with trepidation.

"I'd prefer a more intimate ambience," she disclosed with finality.

"I know just the place," agreed Cuffington, with a wink of the eye.

Cuffington, Fuentes, and Talia Teller turned and faced the front entrance of Brewster's. First-lieutenant Ginger Snapp fluttered her attention towards Patrick Killingsworth.

"Captain, don't you think it's about time we returned to U.S. Capitol Police headquarters and got an update on Special Technician Hightower's progress regarding the data base break-in?" steered the First-Lieutenant.

Killingsworth carefully weighed the options facing him before responding.

"You're absolutely right, First-Lieutenant. The ongoing management of the breach at U.S. Capitol Police headquarters data base demands constant vigilance!"

Captain Patrick Killingsworth looked longingly at the front door of Brewster's Bistro.

"Therefore, I am ordering you back to headquarters to oversee that particular facet of this ongoing investigation," directed the Captain. "In the meanwhile, I shall remain positioned here, on the frontline of possible new leads. It's these very moments that require a proper division of labor approach to law enforcement!" he trumpeted.

First-Lieutenant Ginger Snapp fluttered off with obvious disappointment.

The three police officers and newspaper reporter re-entered the realm of Brewster's Bistro. Toby the Waiter intercepted them as they were about to enter the bar room. He was not his usual cheerful self. Toby was visibly out of sorts.

"Inspector Cuffington, I mistakenly presumed that you had adjourned for the evening," he explained, awkwardly.

"Toby, in the profession of law enforcement, one never knows what may rear its ugly head in the shadows of the after-hours," consoled the Inspector.

Howls of heated reproach could be heard emanating from inside the barroom. At length, a burly member of the restaurant's security staff emerged from the tavern section of the establishment and gave the thumbs up to Toby the Waiter.

"All clear on Cuff-Kill Corner," reported the man from security.

"Right this way, Inspector," motioned the now relieved server.

Once seated, Toby took their drink orders.

"Detective Fuentes, what is your pleasure?"

"Hatuey"

"Of course, please excuse my lapse!" he implored.

"Ms. Teller, what are you drinking tonight?"

"Pinch on the rocks"

"May I pinch you twice?" he giggled, trying to calm himself after the hastily reconfigured "seating arrangement."

"Whatever, Toby," replied Teller, absently.

"And for you, Captain?"

"Death in the Afternoon," ordered Killingsworth.

"Oh, I'm quite sorry Captain," lamented the waiter. "Brewster's Bistro has seen fit not to stock absinthe. Management concluded that the availability of wormwood on site might tend to make potentially sticky situations all the more tenuous," explained Toby.

"I completely understand and laud Team Brewster for doing its utmost to avoid sticky situations!" commended the Captain. "Therefore, given the circumstances, I shall opt for a Double High Jack," compromised Killingsworth.

"Very good sir, a Double High Jack it is!" confirmed the waiter.

"And for the Inspector, a cold can of domestic," presumed the order taker. "I'll be back in a jiff."

Cuffington looked at the Captain and shook his head, smiling.

"Pat, it appears you've decided to spare no prisoners this evening," noted the Inspector.

"Nary a one, Nick," confirmed Killingsworth.

Cuffington shifted his attention to the reporter from *The Washington Rumor*.

"So Talia, how have you decided to blow the whistle on the theory that more than one killer may have been involved in the murders of Congressman Sooner and Senator Ryder?" he inquired with measured aplomb.

"I don't know that I'm going to," she revealed with strained control.

Toby returned with their drinks. After having duly served them, he quickly departed.

Cuffington stared into the face of Talia Teller, trying to get a read on where the young woman was coming from and going to.

"Why the sudden change of heart, Talia," he asked with genuine concern.

Teller did not immediately answer. Instead, she sat quietly, sipping her drink. It was apparent to Cuffington that the reporter was still at odds with herself with whatever it was she had come to discuss. At last, with a final sigh of commitment, Talia Teller extracted a folder from her carry-all and tossed it on the table.

She then focused her attention on Cuffington.

"My change in perspective is a direct result of that," as she motioned towards the file.

"That can only be an advance copy of your "journalistic" endeavor to fan the flames of public hysteria!" derided Detective Fuentes in disgust.

Talia Teller glared at Maria Fuentes.

"As usual, you are just mindlessly banging the bongo of Baba-Lou, Cuban girl!" dismissed the reporter from *The Washington Rumor*.

Fuentes let out a primal scream and made an aborted lunge at Talia Teller. Captain Patrick "Killer" Killingsworth raised an arm, effectively keeping the two would be female combatants separated. With his other hand, Killingsworth downed the remainder of his cocktail and then slammed the emptied glass on top of Teller's folder. He motioned for service.

Toby the Waiter responded post haste.

"Another Double High Jack!" demanded the Captain. "And while you're at it, another round for the table. We wouldn't want a sticky situation on our hands, now would we, Toby?"

"Absolutely not, Captain; I'll be back before I'm gone!" promised the flustered young man.

Inspector Cuffington sat stoically, taking in the events of the evening as they were unfolding.

Toby the Waiter returned with a second round of drinks, effectively ending the cooling off period.

224

Killingsworth picked up the folder and opened it to examine the contents. After reading the dossier's words, the Captain closed the file and looked Talia Teller squarely in the eyes.

"So, you already know," he grimaced.

"And it's not even midnight," replied the reporter for *The Washington Rumor*, ruefully.

Cuffington sat calmly drinking his beer. He immediately realized that whatever the contents of Teller's folder, it was only going to further complicate an already convoluted situation. With deliberate time, the Inspector finally confronted the undivided attention of Captain Patrick Killingsworth.

"What's in the folder, Pat?" Cuffington asked with gritty resolve.

Killingsworth returned the Inspector's gaze with facial malcontent. He swallowed what was left of his second Double High Jack and reported with preemptory professionalism.

"It's an alphabetical listing of every member of the United States Congress," answered the Captain. "The various members of the House of Representatives and Senate have been segregated into two different pages," he detailed.

Cuffington paused to digest the Captain's description of the folder's contents.

"So, Teller has presented us with an alphabetical listing of every member of the United States Congress?" he confirmed with incredulity.

"Yes," reiterated the Captain. "But with four names highlighted," furthered Killingsworth.

Although Cuffington had little doubt as to the identity of those four names, he went through the mechanical protocol, in an attempt to buy some personal processing time.

"Enumerate, Pat," recited the Inspector.

Captain Killingsworth drew a deep breath and continued.

"The four names high-lighted in magic marker are none other than Congressman Sooner, Senator Ryder, Congresswoman Muckler and, Senator Bidwell," listed Killingsworth. "What's more, two of the names are high-lighted in red and two of the names are high-lighted in blue," he elaborated.

Cuffington ruminated over the facts of the Captain's briefing before responding.

"So, in essence, what we are now confronted with is a literal hit list on every member of the United States Congress," summarized the Inspector.

"Precisely," concurred Killingsworth. "

Chapter Forty-Six

Inspector Cuffington, Captain Killingsworth, Detective Fuentes, and Talia Teller remained seated at Brewster's Bistro. Maria Fuentes hissed at Talia Teller with both skepticism and mistrust.

"Why is it, Ms. Reporter for *The Washington Rumor*, that you, of all people, always just happen to be in possession of information no one else seems to have access to?" questioned the Detective.

Talia Teller searched the eyes of Maria Fuentes, plaintively.

"Maria, you have no idea how I wish I could answer that question!"

The reporter began to visibly tremble.

"Do you actually think for a moment I want to be in the middle of this ongoing freak show, playing the role of some out of the loop dupe?" she continued in a barely audible voice.

Inspector Cuffington injected himself into the conversation.

"I've listened long enough to both accusation and self-pity," reproached the Inspector. "Let's, collectively, analyze what's been thrust upon us and try to utilize it to our advantage!" he demanded.

Cuffington centered his attention on Detective Fuentes.

"Maria, in one sentence or less, how does the appearance of this folder help in our investigation of the Congressional murders?" he asked while pointing to Teller's file.

The Detective thought for a moment. She then polished off her Hatuey and addressed the Inspector.

"The alphabetical listing of every member of the United States Congress provides us with a suggested pool of possible future victims," offered Fuentes.

She once again scanned Teller's file.

"The problem that I'm having, Nick, is that when I juxtapose the names of the four dead Congressional members with the alphabetical listing I'm failing to recognize a pattern that might explain the motive for the murders and, more importantly, indicate specific future victims."

Fuentes briefly paused to properly phrase her final words.

"That's assuming, of course, there are any more intended victims."

Cuffington looked at Fuentes and shook his head in agreement.

"Unfortunately, I'm right there with you as far as gaining anymore insight from the Congressional alphabetical listing," admitted the Inspector.

"The only definitive pattern that I can come up with are that the murders occur in pairs and in each instance both major political parties are equally and fairly represented," noted Cuffington.

The Inspector turned towards Captain Killingsworth with intent.

"Pat, what can you contribute to the mix?" summoned Cuffington.

Killingsworth returned Cuffington's stare as he accepted the Inspector's challenge.

"In one sentence or less?" scoffed the Captain. "It won't take me that long! Mr. and Mrs. Hedgegrowth are legitimate suspects in the murders of Congresswoman Muckler and Senator Bidwell, and are circumstantial suspects in the murder of Congressman Sooner."

Captain Killingsworth motioned for service. Their waiter was table-side even before Patrick Killingsworth was afforded the opportunity to carp.

"Another round for those of us working over-time here in Washington D.C. for the protection of those plundering here in Washington D.C.!" ordered the Captain.

"Straight away, sir," complied the young man.

Cuffington mentally rehashed what the others had put forth as "progress in the investigation" and remained dissatisfied.

He could not rid himself of the haunting belief that the ultimate piece to the Congressional murders puzzle was palpably within their grasp.

Toby the Waiter returned and dispensed a fresh round of societal ammunition.

"Can I do anything else for the table at this time?"

"I think we're just fine for right now," dismissed the Captain.

Cuffington studied the faces of the other three people seated at the booth before speaking.

"I believe we must address two salient issues here this evening," he intoned. "First of all, why has Talia been purposefully singled out and dragged into this situation to act as some sort of surrogate conspirator."

The Inspector took a pull on his beer and continued.

"Secondly, when, at midnight this evening, it becomes public record that Congresswoman Muckler and Senator Bidwell must be added to the growing list of Congressional homicides what is our united response going to be?" posited the Inspector.

Detective Fuentes was the first to offer an opinion.

"I believe Talia may have been tapped specifically because, whoever is responsible for the Congressional murders assumed she would do her job as a reporter and make public the information as it was being fed to her," deduced Fuentes.

Teller studied the Detective with anguish in her eyes.

"Maria, are you inferring that I am not living up to my professional responsibilities?" she anguished.

Fuentes calmly surveyed the writer from *The Washington Rumor*.

"Oh no, Talia, quite the contrary," reassured the Detective. "My word was reporter not journalist. I rather doubt those behind the Congressional murders are aware of the distinction. I know I wasn't until I met you," explained Fuentes.

For the first time, the two women smiled at one another. A bridge of mutual respect had finally been forged.

Maria Fuentes re-focused her attention in the direction of Cuffington.

"As for a united response to the news of two more Congressional killings; that will depend entirely on whether we choose to act professionally or politically," she stated, problematically.

That remark got the undivided attention of Captain Killingsworth.

"And what exactly do you mean by that, Detective?" groused the Captain.

"What I am simply saying is that if you are not a current member of the United States Congress, Washington D.C. is still a pretty safe place to live," postulated Fuentes.

"Make your point, damn it!" implored Killingsworth with petulance.

"My point is, professionally, we inform the public that the recent rash of murders committed here in Washington D.C. have been deliberately restricted to current members of the United States Congress. Therefore, between now and the time we apprehend those responsible, the good people of Washington D.C. should go about their normal lives without fear for their own well-being," clarified the Detective.

Captain Patrick "Killer" Killingsworth sat dumbfounded.

He stared at Detective Fuentes with a combination of inner rage, moral angst and bewilderment. His first attempt at words of response failed him. Gathering himself, he reloaded and fired upon his intended target.

"You have lost your senses, Detective! I'm being quite serious, you're profoundly delusional," he seethed in slow burn.

Maria Fuentes, observing the Captain's consternation, smiled impishly.

"Why Captain, if we choose to be ethical, as well as, professional we could also inform the public that we have absolutely no substantial leads in the recent Congressional poisonings," baited the Detective.

This last statement seemed to tip the scale of Killingsworth's emotional equilibrium. He savagely slapped his unoccupied hand on the table top, as his eyes blazed at Fuentes, in rage.

"You, young lady, are obviously ignorant to the nuances that distinguish politics from professionalism here in Washington D.C.!" lambasted the Captain. "I'm going to see to it that you are immediately relieved of any authority you had regarding the investigation into the Congressional assassinations!" he screamed.

"The truth can be hard to swallow, can't it, Captain," provoked the Detective.

"Fuentes, the truth is, you're not only out of an assignment, but you're getting real close to being out of a law enforcement career here in Washington D.C.!" threatened the Captain of U.S. Capitol Police.

Before Inspector Nick Cuffington could intercede as a would-be peace keeper, two events occurred simultaneously. Detective Maria Fuentes' cell phone toned, and First-Lieutenant Ginger Snapp suddenly descended upon the booth at Cuff-Kill Corner.

Snapp eyed the table's congregation with suspicion.

"Captain, I must speak with you immediately," she insisted in loud whisper.

Killingsworth extricated himself from the bistro's booth and huddled with the First-Lieutenant from U.S. Capitol Police just outside of earshot of the people seated at the table. Talia Teller, sensing the moment, excused herself and retreated to the ladies room. Detective Fuentes nodded affirmatively into the cell and then placed it back on the table. Inspector Cuffington carefully gleaned the facial expression of the Detective before speaking.

"So, who called?" he asked with resolve.

"Downtown Metro"

"And?"

"Mr. Russell Hedgegrowth died earlier today of an apparent suicide," related Fuentes without emotion.

The Inspector shook his head, pensively.

"Isn't that just Capitol," he sighed.

Captain Killingsworth returned to Cuff-Kill Corner but remained standing. The smile of a victor covered his face.

"Unfortunately, I must take my leave," he invoked with haughty self-satisfaction. "It seems my professional presence is required elsewhere!"

"And where exactly are you off to, Pat?" asked the Inspector.

"To question Mrs. Rose Hedgegrowth," he answered with a sense of authoritative urgency. "U.S. Capitol Police are escorting her to headquarters as we speak.

"And why has U.S. Capitol Police seen fit to apprehend and question Mrs. Hedgegrowth?" dummied Cuffington.

"Only because Mr. Russell Hedgegrowth decided to commit suicide earlier today," he snickered with self-approval.

Killingsworth beamed at First-Lieutenant Ginger Snapp and sneered at Detective Maria Fuentes.

"Nick, do you want to attend this evening's victory interrogation?" he asked the Inspector, while purposely ignoring Fuentes.

Cuffington eyed the Captain and shook his head.

"No, Pat, I think I'll pass on tonight's festivities."

And with that, Captain Killingsworth and First Lieutenant Snapp were gone.

Talia Teller returned to the booth just as Cuffington and Fuentes were getting up to leave.

"Where did Captain Killingsworth go?" asked the writer for *The Washington Rumor*.

"To a shark feeding frenzy," replied the Inspector.

Chapter Forty-Seven

"So, how do you think she's going to play the situation, Nick?" asked an unusually tense Detective Fuentes.

"Which 'she' are you referring to, Maria," questioned a distracted Inspector Cuffington.

"Why, the journalist from *The Washington Rumor*; what other she did you think I might be talking about?" wondered Fuentes.

"First-Lieutenant Snapp, for starters," reasoned the Inspector.

"I already know how that girl plays it," she asserted with derision in her voice.

"At this juncture, what does it really matter how Talia Teller proceeds," dismissed Cuffington.

Having left Brewster's Bistro, Cuffington and Fuentes were on their way back to the Inspector's home. The hour was approaching eight p.m.

"Honestly, Nick, would it really be so terrible if Killingsworth's initial instincts regarding the Hedgegrowth's involvement in the Congressional murders turned out to be correct?" she put forth. "After all, such a conclusion would prove to be both politically and professionally convenient," she persisted without attempting to shroud the obvious implications.

"Leave it to Pat Killingsworth to force a square peg into a round hole," remarked Cuffington.

"I wouldn't know anything about that aspect of the Captain's personality. Mercifully, that's First-Lieutenant Snap's area of expertise," she laughed.

Nick Cuffington smiled for the first time since their departure from Brewster's. Cuffington's moment of levity was short-lived. He unexpectedly turned in the car's passenger seat to squarely face the Detective.

"Maria, do you, at all, buy into Killingsworth's Hedgegrowth theory?" he asked, somberly.

Fuentes quietly reflected before offering a measured response.

"Truthfully, at this point in time, I would like to," she admitted with candor. "However, objectively, why bother providing Talia Teller with a possible Congressional "hit list" and then go ahead and whack yourself on the same day?" she pondered, dubiously

Inspector Cuffington uttered no response

Fuentes' vehicle rolled to a stop in front of the Cuffington residence.

"I very well may be calling you later this evening," informed the Inspector.

"Well, I think you already have my number," she grinned.

Cuffington entered the side door to the still lighted kitchen. He proceeded down the hallway to Leigh's library. Its door was ajar, and the room unlit. He returned to the kitchen, procured a beer from the refrigerator and retreated to the backyard patio. The Inspector sat down at the table. He took solace in the comfort of the evening's stillness. As he reached for a cigarette, the patio outside lights suddenly illuminated.

Leigh Cuffington emerged from the kitchen. She walked to the patio table, kissed her husband, and then sat down next to him.

Cuffington postponed his smoke.

"I assumed you had gone to bed, Leigh," he explained.

"No, I was taking a shower. I saw Maria's headlights and decided to come downstairs to say hello," she smiled.

"How was dinner with the girls?" he asked, perfunctorily.

"Dinner with the girls," she dismissed with a wave of her hand.

Leigh Cuffington wordlessly tried to read the mood of her husband.

"Did you make any progress in the Congressional murders today?" she asked with keen interest.

"Some believe we did," he answered with non-commitment.

Mrs. Cuffington turned to stare directly into the face of her husband.

"I can only assume that you don't share that point of view," she concluded.

"No, I do not," he replied.

"And why not?" continued the Inspector's wife.

"Because, I don't believe Rose Hedgegrowth to be a credible suspect," he replied tersely.

Leigh Cuffington offered no immediate reaction. Instead, she, once again, studied her husband and then shook her head with disapproval.

"Nick, that's not close to being humorous. In fact, even by your standards, Inspector, it's just plain dumb!" she lectured with annoyance.

Nick Cuffington remained stoically silent. He pulled out the awaiting cigarette, lit it, and exhaled a plume of socially unacceptable smoke into the overly regulated atmosphere of Washington D.C.

With her husband's lingering silence, Leigh became apprehensively aware of the gravity of his mood.

"Nick, tell me exactly what the hell you're talking about," she exhorted weakly.

"U.S. Capitol Police has seen fit to apprehend Rose Hedgegrowth for questioning in the murders of Congresswoman Muckler and Senator Bidwell," he conveyed with practiced indifference.

"They were both murdered?" she gasped while trying to shake off the revelation's mind-numbing impact.

Cuffington sat quietly, affording his wife time to fully absorb the news.

"Yes, murdered; both Muckler and Bidwell were poisoned. In fact, they were killed with the same toxin used in the murders of Congressman Sooner and Senator Ryder," he detailed.

Leigh Cuffington's jaw slackened agape in utter disbelief. After gathering her thoughts, Mrs. Cuffington riveted her eyes on her husband. She quivered with non-acceptance.

"I know Rose Hedgegrowth! She is absolutely not capable of such evil acts!" she tried to convince herself. "Nick, how could you let such an innocent individual be dragged into this nightmare!" she beseeched with outrage.

Cuffington quietly sipped his beer, smoked his cigarette, and patiently waited for his wife to calm herself.

"Who's responsible for Rose's incarceration?" demanded Mrs. Cuffington.

"She hasn't been incarcerated. She is merely being questioned," mildly corrected the Inspector.

"Whatever!" she cast aside the distinction with impatience." Who's behind Rose being picked up for questioning?"

"U.S. Capitol Police," he answered.

"And what makes them think that Rose had anything to do with either Congressional murder?" Leigh persisted.

"For starters, Mrs. Hedgegrowth was dining with Congresswoman Muckler at the time she dropped dead. Furthermore, Mr. Hedgegrowth had been seated with Bidwell just prior to the Senator's mortal collapse," explained the Inspector.

Nick paused before continuing his explanation.

"But, what precipitated U.S. Capitol Police to bring Mrs. Hedgegrowth in for questioning this evening was the apparent suicide of Mr. Russell Hedgegrowth earlier today," elaborated the Inspector.

"The what?" struggled Leigh Cuffington.

"Glad you decided to come downstairs this evening, dear?"

Nick Cuffington smiled for the first time since arriving home; thus proving once and for all, the age old axiom that misery does, indeed, love company.

"You heard me correctly," confirmed the Inspector. "The word is that Russell Hedgegrowth saw fit to take his own life earlier today."

Leigh Cuffington lowered her head dispiritedly.

"What the hell has gone so terribly wrong with this city?" she asked, whimsically.

"What the hell hasn't?" countered the jaded Inspector from Metro.

Leigh Cuffington tilted her head to look at her husband.

"Unless you have any more uplifting news you want to lay on me, I'm going to bed," she said while rising from the patio table.

"Have I told you the one about the Key Lime Pie Line?" he asked, trying to elicit a smile from his wife.

"No! And I'm not in the mood to hear about it."

Nick swilled the remainder of his beer, snuffed his smoke, and followed Leigh into the kitchen.

"Are you coming to bed, Nick?" she asked with a yawn.

"Not quite yet; I have to get on the computer. Besides, I'm anticipating a phone call," advised the Inspector.

Nick kissed his wife good night, and headed to his office. He fired up the desk top and with great reluctance began trying to link the late Congresswoman Muckler to the Key Lime Pie Line legislation. As he had expected, his cell phone beckoned slightly past midnight.

"Why Emma, I was just about to call you," he postured.

"Oh, I'm quite certain you had the phone in your hand, Nick," replied Emma Teasedale, Chief of Metro Police. "Sorry to be calling you at such a late hour, however, I just got off the phone with Chief O'Toole," she imparted.

"And how is the Chief of U.S. Capitol Police this evening?" inquired Cuffington

"His general mood has improved markedly tonight," responded Teasedale. "Hank is quite impressed with the outstanding investigative work of his Captain, Patrick Killingsworth," revealed the Chief of Metro.

"As well he might be, given the current circumstances," agreed Cuffington.

"Don't get cute with me, Inspector," warned his superior officer. "After speaking with Chief O'Toole, I can only surmise that the dead ends you alluded to during out last conversation were none other than Russell and Rose Hedgegrowth," she ventured.

"The very same dead ends," verified the Inspector.

"That notwithstanding, Chief O'Toole and I have scheduled a meeting to be held this morning at ten a.m. in his office at U.S. Capitol Police headquarters," informed Teasedale. "I expect you to not only be present, but punctual, as well," ordered the Chief of Metro.

"And what will we be discussing at this morning's meeting?" pandered the Inspector

"Why, putting these Congressional murders in their proper perspective, of course," she answered, obliquely.

"Of course," echoed Cuffington. "In that case, I look forward to seeing you promptly at ten a.m.," confirmed the Inspector.

Teasedale abruptly terminated the conversation.

Cuffington placed a call to Detective Maria Fuentes.

Chapter Forty-Eight

"You're up bright and early this morning," smiled Leigh Cuffington as her husband walked into the kitchen.

Nick went over to kiss his wife and then secured his usual two glasses.

"I have a meeting at U.S. Capitol headquarters later this morning," explained Cuffington.

"I assume that was the phone call you were waiting for?"

"Yes," acknowledged Cuffington.

"And how is the inimitable Emma Teasedale holding up under the current circumstances?" queried Mrs. Cuffington.

"Emma is Emma. However, I would imagine this particular morning has been a rather rough one for her," speculated the Inspector.

"So you suspect, Inspector, that Chief Teasedale may be receiving a few calls, texts, and tweets this morning?" grinned Leigh, puckishly.

"I wouldn't at all be surprised if she has been contacted by more than one concerned elected official here in Washington D.C. since the Muckler and Bidwell autopsies went public," speculated Cuffington.

"What time is your meeting this morning, Nick?"

"Ten a.m."

"What time is Detective Fuentes picking you up?"

"Another pending phone call," he answered with distraction.

The Inspector had turned his attention to the kitchen counter's flat screen.

"Leigh, what has been the media's initial reaction to the news that both Congresswoman Muckler and Senator Bidwell were poisoned?" he asked between sips of grapefruit juice.

"Well, I guess their morning's theme can be best described as, "Who has declared war on the members of the United States Congress," she summarized.

"That's not a far-fetched story line," admitted Cuffington. "Tell me, has there been any buzz about the possibility of multiple murderers?" he questioned with particular interest.

"No, not really; the media seems convinced that the Congressional fatalities are the work of a lone assassin," replied Leigh. "However, given the disparate backgrounds of the four murdered Congressional members, they have not been able to arrive at a discernible political configuration to explain the whys and wherefores," was her morning recap.

"The Pattern of the Unfathomable," the Inspector mused to himself.

"What did you just say, Nick?" questioned his wife.

"Nothing, Dear"

Nick Cuffington's cell phone toned. He checked the incoming number and picked-up.

"Yes, Maria?"

The Inspector listened carefully, shook his head, and clicked-off.

"She's going to be here at nine a.m.," advised the Inspector.

"An hour to get from our house to U.S. Capitol Police headquarters," questioned a leery Mrs. Cuffington.

"According to Maria, the downtown D.C. traffic is crazy and is going to get crazier as the day goes on," explained Nick.

"That reminds me," remembered Leigh. "They were saying earlier on the news that the protestors are erecting two speaking platforms from which they will deliver speeches that will be audible to anyone inside the U.S. Capitol Building."

"A nod is as good as a wink to a blind horse," was Cuffington's only comment.

"Oh, Nick, there is something I was thinking of not mentioning to you," confided his wife.

"And what is that?" he responded with theatric chagrin.

"There were several distraught members of Congress doing the rounds on the morning cable newscasts this morning," she divulged, reluctantly.

"I can't even begin to imagine what might have been on their minds this morning," he brushed off, sardonically.

"Essentially, they were expressing their frustration and disappointment at the Washington D.C. law enforcement community's apparent inability to get a handle on who's behind the Congressional killings," briefed Mrs. Cuffington.

She paused to sip from her coffee mug.

"Furthermore, if, in their words, these law enforcement departments continue to bumble along ineptly, seemingly incapable of doing the job they are being paid to do, heads are going to roll!" she paraphrased.

The Inspector turned Leigh's words over in his mind and then shook his he head, smiling.

"If everyone in Washington D.C. was fired for bumbling along ineptly, seemingly incapable of doing the job they are being paid to do, Washington D.C. would be a very desolate place, indeed."

"Nick, there is one more thing."

Cuffington peered into his wife's eyes and knew immediately she was troubled.

"What's the matter, Leigh?"

"It's Rose Hedgegrowth, Nick. After our conversation last night, I thought it might be a good idea for me to call Rose and just see how the poor dear is doing."

Inspector Cuffington thought for a moment and then shook head.

"Leigh, I think it might be in Rose's better interest if you hold off contacting her for now," he stated with well-meaning conviction." Wait until you hear from me. I'll know more about Mrs. Hedgegrowth's present predicament after this morning's meeting," he stated, emphatically.

Leigh Cuffington looked at her husband with an unwavering trust in his instincts.

"Then I'll wait to hear from you, Nick."

Nick Cuffington glanced at his watch and then waked to the kitchen window. As always, Detective Fuentes was on time and waiting curbside.

"Leigh, I've got to go."

He kissed his wife and then disappeared out the side door.

Inspector Cuffington slid into the passenger seat of Fuentes' cruiser.

"And how are you this morning, Maria?"

"Better than these damn roads, I suppose," she griped and threw the car into gear. "Are we still bound for U.S. Capitol Police headquarters?" she asked.

"Yes"

Maria Fuentes did not hesitate with her next question.

"What are we walking into, Nick?"

"I'm not sure. I do know that Chief O'Toole is quite pleased with Captain Killingsworth's "investigative" results in the circumstances explaining the murders of Congresswoman Muckler and Senator Bidwell," he offered.

"So obviously, Killingsworth's contention that Russell and Rose Hedgegrowth were involved in those killings has grown legs," she concluded, contemptuously.

"That would be my assumption," he nodded, sullenly.

The gridlocked traffic to and through downtown Washington D.C. was everything Detective Fuentes had described it would be. They approached the restricted parking lot of U.S. Capitol Police headquarters and stopped at the security check-point. The guards recognized the two officers from Metro Police.

"Go right on through, Inspector. Chief O'Toole is expecting you," acknowledged the Charlie.

After obediently parking in the "guests only" zone, Cuffington and Fuentes walked towards the rear entrance of the building. At once, the Inspector picked-up on the first red flag. Unlike their first meeting at U.S. Capitol Police headquarters, Pat Killingsworth was not waiting outside to greet them.

242

"It appears that the battle lines have already been drawn," Cuffington reflected aloud.

Detective Fuentes nodded, in silent agreement.

At the back door, a freshly scrubbed cadet opened it, to allow them access.

"The Chief has given the okay for you to use "his" elevator," beamed the rookie.

"That was big of him," needled the Detective from Metro.

They entered "his" elevator and ascended to the top floor.

"How do you want me to play this one, Nick?" she asked with loyal cooperation.

The Inspector looked at the Detective with professional respect.

"Maria, always go with your gut."

The elevator door opened, depositing them directly into Chief O'Toole's spacious penthouse office. The young male administrative assistant was still seated at his desk, glued to the screen of his desk top. Once again, he did not bother to look up.

Without hesitation, Cuffington walked to the Chief's closed door and knocked.

"C'mon in." was the muffled "welcome."

Nick Cuffington and Maria Fuentes entered the impressive windowed office.

"Inspector Cuffington, how gracious of you to join us!" welcomed Chief Henry "Hammerin Hank" O'Toole, Chief of U.S. Capitol Police. "And right on time!"

Nick Cuffington walked confidently towards the Chief of U.S. Capitol Police and stopped just a bit too close to the superior officer. He leaned down, to get into the Chief's face.

"Hank, I wouldn't have missed your meeting for all the T-Bills in China," he smiled, pugnaciously.

Chapter Forty-Nine

Seated with Henry O'Toole at the Chief's impressive conference table were Emma Teasedale, Chief of Metro Police, Captain Patrick Killingsworth, First-Lieutenant Ginger Snapp, and two men Cuffington recognized, but did not know personally.

The elder of the two men was United States Senator Wendell Keeper. Keeper appeared to be in his late seventies. He was of both average height and weight. His most distinguishing physical feature was the shock of silver-white hair that was plastered in place with utmost perfection. The elder "statesman" of the Senate was approaching the last year of his sixth term. He was already gearing up for a re-election bid the following November.

"My work here in Washington for both my state and my country has only just begun," was his well-worn political slogan.

The gentleman seated next to the "Mustafa of the Senate" was United States Congressman Peter "Tweet Pete" Poseur. Poseur, although not yet fifty years of age, was hungrily seeking his eleventh term as a member of the U.S. House of Representatives in the following year's looming election. Tall, svelte, and attractive to both sides of the aisle, Poseur had made no secret of his ambition of becoming Speaker of the House.

Cuffington and Fuentes sat down next to each other directly facing Captain Killingsworth and First-Lieutenant Ginger Snapp.

Chief O'Toole officially convened the morning's meeting.

"Inspector Cuffington, just to bring you up to date, Senator Keeper and Congressman Poseur are present this morning at the behest of the United States Congress," he opened.

The Chief paused to dutifully pay tribute to the two Congressional member's presence. He then continued.

"Both chambers feel it their foremost responsibility to monitor the progress being made by law enforcement in apprehending

244

those responsible for the murders of their fellow Congressional colleagues," explained Chief O'Toole.

"I can well understand their sense of urgency," acknowledged the Inspector.

Chief O'Toole paused to glance at Emma Teasedale, who was seated at the other end of the table, before continuing.

"Therefore, I shall now turn the proceedings of this meeting over to Captain Patrick Killingsworth. He will detail the headway our department has made as it pertains to the deaths of the late Congresswoman Muckler and the late Senator Bidwell."

Pat Killingsworth intentionally avoided eye contact with Nick Cuffington. Captain Killingsworth looked the two Congressional emissaries squarely in the eyes and began.

"Distinguished members of Congress, I have no way to make what I'm about to report to you any more palatable than what the realty of the situation demands!" blustered the Captain from U.S. Capitol Police.

Keeper and Poseur looked at one another and nodded in bi-partisan agreement.

"Go on, Captain, but with a careful eye on the facts," implored the Senator.

Patrick Killingsworth gathered his thoughts before continuing.

"Senator John Bidwell was operating nefariously behind the scenes of the proposed Key Lime Pie Line legislation!" exposed the Captain.

"Why, I find that rather hard to believe, Captain," contended the silver haired Senator.

"No, it's true," insisted the Captain.

Killingsworth then seized the moment. He stood up and glowered at Senator Wendell Keeper

"Senator John "Black Jack" Bidwell was "riding dirty" on the Key Lime Pie Line!" slammed home the Captain.

"Oh my God, do you have any idea what the political ramifications of this disclosure could do to my Senate re-election efforts next fall?" bemoaned Keeper.

Captain Killingsworth paused for deliberate dramatic effect.

"Not to worry, sir," he reassured, obsequiously.

"And why the hell not, Captain!" demanded the Senator.

"Because, sir, not only has Senator Bidwell's murderer already committed suicide, but his accomplice in the execution of the late Congresswoman Mindy Muckler is already in the custody of U.S. Capitol Police!" he confirmed with pride.

"And how does that help my bid for re-election, Captain?"

"Think about it for a moment, Senator. Thanks to the fast and efficient work of U.S. Capitol Police, by the time of your re-election bid, this tawdry little episode will have been long forgotten by the voting public," explained Killingsworth.

The senior Senator took a moment to weigh the Captain's words.

"Yes, that does start to make some sense. In fact, Captain, your entire explanation, thus far, is quite logical to me," admitted Keeper. "And tell me, Captain, what are the identities of these devils incarnate?" asked the now more relieved six term Senator.

Captain Patrick Killingsworth swelled with hubris.

"A married couple, Senator; Russell and Rose Hedgegrowth," clucked Killingsworth.

Congressman Peter Poseur looked at Senator Keeper. He nodded in recognition of the name.

"Hedgegrowth was a notorious Washington D.C. lobbyist," he seethed.

The Congressman was starting to feel a bit more confident.

"If my memory serves, he works, or more deservedly, worked for the "P" in Public Means Profit group," he hissed with contempt. "I, for one, discontinued accepting their contributions after those donations began to exceed the legal limits, as mandated by your landmark legislation, Senator Keeper."

"Refresh my memory, son. To which piece of legislation are you referring?" fumbled a charter member of the gang of 20/20.

"Why Senator, your ground breaking bill "You Can't Buy a Vote in Washington D.C. Anymore," reminded the younger Congressman.

"Oh yes, now I remember. That piece of legislation seems like such a long time ago," as his voice trailed off.

Congressman Peter Poseur narrowed his hawkish eyes on Captain Killingsworth.

"Pat, how does your explanation of the unfortunate murder of Senator Bidwell tie into the murders of Congresswoman Muckler and Congressman Barry Sooner?" he demanded, authoritatively.

Captain Killingsworth hesitated momentarily, and then fixed his stare at First-Lieutenant Ginger Snapp.

"First-Lieutenant, please brief Congressman Poseur on how Congressman Sooner's and Congresswoman Muckler's murders tie into the killing of Senator Bidwell," ordered the Captain.

Ginger Snapp appeared ill at ease. She hesitated, and then launched into an unscripted explanation.

"Well, Mr. Congressman, the late Congresswoman Muckler and the late Congressman Sooner were definitely involved, in some way, with the Key Lime Pie Line fraud," she sputtered.

"In specifically what way, First-Lieutenant?" asked the Congressman in a matter of fact tone of voice.

"Well, you see Mr. Congressman, the late Mindy Muckler and the late Barry Sooner were members of the Mount Olympus Wealth and Racket Club," she revealed with growing self-confidence. "Furthermore, Senator Bidwell and Lobbyist Hedgegrowth were also members of said club."

First-Lieutenant Ginger Snapp continued.

"Anyway, it was at the Mount Olympus Wealth and Racket Club, in particular, the Parthenon Tap Room, that they hatched the scheme to illegally profit from the Key Lime Pie Line legislation," she explained.

"The involvement of members of the Mount Olympus Wealth and Racket Club does, indeed, begin to bring these Congressional murders into their proper perspective!" agreed the Congressman with an enthusiastic nod of the head.

Suddenly, Poseur's face darkened with doubt. Something had occurred to him that he had failed to take into consideration just moments earlier. He turned towards Ginger Snapp and began to interrogate her with a line of questioning reminiscent of his days at the prestigious northeastern law school he had attended.

"First-Lieutenant Snapp, your contention is that the Congressional murders were the direct result of illegal activities involving the Key Lime Pie Line legislation, is that correct?"

"Yes"

"You are also alleging that these illicit goings on took place exclusively within the domain of the Mount Olympus Wealth and Racket Club, is that also correct?"

"Yes"

"First Lieutenant Snapp, are you aware that the Mount Olympus Wealth and Racket Club is a males only establishment?"

"Yes'

Congressman Peter Poseur, graduate of one of the most esteemed law schools in the land was now confidently ready to call into question and possibly discredit the words of First-Lieutenant Ginger Snapp.

"So then I ask you, First-Lieutenant, how in the world would it be possible that Congresswoman Mindy Muckler could have been privy to, let alone party to, the shenanigans being perpetrated at the all-male Mount Olympus Wealth and Racket Club?" he demanded arrogantly.

"Oh, that's an easy one, Mr. Congressman," fluttered a now relaxed Ginger Snapp. "Thanks to Senator Keeper's recent legislation banning the War on Women here in Washington D.C., Congresswoman Muckler was provided full guest privileges with an option to apply for permanent membership," she fluttered.

"Hear, Hear." mumbled the senior Senator.

"Well, that does appear to explain things satisfactorily," smiled Congressman Poseur. "I have but one last question for you, First-

Lieutenant. How does the murder of Senator William Ryder tie into the attempted Key Lime Pie Line swindle? Was the Senator also a member of the Mount Olympus Club?"

This last question seemed to stump the First-Lieutenant.

Without hesitation, Captain Killingsworth asserted himself into the proceedings.

Unexpectedly, the senior Senator roused himself from what had been a mid-morning doze.

Killingsworth chose the easier mark.

"Senator Keeper, the murder of Senator William Ryder was totally unrelated to the Key Lime Line incident. In point of fact, the late Senator was not even a member of the Mount Olympus Wealth and Racket Club," confirmed the Captain from U.S. Capitol Police.

"Then who the hell did kill him!" shouted the rejuvenated Senator.

Patrick Killingsworth broke into his best Irish jig.

"Senator, I don't think that even you have to be reminded of the rather, how should I properly phrase this, the Avant-Garde life-style the late Senator Ryder led.

A look of anguish swept across Senator Keeper's face.

"No, Captain Killingsworth, not even I have to be reminded of Billy's "eccentricities" he agreed.

Keeper then looked long and hard at Killingsworth.

"Captain, are you suggesting that Senator Ryder's death was related to his after -hour activities?" questioned the elder man.

"I am more than suggesting, Senator," replied Killingsworth. "In fact, U.S. Capitol Police is in the process of apprehending the suspect for questioning as we speak," asserted the Captain.

Senator Wendell Keeper shook his head forlornly.

"Sadly, none of this surprises me about Billy's ultimate fate, Captain Killingsworth; and I rather doubt the news will shock many of my colleagues in the Senate. "By the way, who was Billy's assailant?" inquired Senator Keeper.

"One Terrence Frailey," answered Killingsworth. "And, I might add, known to be a regular consort of the late Senator Ryder."

Congressman Peter Poseur looked at Inspector Nick Cuffington.

"Inspector, do you concur with the findings of U.S. Capitol Police as presented here at this morning's meeting?" he asked.

"No," he answered without hesitation nor regret.

With the swiftness of a cougar in season, Chief Emma Teasedale exerted her presence and invoked her authority.

"Congressman Poseur, Inspector Cuffington no longer has an official involvement in the Congressional murders investigation," she stated with immediate finality. "In fact, as of this morning, the Inspector has been placed on a leave of absence."

Detective Maria Fuentes rolled her eyes in disgust but remained silent.

Senator Wendell Keeper shifted his attention to his old friend Henry O'Toole, Chief of U.S. Capitol Police.

"Hank, do I have your seal of approval on these findings?" he demanded.

"I don't doubt for a moment, the competence of Chief Killingsworth and First-Lieutenant Snapp," replied "Hammerin Hank" O'Toole.

Senator Keeper and Congressman Poseur exchanged glances and stood up to leave.

It was the Congressman who addressed the people still seated at the conference table.

"After this morning's proceedings, both Senator Keeper and I can report to our respective chambers with the utmost confidence that U.S. Capitol Police have the matter of the Congressional murders well in hand, indeed."

Chapter Fifty

Inspector Nick Cuffington and Detective Maria Fuentes were mired in traffic. The increasing and ongoing demonstrations were beginning to bring Washington D.C. to a near stand-still. They had left Chief O'Toole's office without uttering a word to their fellow law enforcement officers in the wake of Chief Teasedale's leave of absence pronouncement.

Even after getting on the road to Foggy Bottom, they had remained silent; preferring the privacy of their own thoughts and reflections on what had just taken place at U.S. Capitol Police headquarters. As usual, it was Maria Fuentes that broke the barrier of their frequent lapses in conversation.

"Nick, do you think she actually meant what she said?" asked the Detective.

"Absolutely, Maria; First-Lieutenant Ginger Snapp genuinely believes that the War on Women here in Washington D.C. has been brought to its rightful conclusion," he stated with a straight face.

In spite of the situation, Fuentes found herself laughing.

"No Nick, I was referring to Chief Teasedale's avowal that you are now on a leave of absence," she clarified. "I'd like to think it just was one of her theatrical stunts used in the heat of the moment to pacify the two stooges from Congress."

"Honestly, I don't know. What's more, I no longer really care," he revealed with unusual frankness.

Sensing a first time vulnerability in the Inspector's mood Fuentes nurtured the dialogue.

"Nick, did Captain Killingsworth's conduct at this morning's charade take you by surprise?"

"No"

"And why not?" pressed Maria, as she began to anger, once again, at the recollection of what had gone down at the morning's meeting.

"Because Pat Killingsworth has mutated into the consummate politician," professed the Inspector.

"But Captain Killingsworth is a police officer, not an elected official, she countered.

Inspector Cuffington smiled at Detective Fuentes with the affectionate benevolence of a surrogate father.

"Maria, are you at all interested in a long and successful career here in Washington D.C. be it law enforcement or otherwise?" he asked, quietly.

"After this morning's nonsense, Nick, I really don't know," she acknowledged with a shake of her head.

The Inspector nodded with the empathy of one who had already experienced Maria's current disillusionment with "friends" in Washington D.C.

"Detective!" he suddenly barked with authority. "If you learn absolutely nothing else from me, pick-up on this one indisputable fact; anyone who makes their living in Washington D.C. at the American taxpayer's expense is, by definition, a politician!"

He stopped to let his words sink in before continuing.

"Those who understand, accept, and live by this immutable truism of life, here in Washington D.C. will ultimately grow and prosper faster than their counterparts in the private sector!"

Maria Fuentes carefully considered Cuffington's words for several moments before reacting.

"Well, if just about everyone in Washington D.C. is a politician, what does that make the actual politicians?" she questioned with growing interest.

"Maria, over the years, Washington D.C. has morphed into a world unto itself," averred Cuffington. "The elected officials and non-elected bureaucrats have assumed the position of the ruling elite in their "realm of delusion." And anyone or anything that becomes a perceived threat to their Land of Distortion will be dealt with accordingly."

The Detective looked at the Inspector and smiled.

"Nick, don't you think you might be getting a wee bit too Orwellian?" she asked, good-naturedly.

Cuffington looked askance.

"Maria, I've heard you express very similar sentiments," the Inspector reminded her.

"Yes, but that was in the context of explaining to you the reasons why the Squatting On Whore Street Movement and the Herbal Brigade are here demonstrating in Washington D.C.," she sorted. "Besides, in that instance, we were only talking politics. This morning, we were dealing with murder, cops, and cover-up; big differences, Nick!"

"Really, Maria, name **one**," challenged the Inspector.

While Fuentes ruminated, Cuffington continued.

"In point of fact, Maria, you witnessed Washington D.C.'s obligatory doctrine of self-insulation in action during this morning's meeting," advised the Inspector.

"And what's that supposed to mean?" she asked with a hint of edge in her voice.

Cuffington surveyed the countenance of Maria Fuentes. He was at odds with himself. The Inspector was questioning in his mind, the merits, if any, of continuing the current line of discourse. He ventured forth.

"Maria, do you still believe that Senator Keeper and Congressman Poseur attended this morning's meeting at U.S. Capitol Police headquarters in search of facts and the truth surrounding the four Congressional murders?" he asked, pointedly.

"Why else would they have bothered to show up?" she countered with curiosity.

"To receive exactly what Captain Killingsworth provided for them, reassurance," the Inspector said, emphatically. "You must try to understand, Detective, that not providing them with an explanation, even the one fed to them by Killingsworth, would have been perceived as a threat to their now accustomed and cherished way of life here in Washington D.C.; one they have come to expect."

Maria Fuentes remained silent.

Cuffington pressed forward.

"Maria, if you doubt what I am saying to you, please try to explain to me why neither Senator Keeper nor Congressman Poseur questioned my opinion of dissent when asked if I concurred with the findings of U.S. Capitol Police regarding the Congressional killings?" he entreated.

Detective Maria Fuentes explored the eyes of her professional mentor.

"It's because they are delusional!" she laughed, shaking her head.

"I rest my case."

As they continued their traffic crawl through the mid-day convergence of political protestation, Maria turned to look at the Inspector.

"Nick, do you think that Pat Killingsworth feels any guilt or harbors any remorse about hanging you out to dry at this morning's meeting?" she asked with an evolving sense of already knowing the answer to her own question.

"None whatsoever," the Inspector replied, jauntily. "As I told you earlier, Maria, Pat Killingsworth has mutated into a consummate Washington D.C. politician; if it comes down to his survival here in Washington D.C. or the truth be told, let the truth be damned. Besides, in the now immortal words of a not so long ago past President of the United States, "when it comes to politics, the word loyalty doesn't even exist."

Maria Fuentes cautiously eyed Nick Cuffington; yearning to ask him the question that had beguiled both her father and uncles over the years. Cuffington noticed Fuentes' rare hesitancy when it came to saying what was on her mind. The Inspector answered her unasked question with an inquiry of his own.

"Detective, do you happen to be curious about my unexplained departure from New York City and my equally curious arrival here in Washington D.C.?" he dangled, playfully.

"Kind of," she admitted with some trepidation.

The Inspector turned his head from side to side, feigning the pretense of ensuring secrecy.

"Truth be told, Detective, it was coincidental dumb-luck," declared a now smiling Nick Cuffington.

Although Maria Fuentes did not buy the Inspector's explanation, she chose not to challenge it. The Detective's obviously unmarked police cruiser pulled to a gentle stop in front of the Cuffington's residence.

"Maria, as soon as I learn of anything newsworthy, I'll be in touch," he instructed.

Fuentes turned in her seat and fixed her eyes on Cuffington's.

"Regardless of how, this whole Congressional murder mess turns out, I want you to know that I've come to respect, and yes, even like you Mr. Inspector," she fluttered with affection.

Cuffington climbed out of the passenger seat. Before closing the door behind him, the Inspector stared at Maria Fuentes.

"Detective, I have a feeling that the end-game to "this whole Congressional murder mess" is just about to get under way."

Nick entered his house through the kitchen's side door.

Leigh was busily checking and then re-checking to make certain the stove and oven were turned off. When she turned around, Mrs. Cuffington was quite surprised to see her husband standing there.

"Nick, what in the world are you doing home at one in the afternoon?"

"I'm here to take you to lunch," he smiled as he kissed his wife.

"Well, you're too late, would-be suitor!" "I already have a hot date," she declined, demurely.

Leigh Cuffington was already dressed and ready to leave the house.

"Actually Nick, I am literally out the door. Several weeks ago I committed my attendance to a charity luncheon for the aid of the legally-blind here in Washington D.C.," she explained.

"Well, in that case I hope you packed for dinner and an over-night stay," commented the Inspector.

Mrs. Cuffington studied her husband with increased uneasiness.

"No, really Nick, why are you home," she asked with growing concern

"Because I've been placed on a leave of absence," he answered, bluntly.

"Why, for God sakes?" her voice beginning to rise in both pitch and volume.

"Might I suggest you turn on the TV; I'd be quite surprised if a news conference wasn't already in progress, outlining the success of Washington D.C. law enforcement as it pertains to the Congressional murders," conjectured Cuffington.

Leigh quickly clicked the flat screen's remote.

The Inspector made his way to the refrigerator, retrieved a cold one, and started towards the kitchen door. As he passed the set, Captain Patrick Killingsworth's talking head was enveloping the screen. Once seated outside on the patio, Cuffington lit a cigarette and began to mentally revisit the events that had taken place subsequent to the initial Congressional poisonings. He remained convinced that a thread of commonality existed that would ultimately manifest itself and bring explanation and closure to the Congressional murders. Unfortunately for Cuffington, time had "officially" expired as far as his attempt to unearth that answer was concerned.

Moments later, Leigh Cuffington stormed out onto the patio. She confronted her husband with arms folded in suppressed rage.

"So let me get this straight. Thanks to the vaunted efforts of U.S. Capitol Police, those responsible for the Congressional murders are now in custody, and all is well, once again, in Washington D.C.," she hissed with unmitigated venom.

The seated Inspector calmly looked up at his wife.

"Did Killingsworth get into any specifics?" he inquired without a trace of emotion in his voice.

"If you're asking me whether or not he dropped any names, the answer is no," she reported.

Suddenly, as if she had been slapped in the face, Mrs. Cuffington's eyes widened and her entire body began to convulse.

"You are not going to tell me that these bastards are trying to pin this whole thing on poor Rose Hedgegrowth!" she screamed.

Immediately, the Inspector was on his feet. He grabbed his wife's shoulders and shook her once. She looked up at him. His face was expressionless. His voice was indurate. And the eyes were something that not even she had ever seen before.

"You listen to me. This thing is not over. And it won't be over until I say it is. Do you understand?"

Leigh Cuffington nodded her silent assent. Nick Cuffington, seemingly turning on a dime, reverted back to the "same old Nick."

"Leigh, the best way you can help matters in general, and myself in particular, is to calm down. Try, as best you can, to put this entire matter out of your mind. I suggest you get going to your luncheon," he encouraged.

Again, she nodded in taciturn agreement. Nick Cuffington looked at his wife with the love he had felt for her since the day they had met.

"Besides, over the years, I've done some of my very best work while on mandatory leaves of absences," he grinned.

"Yes, that's quite true, dear.

Mrs. Leigh Cuffington was, once again, smiling.

Chapter Fifty-One

Vice-President of the United States Frank Bentklin sat at the head of the table. To his left were seated Senate Majority Leader Morey Drainer and Minority Leader of the House Fanny NoGosi. Speaker of the House Jim Spendforth and Senate Minority Leader Steve "Pitch" Middleton were situated to the Vice-President's right.

The meeting was taking place in a subterranean office located beneath the ground floor of the U.S. Capitol Building.

"I just got off the phone with the Big Guy," smiled Vice-President Bentklin. "He sends his regards to all of you."

"What leg of his Re-election Extravaganza Tour is he on?" inquired Senate Minority Leader Middleton.

"Actually, the Big Guy is taking a few days off from the rigors of the campaign trail for some well-deserved R&R," informed Bentklin.

"Slow and steady wins the race," agreed "Pitch" Middleton.

"In fact, he should be touching down in Hollywood within the hour," continued the Vice-President. "From there, it's off to the Walk of Fame for photographs with his recently embedded star. After that, Grauman's Chinese is on the menu," elaborated Bentklin.

"Oh, is he going to leave his fingerprints in the wet cement?" asked an anxious Fanny NoGosi.

"Heavens no!" shuddered Bentklin. "Actually, Fanny, he's going to leave an impression of one of his golf clubs in the cement," informed the Vice-President. "And he did confide to me that he is still uncertain which club that will be," revealed Bentklin.

"That will depend entirely upon which way the wind is blowing at the time," declared Morey Drainer.

"But the Big Guy's day of rest doesn't end there," resumed Bentklin. "This evening he will be in Beverly Hills attending a dinner party for 'superstars only' as their guest of honor," informed the Vice-President.

"Only the Big Guy would consider such an event filled day to be one of leisure," marveled an awed Fanny NoGosi.

The Speaker of the House, Jim Spendforth, spoke for the first time.

"I hate to interrupt, but I think we should be discussing the situation that has necessitated this meeting. After all, there is a rare joint session of Congress scheduled to begin in several hours," he reminded them.

"That's right!" remembered Bentklin. "Senator Keeper and Congressman Poseur will be updating the entire Congressional body on the progress that U.S. Capitol Police has made in the investigation of the four Congressional murders."

"By the way, Frank, what is the skinny on those killings?" asked the Senate Minority Leader.

The Vice-President looked at Middleton, smiled, and then winked.

"Steve, let me just say that my old golfing buddy, Chief O'Toole of U.S. Capitol Police, already has that would be bugaboo in the bag!" reassured Bentklin.

"Say, that is good news!" responded Middleton, approvingly.

The Vice-President glanced at his watch.

"Let's get down to why we are here this afternoon and start addressing these damn federal spending cuts being forced upon us," he insisted.

Before anyone had the opportunity to respond, there was a knock on the conference room's door.

Vice-President Bentklin smiled, agreeably.

"Enter"

The door opened. Standing there was a bespectacled man in his early forties. He was medium in height, slight of frame, and had thinning hair. His suit was rumpled.

"Professor, good to see you," greeted the Vice-President. "Please, take the seat facing me at the end of the table."

Professor Thaddeus "The Source" Sagerman taught Constitutional law at a local university. However, his true area of expertise was in the governing body of laws and by-laws pertaining to the enactment of Congressional legislation.

"I asked the Professor to join us today to see what options we might have at our disposal to reverse these treasonous spending cuts," informed Bentklin.

"And not a moment too soon!" agreed House Minority Leader Fanny NoGosi. I, for one, only found out about these nonsensical reductions in domestic spending because my phone has not stopped ringing since those unfortunate announcements were made public!"

"Fanny, you're preaching to the choir," rued the Speaker of the House. "The recently publicized mandated cuts in military spending have ruffled more feathers than I even knew existed!" carped Jim Spendforth.

Professor Sagerman afforded the people seated at the table a "cooling off" period before entering the dialogue.

"It is my understanding that the Vice-President has requested my presence here this afternoon to explain the origin of these obligatory slashes in spending to both domestic and military programs," he began, pedantically.

"Federal spending cuts that no one seated at this table approved!" objected Fanny NoGosi.

The Professor looked patiently at the House Minority Leader before he continued.

"I beg to differ with you Congresswoman NoGosi," said Sagerman. He did so without contention, but rather, with erudite detachment.

"But how can that be possible?" demanded the Speaker of the House, Jim Spendforth.

Again, the Professor paused before responding.

"Was it not the very people in attendance here today who authorized the creation of the Mega Committee to oversee future spending cuts at some time in the future?" he asked with indulgence.

260

"Yes!" was the unanimous, bi-partisan voice of affirmation.

Professor Sagerman acknowledged their united agreement and, with scholastic pace, resumed.

"As it turned out, the Mega Committee failed to achieve any bi-partisan agreement on specific spending cuts as was mandated by its very creation. The direct result of this breakdown was an automatic 10% across the board reduction in spending that has now been set into motion," instructed the Professor.

"How the hell could such an event take place without our approval?" demanded a now irate Morey Drainer, Senate Majority Leader.

"Why Senator, the automatic spending cuts have been triggered by your *tacit* approval," corrected "The Source".

"Professor, I must confess that I have no idea what you're talking about," conceded Morey Drainer.

Professor Sagerman looked benignly upon the ignorance of his ill-prepared "students".

"In a word, the term is referred to as 'sequester', enlightened the instructor-or 'sequestration', depending upon which Ivy League school one attended."

"It's called what?" thundered the voice of Frank Bentklin. "I've been here in Washington D.C. for nearly forty years and that's one "S" word I've never heard before!"

The professor patiently persevered.

"The legislation that approved the formation of the "ad hoc" committee to oversee future spending cuts specifically stipulated that if said committee failed to come to agreement on future spending reductions, 10% sequester on all spending would be activated," explained the Professor.

"I, for one, didn't see that fine print in our resolution," objected Fanny NoGosi.

"Did you take the time to read your proposed resolution, Congresswoman?" asked the Professor.

Fanny NoGosi sneered at Thaddeus Sagerman.

"Professor," she huffed, "my overloaded Congressional calendar doesn't permit me the luxury of reading every piece of paper that clutters my desk. Besides, Einstein, as a member of the United States Congress, my solemn duty is not to read legislation, but to pass legislation!"

An uneasy pall silenced the room. Senate Majority Leader Morey Drainer was the first to speak.

"Professor, what Congressional loopholes exist that might enable us to postpone these distasteful reductions in federal spending?" he coaxed.

Thaddeus Sagerman momentarily suspended himself into arcane reflection before responding.

"Theoretically, if new legislation designed to replace the current domestic and military programs was to bog down in both houses of Congress, simultaneously, the resulting gridlock would allow for the "M Option".

"The "M Option?" puzzled Morey Drainer.

"The **Monetary** decision to create more money to fund *existing* programs at *existing* levels would then fall into the hands of Treasury Secretary Skim Lighter and Federal Reserve Board Chairman Bend Vernacular," explained "The Source."

The Senate Majority Leader nodded his approval.

"We can always count on those two," he grinned.

Jim Spendforth began to wipe away his tears.

"And the added bonus to this approach is that it leaves all of us out of the loop of responsibility when it comes to next year's elections," smiled the Speaker of the House.

Vice-President Frank Bentklin finally, weighed in.

"You know, I think we just managed to achieve what the polls have been telling us the American people expect and demand from their Congress; good old-fashioned bi-partisan compromise. Therefore, I hereby declare this meeting adjourned to allow ample time to dress for tonight's joint session of Congress; which will be followed immediately by cocktails and dinner."

"Hear, hear!"

Chapter Fifty-Two

Inspector Nick Cuffington was at home seated in front of his office desk top. He had been futilely attempting to find a thread of commonality that might help explain the motive behind the four Congressional murders. Hours earlier, Leigh had decided to attend her charity event. Finally, he rose from his desk and walked to the kitchen. Cuffington picked up the T.V. remote and clicked on the flat screen. The U.S. Capitol Building was in the center of the picture. As the T.V. camera pulled back to afford a more expansive angle, the vast number of demonstrators that had converged on the grounds came into view. The protestors appeared to have completely surrounded "The Dome." Two make-shift platforms had been erected to allow the various "leaders" of the people the opportunity to have their voices, be heard.

Nick grabbed a beer from the fridge and ambled outside onto the patio. He sat down at the table and lit a smoke. The hour was just after four in the afternoon. Something was tugging at the Inspector even more than his seeming inability to connect the dots leading to the explanation for the Congressional killings. He had been home well over three hours since leaving U.S. Capitol Police headquarters. During that period of time, he had not received a single piece of outside communication; not one phone call, text, email, or tweet. This struck Cuffington as somehow "not right."

"But then again," he thought to himself," may be this is the new norm, in the wake of my leave of absence."

As if eerily on cue, Cuffington's cell phone toned. He checked caller I.D. "Private caller" The Inspector picked up the call.

"Yes"

"Nick, is that you?" questioned the voice on the other end.

"Yes"

"Seymour Savage, here"

Cuffington remained silent.

"I heard about your hastily arranged sabbatical; can't say that I'm surprised," admitted the Doctor.

"Good news always travels quickly in Washington D.C."

There was silence on Savage's end of the line.

"Why did you call, Sy?"

"Inspector, we must speak, immediately!"

Cuffington, already familiar with Savage's quirky qualms regarding phone conversations proceeded accordingly.

"Okay, Doc, I'll meet you at Metro Morgue. I will leave here as soon as possible but, my time of arrival is going to depend upon traffic," committed the Inspector.

"No, not Metro Morgue; the location is no longer secure. Hell, that place is starting to give me the creeps! No, we will be better served at a neutral site," recommended Savage.

Cuffington thought for a moment.

"Sy, are you familiar with Brewster's Bistro?"

"No, but I'll find it," asserted the Doctor.

"Alright then, I'll meet you there as close to five p.m. as possible. I will be waiting for you outside. Should you arrive before me, ask for Toby the Waiter. Tell him you're meeting me. He'll take things from there," instructed the Inspector.

Cuffington immediately terminated the connection and punched speed dial.

Detective Maria Fuentes did not pick up.

The Inspector disengaged, and then accessed the number manually. This time, a voice answered.

"The number you have reached is not in service at this time. Please check the listing. . . ."

Cuffington did not waste the time. Instead, he returned to the kitchen. After shutting down the flat screen, he rifled through a kitchen drawer and plucked a set of car keys. As he passed the refrigerator, he pilfered a cold one and then opened the door to the garage. Once inside, he initiated the automatic door opener and climbed into his personal automobile. He fired up the car's seldom used engine. Two of the things Nick Cuffington found most distasteful in Life were driving on public thoroughfares and drinking warm beer. Fortunately for the Inspector, he was experiencing only one of those dislikes that late afternoon. Cuffington's car of choice was a 1970 Olds 442 convertible. It was equipped with the W-30 Package and a Hurst "his and hers" slap stick shifter. As he eased out of the garage and down the driveway, Cuffington popped both tops and began the drive to Brewster's Bistro. Rumbling down the roadways, the Inspector quickly noticed the lighter volume of traffic congestion. This he attributed to the mass convergence of protestors currently assailing the U.S. Capitol Building. While driving, Cuffington's mind continually shifted gears between Fuentes' disconnected phone service and Savages' yet to be explained contact.

Nearing Brewster's, he began to look for a parking space. To his pleasant surprise, available parking was in abundance. Cuffington parked outside the front entrance of his point of rendezvous. He raised the rag-top and buried the dead soldier underneath a rear seat. As he hit the sidewalk, a uniformed Metro uniformed officer accosted him.

"Nice wheels, Inspector"

"Well, it manages to get me to and from church on Sundays," admitted the owner.

"Don't worry, Sir, I'll keep an eye on her," volunteered the young man.

"I appreciate that, Officer," acknowledged the Inspector.

"Say, I've noticed that there's not too much going on in this part of town tonight," observed Cuffington.

"No, Sir, all the action is over at the "Dome" this evening," reported the patrolman.

"And justifiably so," confirmed Cuffington.

"I guess," was the Metro cop's vapid response.

As the Inspector neared the front entrance of Brewster's, his cell phone belched its obtrusive presence.

"Yes"

"Nick?"

"You've got him"

"Nick, it's, Nelson. May I have a word with you?" implored the Patron of the Arts.

"Nelson, right now, I'm a little pressed for time," fended off the Inspector.

"It may very well be important, Nick," dogged Nelson Lloyd Sinclair.

Cuffington paused to consider the possible ramifications of not agreeing to a meeting.

"Are you acquainted with Brewster's Bistro?"

"Yes, but it's not exactly one of my haunts," objected the Gentleman of Upper Land.

"Well, it's one of mine, so if you want to talk, you'll know where to find me."

Cuffington pocketed his phone and slammed through the front doors of Brewster's.

Toby the Waiter was standing in the front entrance, anticipating his arrival.

"Inspector I'm so glad you are here! There's some guy that says he's supposed to meet you. I seated him at Cuff-Kill Corner," was the server's update.

"Yes, I was expecting his arrival, Toby," was all that the Inspector said.

As they walked towards the bar room area, Toby shook his head in disquieted consternation.

"He's one spooky looking little dude, Inspector. I mean, where, did you meet him, Doctor Moreau's Island?" asked the young man with genuine apprehension.

"No, Toby, not on that particular island," glibly replied the Inspector.

"Does he bite?" asked the young man with an ill at ease smile.

"Only when angered"

Cuffington suddenly stopped and confronted the waiter with narrowed eyes and a straight face.

"Toby, please don't tell me you got him mad!" chided the elder man.

Toby's eyes ogled and his mouth dropped.

"Get him mad, hell, I don't want to get anywhere near him!" he confessed and stopped just short of the booth.

"I'll be right back with your beer, Inspector."

Cuffington sat down facing Savage. Neither hands nor small talk were exchanged.

"I want you to know, Inspector, that after our last meeting, I came to the conclusion that your abrupt manner with me was justified. Anyway, at long last, I now possess the information you were seeking that afternoon," offered Doctor Seymour Savage.

"You've identified the toxin that killed the four members of Congress?"

"Yes"

"Did you know what it was the last time we met?"

"Absolutely not; whether it was your curtness or simply dumb luck, its identification was confirmed only hours ago."

Toby the Waiter returned with Cuffington's beer.

"Sy, what are you drinking?" asked Cuffington.

The Doctor stared at the young man.

"I shall have a double Beefeater's on the rocks with two wedges," ordered Savage.

"Very good, sir; can I get you anything else while I'm here, sir?"

"No"

"I'm already on my way back!" he exclaimed and broke into a trot towards the bar.

The two men sat in silence until Toby returned. He quickly served Savage his drink and disappeared. The Doctor raised his glass.

"To old times"

The Inspector followed suit.

"To old times"

Savage took a healthy pull and then fixed his eyes on Cuffington.

"The toxin is known by the name Negra Veneno; it's Spanish for "Black Poison." What made it so difficult to track down was the fact that the plant used to make the stuff grows in only one place in the entire world," explained the Doctor.

"And where might that be, Doc?" demanded the Inspector.

"The Sierra Maestra Mountains of Cuba. More specifically, in the foothills just outside Santiago de Cuba."

Although Cuffington didn't blink, his mind was racing at the speed of sound. He calmly sipped his beer for the appearance of nonchalance.

"I sincerely hope that this information proves useful to you in your murder investigations, Inspector."

"Obviously, it's too early to tell," was Cuffington's robotic response.

Savage took another drink of gin and continued.

"Just for the record, the Russell Hedgegrowth autopsy has been completed."

Cuffington immediately mentally compartmentalized and focused solely on what Savage was now saying.

"And what were the results of those findings?"

"It seems Mr. Hedgegrowth decided to commit suicide by ingesting Negra Veneno," revealed the Doctor.

"Who else is privy to this information?" demanded the Inspector.

"We are a club of two; at least until midnight," assured Doctor Savage.

Immediately, Cuffington silently sorted through the information presented by Savage hastily attempting to make any sense of it.

Savage sipped the gin and resumed his dialogue.

"And even after midnight, I wouldn't be terribly surprised if our club's membership remains rather small."

"And why might that be, Doc," he asked, curiously.

"Because, no one, over at U.S. Capitol Police seems overly anxious or interested in the results of the Hedgegrowth autopsy."

Cuffington thought for a moment and then shook his head.

"They're delusional."

"Be that as it may, I've got to go."

Doctor Savage finished his drink stood up to leave.

"Until next time, Inspector"

Nick Cuffington looked at the Doctor.

"Maybe there won't be a next time," he offered, rhetorically.

Savage let out a loud jackal-like cackle.

"Now who's being delusional, Inspector!"

As he walked away, Doctor Seymour Savage stopped and turned to face Cuffington.

"Nick, I would like to think that after our little get together today, I am now even with you as far as the help you so graciously extended to me in New York City all those years ago."

Inspector Nick Cuffington looked at Savage and raised his beer.

"Doc, as far as I'm concerned, you and I are all square."

Chapter Fifty-Three

After Savage's exit, Nick Cuffington, once again, sat alone in the booth at Brewster's. He was desperately trying to align the facts the Doctor had given him into some sort logical configuration.

Without prompting, Toby the Waiter approached the table and replaced Cuffington's beer with a fresh one.

"Inspector, Nelson Lloyd Sinclair is out front. He wants to know if you are here," he reported, excitedly. "What do you want me to tell him?"

"Let him know that, yes, I am here and then escort him to my booth," were Cuffington's instructions.

"At once," acknowledged the young man.

He scampered off with relished purpose. Moments later Toby the Waiter returned with Sinclair in tow.

"Nelson, I trust you had no problem finding my little "haunt" greeted the Inspector as he extended his hand.

"None whatsoever," retorted the Patron of the Arts, as he sat down adjacent to Cuffington.

"Nelson, what's your pleasure?" beckoned the impromptu host.

"A glass of the house's very finest cognac," requested the heir to the heir to the heir.

"Right away, Mr. Sinclair," assured the waiter.

"So Nelson, what brings you to my neck of the woods?" Cuffington wondered aloud.

Before Sinclair had time to formulate a response, Toby the Waiter returned with his drink. The Inspector, noticing the young man's awe, in the presence of the Patron of the Arts, initiated a formal introduction.

"Nelson, our waiter's name is Toby.

I find him to be attentive, sociable, and above all else, competent."

"I'm also a painter, Mr. Sinclair," added their server.

"Toby, you never mentioned that to me," remarked Cuffington; how fortuitous. Nelson, give Toby one of your cards," insisted the Inspector.

"But, of course"

Nelson Lloyd Sinclair proffered a card with proviso.

"Toby, call me only after you have at least three paintings that *you* are quite pleased with," he counseled.

"Alright, sir," obeyed the young man as he left, floating.

No longer encumbered by an audience, Sinclair abandoned all pretenses.

"Nick, this may be nothing, but I thought you should know about it."

"Please, continue Nelson"

"When the family relocated from New York City to D.C., my grandfather mandated that I assume a sort of "hands on" role in one of our business enterprises. I chose to "manage" the local real estate operation here in D.C.

Sinclair paused to taste the cognac and then continued.

"By manage, I mean, having to sit in on a weekly meeting to review sales, acquisitions, property inventories, and the like."

The Inspector made no attempt to disguise his boredom. Noting this, Sinclair cut to the chase.

"Anyway, at this afternoon's meeting, it was brought to my attention that we just purchased a property in DuPont Circle."

"So?"

"So, the seller's name was Detective Maria Fuentes."

Suddenly, Cuffington was keenly interested.

"When did the property close?" confronted the Inspector.

"The day before yesterday," answered Sinclair.

"Did she provide a forwarding address?" questioned Cuffington.

"No"

"And why not?" pressed the Inspector.

"According to the person handling the purchase, Detective Fuentes said that she is relocating outside the D.C. area and saw no need to provide one," he explained.

Nelson Lloyd Sinclair looked at his watch.

He finished the cognac and got up to leave.

"Listen, Nick, I've got to run. But please check with Leigh and let me know when the two of you are free for lunch."

"I'll check our social calendar and see when we might be able to squeeze you in," he smiled.

And with that, Nelson Lloyd Sinclair was gone.

Inspector Nick Cuffington was left with only unanswered questions to provide him company. However, he was no longer actively inputting, processing, and interpreting data. He was merely sitting, consciously attempting to take some mental time off. Cuffington slid out of the booth and headed for the front door of Brewster's.

"Inspector, are you leaving for the evening?" asked Toby the Waiter.

"No, I'll be right back."

Once outside, he lit a cigarette. Immediately, an overwhelming volume of noise could be heard emanating from the direction of the U.S. Capitol Building. Seconds later, two uniformed Metro cops were running down the sidewalk in his direction, brandishing flashlights and shouting; "two more are dead, two more are dead!"

One of the officers, recognizing Cuffington stopped to personally deliver the news.

"Inspector, two more Members just dropped dead on the floor of Congress!"

"When did this occur?"

"Just happened moments ago, Sir," he replied and then continued forward with his public announcements.

Cuffington made no initial move. He stood calmly smoking and weighing his best course of action. After finishing his cigarette, the Inspector re-entered Brewster's Bistro and made his way to the now crowded bar. One large flat screen was hung on the wall behind the trough of libation. A nationally televised baseball game was in progress. Cuffington pushed his way to the front and motioned for the bartender's attention.

"What can I do for you, buddy?" asked the dispenser of the holy water.

"I want you to change the channel," instructed Cuffington as he nodded towards the big screen.

A bar patron seated next to where Cuffington was standing voiced his objection.

"Hey, I'm watching this game!" he complained.

Undaunted, the Inspector persisted.

"I said change the channel!"

The seated patron stood up to get into Cuffington's face. He was young, powerfully built, and pissed off.

"Listen to me, Dad, if you're looking to get into real trouble, real fast you've come knocking on the right hombre's door!" he menaced.

Before Cuffington could respond, a voice from behind the two would be combatants boomed through the loud din of the room, quickly rendering it to muted curiosity.

"From where I'm standing, the only one in this place that's real close to getting busted up real bad, real fast, is you, Panty Boy!"

Both Cuffington and his irate adversary turned around to face the "voice." It was the Burly Bouncer of Brewster's Bistro, who had already been of assistance in the recent past. Standing beside him was Toby the Waiter.

"So, what's it going to be Maidenform?" demanded the all too anxious gladiator.

The young man responded without hesitation.

"I think it would be a good idea if we change the channel," agreed the now deflated fun-seeker.

"Inspector, what station do you want to watch solicited the "Enforcer."

"C-SPAN" answered Cuffington.

"C-SPAN it is!" announced the keeper of the peace.

As the satellite honed in on its designated target, Cuffington looked at the bartender and extended his hand.

"I'm Nick"

"They call me Slinger," responded the man.

"Well, Slinger, I'll take a Bud. Also, back up my newly found friend here," as he tapped "Maidenform" on the shoulder. In fact, while you're at it, Slinger, buy the bar a round on me," declared Cuffington.

An ovation of appreciation resounded throughout the barroom.

"Hey Inspector, what's so important about C-Span tonight?" asked a voice in the crowd.

"I'm paid to follow a far more violent game than baseball," he replied.

"And what's that?" inquired another voice at the bar.

Cuffington turned to face the jam packed room.

"Two more members of Congress just dropped dead inside the U.S. Capitol Building," he informed those present.

There ensued a stir of eager anticipation.

"Hey, Inspector, does C-SPAN have instant replay?" asked another voice from the crowd.

"Yea, and Slo-Mo?" added another.

"We can only hope," responded Cuffington for differing reasons than those of the thirsty patrons at Brewster's.

The television's satellite located it's sought after prey. On the screen are two men standing behind separate podiums. They are facing the camera as if in debate format.

"Hey, turn up the volume!" shouted someone.

Slinger, the bartender, adjusted the remote's volume button, but the T.V. remained silent.

Inspector Nick Cuffington, in a glance, recognized the two speakers about to address the joint session of Congress. On the left is Senator Wendell Keeper and on the right side of the screen is Congressman Peter Poseur. Both men appear to exchange pleasantries and then it is Congressman Poseur who defers to the senior Congressional member as to who is going to address the joint session of Congress first.

As the Senator begins to speak he becomes unsteady. Suddenly, he begins to claw violently at his throat. The Senator, then crashes into the podium and spills awkwardly onto the floor of Congress.

Congressman Poseur's initial reaction is to come to the aid of his fallen Fraternity Brother. However, he too begins to frantically rip at his throat. He sinks to his knees, and then topples unceremoniously on top of Senator Keeper.

The camera quickly shifts angles to avoid further viewing of the two now limp Members. Instead, what comes into focus is the picture of Congressional members abandoning their seats and frantically trying to exit the room in flight for their own safety. The last image before the screen turns to snow is one of utter mayhem!

Suddenly, the T.V.'s volume is back and blaring at full-tilt. The coverage is now live. The footage is being shot from outside the U.S. Capitol Building

"It's absolute madness here outside the Capitol Building," shrieks one news commentator. "The People have absolutely lost their minds over the news of two more Congressional deaths!"

Inspector Nick Cuffington signaled Slinger the Bartender.

"Hold my spot."

"It's all yours, Inspector," he obliged while remaining riveted to the television.

Cuffington picked up his beer and walked outside the bistro. He reached into his pocket and retrieved his phone and a piece of paper. He punched the scribbled phone number.

"Yes?" responded a person on the other end.

"Talia Teller, please"

"This is she."

"Talia, Nick Cuffington"

"Oh Inspector, I can't talk now. I'm on my way to the Capitol Building to cover a story. Did you hear that two more members of Congress have just died?"

He ignored her question

"Talia, let me ask you something. Do you want to cover a story or would you prefer to write one, Ms. Journalist?"

There was a pause.

"Where are you?" she asked with resolve.

"Brewster's"

"I'll be there in fifteen minutes."

Cuffington walked back inside the Bistro and sat down in Cuff-Kill Corner to wait for the reporter from *The Washington Rumor*. The Inspector was calmly placing, in order, the pieces of the puzzle that had, heretofore, so successfully eluded him.

Toby the Waiter led Talia Teller to where the Inspector was seated. She sat down facing Cuffington. She was early.

"May I get you something from the bar, Ms. Teller?" asked the waiter.

"No thank you, Toby,"

With that, he disappeared into the adjoining room to continue watching the show.

"So, what's the story, Inspector?" she asked, anxiously.

"Do you have your "hit list" on you?"

"Of course"

"Let me see it," urged the Inspector.

Teller reached for her carry-all. She pulled out the requested file and handed it to Cuffington. He placed it on the table and began an intense examination. Moments later he looked up at Teller.

"Talia, do you have a high-lighter?"

She did, and gave it to the Inspector.

He continued his analysis.

"That's it!" he said nodding his head in self-approval.

He turned the file around and pushed it towards Teller.

"Look at the two lines I just highlighted over Congressman Poseur and Senator Keeper; and then compare those to the already highlighted lines of Congressman Sooner, Congresswoman Muckler , and Senators Ryder and Bidwell."

Teller complied as requested, but after several minutes she looked at the Inspector shaking her head.

"I give up," she conceded. "Inspector what do you see?"

"I see the Pattern of the Unfathomable," he responded.

"The what?" she questioned, now beginning to think her time would have been better spent covering the events unfolding over at the U.S. Capitol Building.

"If, you study the highlighted lines of the six members of Congress who have been murdered, there exists two commonalties that each of them shared," declared the Inspector.

"And what were those?" pressed the now more interested journalist.

"The first was that all six of them had spent at least twenty years holding on to their seats of power here in Washington D.C.

"And the second?" she implored.

"All six were actively seeking another term in next year's elections," he concluded with finality.

Talia Teller quietly reflected on Cuffington's conclusion. At length, she nodded her skepticism.

"But, Inspector every member of the House is up for re-election next year" she rebuked.

"Yes, but not every Senator"

He continued.

"Senators Ryder, Bidwell, and Keeper were all members of the Senate for over twenty years, and actively seeking their re-elections," countered the Inspector.

"That could be mere coincidence," counter-punched the journalist.

Cuffington looked benignly at the writer from *The Washington Rumor*.

"In the business of law enforcement the word "coincidence" doesn't exist," he dismissed with finality.

Talia Teller considered Cuffington's hypothesis.

"But Inspector, even if you've successfully uncovered the motive for the Congressional murders, you still haven't determined who's responsible for those murders," she pointed out.

Cuffington carefully weighed the young journalist's observation.

"Yes, but, by now knowing the motive for the Congressional murders I have successfully shortened the list of possible future targets and at the same time shortened the list of possible future suspects," rationalized Cuffington.

"And who is still on that now shortened list of possible future suspects," questioned the young woman from *The Washington Rumor*.

"On that list is only anyone angry enough to kill any current member of the United States Congress who has been in Washington D.C. for twenty years or more and is actively seeking to overstay his or her already worn out welcome in next year's elections," concluded the Inspector.

"That may very well prove to be an exhaustive investigation," sighed the Journalist.

'Well, on the positive side, Talia, I just happen to be on an extended leave of absence," smiled Cuffington.

The Inspector stood up.

"Come on, let's go join the party. If you're off the sauce tonight I'll buy you a 16 oz. Diet Coke," invited the Inspector.

"Actually, I think I'm in the mood for a cocktail or two," she confessed.

As they walked into the packed, awe-struck bar room, all eyes were glued to the face of a young man on the giant flat screen.

The advancing throng of protestors was marching steadily towards the front steps of the Capitol Building. Riot Police had circled the structure and were standing at the ready.

The young Captain stood stoically in front of the edifice. He was flanked by two Lieutenants, awaiting his order. To his rear was the incessant shrill of old, withered, and panicked politicians; no longer demanding that their authority be invoked, but , rather their very existences be preserved. To his front, the young officer did not see "Terrorists and Traitors, but rather familiar faces. In his mind's eye he saw his parents, his brothers and sisters, and life-long friends. As the crowd drew closer, he could now peer into the eyes of his high school teachers, local merchants, and community professionals. In essence, he was staring at his people; the very same persons he had known throughout his entire life.

In the blink of a decision in command, the young Captain gave his order; one that would leave an indelible mark on his country's future political landscape.

"Stand Down!"

His two Lieutenants looked at one another and then at their Captain for re-affirmation of his order.

The young officer did not waver.

"I said, Stand Down!" he commanded.

His order was passed down the line.

Weapons were lowered and visors were raised. The demonstrators continued to surge towards the U.S. Capitol Building. On that particular night, the only sound that could be heard ringing throughout all of Washington D.C. was the People's united cry for:

"Scope and Range! Scope and Range! Scope and Range!"

Epilogue

After the Captain's order to "stand down," there was no ensuing violence. The deaths of Senator Keeper and Congressman Poseur were the final casualties in what some were now referring to as the "Declaration of Reclamation."

The People, on that evening, had granted the now shell-shocked puppet-like politicians permission to leave the United States Capitol Building without the threat of bodily harm and with no strings attached.

The departure of the long-time political hacks cleansed the once fouled atmosphere of the United States Capitol Building with a renewed sense of fresh beginning and future prosperity.

Talia Teller's landmark article appeared in *The Washington Rumor* the following day. She had entitled the piece, "Solving the Mystery of the Pattern of the Unfathomable."

After the column's publication, the vast majority of those members of Congress who had been in office twenty years or longer and had been seeking re-election in the following year's referendum "decided" it would be in the *country's* best interest not to do so. Instead, for the most part, they returned to their home states hoping to continue their careers as public servants at the state and local troughs. For the most part, these efforts were met with vehement grass roots resistance.

In the absence of the atrophied political aristocracy of the past, a new wave of Congressional membership descended upon Washington D.C. Though their political perspectives invariably differed and always would, their commitment to "Country First" never did. This new breed of Congressional membership had learned from the mistakes of the past.

They realized full well, that by always putting the interests of the People first, all "parties" concerned would be better served in the long run.

280

With time and a relentless pursuit of the truth, Talia Teller went on to become Editor and Chief of *The Washington Rumor*. For decades to come, thereafter, she was widely recognized as one of the most influential Journalists in Washington D.C..

Shortly after Teller's story broke, Rose Hedgegrowth was exonerated and released from jail. In lieu of a lengthy law suit, Rose had settled out of court for an undisclosed sum of money and a legally binding commitment that the law enforcement practices of U.S. Capitol Police be thoroughly investigated.

Chief Henry O'Toole and Chief Emma Teasedale had a one-time fling. Unfortunately for "Hammerin Hank," the episode resulted in a life ending stroke on the couch in his spacious office at U.S. Capitol Police headquarters.

Emma, always one to pounce on opportunity, convinced the "powers to be" that a merger of U.S. Capitol Police and the Metro Police Department would be in the best interests of all concerned about "law enforcement" in Washington D.C.. She was then given the newly created position of Czar of the Washington D.C. Police Overlords. However, in the wake of the Rose Hedgegrowth Investigation, both the merger and the position were quickly abolished. Under mounting pressure, Teasedale opted for early retirement with the "full Monty" life-time benefit package. Rumor had it, she went on to marry the "Sheik of Physique," the then reigning champion of the WWE.

Captain Patrick Killingsworth was also ensnared by the Rose Hedgegrowth Investigation. After a long and deliberate consideration, the Commission saw fit to terminate the Captain for "cause." His firing specifically denied him both life-time pension and medical benefits. To make matters stickier for "The Killer," after one too many Death in the Afternoons, he proposed to First-Lieutenant Ginger Snapp. It was a marriage of misery. After three tumultuous months, the couple had called it quits. Divorce papers were filed on the grounds of "irreconcilable similarities."

Toby the Waiter, through continued hard work and talent went on to become the owner of Brewster's Bistro. His first official act as proprietor was to rename Cuff-Kill Corner. Henceforth, the plaque displayed over the now revered booth was inscribed "Cuffington's Place."

Toby, with the backing of his financial "partner," Nelson Lloyd Sinclair, went on to become known as the "Restaurateur of Washington D.C.."

Shortly after the Declaration of Reclamation, Nick and Leigh Cuffington left Washington D.C.. They relocated to Montego Bay, Jamaica, W.I. There, in the tranquility and natural beauty of that island, Leigh's career as a writer of fiction flourished.

Their new location also appealed to Nick.

Jamaica afforded him swift, discreet, and legal entry into Cuba; where the Inspector had unfinished business.

P.S. Doctor Seymour Savage and Laboratory-Assistant Betty Ann Norge are still at large.

David Moffatt

David B. Moffatt is a former career professional in the field of financial services.

He currently resides on Long Island with his wife, Cynthia, and the cat of mystery and mayhem, Mc Pherson.

The author, to the chagrin of his publisher and readers alike, is alive and currently writing.

www.ingramcontent.com/pod-product-compliance
Lightning Source LLC
Chambersburg PA
CBHW052019020726
47501CB00004B/1138